DECODED

by

Sara Marx

Bella
BOOK
2011

Bella Books, Inc.
P.O. Box 10543
Tallahassee, FL 32302

Printed in the United States of America on acid-free paper
First published 2011

Editor: Katherine V. Forrest
Cover Designer: Judy Fellows

ISBN 13: 978-1-59493-258-8

Other Bella Books By Sara Marx

Before I Died

Insight of the Seer

Acknowledgment

I would like to thank my dear editor, Katherine V. Forrest for the real work she put into this book. I hope we've created something they'll love. I like our chances.

Dedication

To Mary, Christian, Macy and Roxy, of course.

About The Author

Sara Marx lives on a Florida beach with her partner, Mary. They are parents to a brood that include two political/peace activists, an actor and a United States presidential candidate for 2044.

CHAPTER ONE

Fifteen years Special Agent Shay Cooper had known Roger Holloway. For fifteen years he'd dragged her from one haphazard, dangerous assignment to another until she wondered why she still considered him to be her mentor and friend. Holloway painted the events as "career opportunities," but she had a different name for it: The Old Holloway Maneuver. It was a miracle she'd survived their relationship to this point.

Shay—or Coop, as she was called—no longer reported to Assistant Director Holloway and figured a wiser woman probably would have changed her number at least thirteen years ago. So why she was standing in line for a security check at the Bureau's Chicago Division instead of preparing training assignments for a batch of Academy new bloods, she couldn't say. He'd said lunch, what could go wrong?

"The Old Holloway Maneuver," she muttered to no one.

The agent manning security regarded her with obvious mistrust when she set off the walk-through detector. Shay knew the drill, dumped the contents of every pocket into a silver dish and fished out her badge that identified her as brethren. Despite it all, she didn't seem to be winning any confidence from him. Post 9/11, nobody took chances. She jumped through the additional security measures hoops like a trained circus cat, but shifted impatiently as he repeatedly waved his wand near her nether regions.

"Belt," he declared. Disappointed at the mundane nature of the security flag, he waved her through.

Shay collected her things and moved aside to re-shoe, re-dress and reload her pockets. She looked around for any sign of her old AD. He'd promised her he'd meet her in the lobby promptly at noon. At ten after twelve, she took matters into her own hands and forged through the crowd on a mission to hunt him down. Holloway caught her before she hit the directory. He placed his hand on the small of her back and guided her through a group of college interns, toward a bank of elevators.

"I don't see you for six years and you welcome me back to the state with a cafeteria lunch?" she asked with faux annoyance. "What a guy."

"Welcome to Chicago." He grinned, but didn't look at her directly. "How's life in the little burg—what's it called?"

"Pleasant."

"Ah yes, Pleasant." His tone turned whimsical and he sounded like a commercial announcer when he said, "Home to the plush new Agent Training Academy."

The ATA was actually a former drug warehouse seized by the government and converted to a training facility for the FBI. With its high ceilings, mismatched plank floors and outdated, drafty windows, it was the furthest thing from plush. Shay thought about Pleasant, a burg, just as he'd called it, population of only a few thousand residents. The measly forty miles that separated it from Chicago might as well have been an entire world. She actually relished her new slow-lane lifestyle and it was evident in her relieved tone when she mumbled, "I can tell you that I don't miss this place."

Holloway patiently waited for the doors to close before swiping his ID card through a reader. The car lurched unexpectedly, causing her knees to wobble. She leaned against the metal railing to steady herself. The light feeling in her stomach said they were descending, though the illuminated floor numbers didn't indicate that there existed a basement level. Her eyes flicked to his.

"Secret downstairs? Seriously, James Bond much?"

"I want you to meet someone." He looked across the dimly lit car as if he were seeing Shay for the first time. His features softened somewhat as he remembered his manners. "You look good. Has it really been six years?"

"I would know," she answered dryly. The last time they'd laid eyes on each other had been a grim day in New York in what seemed like another lifetime. She didn't care to discuss it now. Instead, she gave her old boss the once-over, took inventory of his full head of dark hair, spray-tanned skin, and a hard-earned physique that was evident even under drab FBI blues. He looked too good for a man approaching sixty. She made a playful smirk. "You look wretched as hell."

Holloway gave her a stunning grin.

"Love the tie."

He toyed with the knot of his designer paisley blue tie. "Armani."

"Brought to you by Simon and Schuster, I suppose?" Shay grinned at him. "How is the big tell-all, anyway?"

"Number eight on the *New York Times* bestseller list, six weeks running." He shot her a look. "I sent you a signed copy."

"Yeah." She nodded. "It's number eight on my to-do list, also six weeks running."

A grin flashed across his face, but disappeared as the doors opened and he was instantly refocused on their journey. "This way."

The air felt cooler, recycled, like inside an airplane cabin. High ceilings were congested with extensive ductwork and oversized ancient pipes that Shay assumed were plumbing. A loud noise tunneled toward them, growing louder upon its approach before sounding with a twanging shot directly above them. Her knee-jerk response caused her to slightly duck as the sound traveled past them.

"Capsular messaging system," Roger vaguely explained the racket as he walked on.

"Isn't there some OSHA policy requiring hard hats at these depths?"

"Nobody's got a harder head than you do, Coop."

An evenly spaced line of neon bulbs sizzled overhead casting one perfect spotlight after another, dotting an otherwise dark, narrow passage. Adding to the ominous atmosphere was the deep hum of the ventilation system as it started up and vibrated through them to their bones. Holloway calmly raised his voice to be heard over the sound. "Few years back we were forced to absorb a local field office thanks to a budget reallocation." He sarcastically finished with, "Thank you, Homeland Security."

"Yes. The same budget reallocation that founded our own little Agent Training Academy right here in Illinois—*my* new job." Shay smiled and smugly added, "Thank you, Homeland Security."

He ignored her. "Anyway, we had to set them up in the basement."

"I'll bet that made them feel right at home."

Holloway marched on, his words matching the same business-like syncopation as his footsteps. "Tony Williams—they called him Iron Will, you know where you've heard that name?"

She summarily recounted the story. "Agent disappears, no leads, no evidence." Shay's eyes weren't adjusting quickly enough to the low light and she lumbered along gracelessly, almost blindly behind him. A different thought occurred to her. "Are there rats down here?"

"Might have been." Holloway's answer insinuated a different kind of rat.

Just ahead was an office door and she wondered if they'd finally reached their destination.

"I'm taking you to meet Agent Kate Harris, Williams' partner. Her office is a little farther down."

They bypassed the door and wound around another corner, down yet another similarly darkened hallway toward what was quite possibly the remotest office in the building. They were literally in the bowels of the Bureau.

"Jesus, Rog, did she do something wrong?" The ventilation system decided to cycle and went abruptly silent in the middle of the question she'd yelled over the noise. Shay heard the tinny echo of her own voice as it bounced off the cement and metal ductwork all around them. She felt her cheeks grow warm and her voice dropped to a whisper. "Why the isolation?"

Holloway stopped so suddenly she nearly smacked into him. He turned around, inhaled deeply, puffing his cheeks with air. In the shadowy hallway she could see his eyes flit upward then to the left, and Shay wondered if she was about to hear a lie. He did an exhale and eye-roll combo making it difficult to analyze. She could only assume that while Agent Harris might not have necessarily done anything wrong, she probably hadn't done anything altogether right.

After several seconds, Holloway found his voice. "Agent Harris is complicated."

"How so?"

"She was Williams' big defender here at the Bureau. He had a habit of operating so far beneath the radar he was barely detectable. In turn, Harris had mastered every trick shot in the Bureau bylaws to keep his ass out of hot water."

"Behavioral science, right?"

"Specializing in missing persons," he clarified.

"Were they any good?"

Holloway smirked. "He was good at getting into trouble. And out of it, thanks to Harris. When Williams' case leads ran dry, we shelved it. Harris never forgave me for that."

Shay shrugged. "Well, it doesn't exactly validate that theory about the Bureau taking care of its own."

"Exactly what she said. But that case is ice cold. No evidence to speak of. Nothing."

Shay thought it was absurd that they were whispering in the hallway only feet away from Harris's office. The soft glow that emanated from the marbled glass window gave the hallway an even creepier feeling. "When you say she never forgave you, why you, specifically?"

Commencing the aforementioned complications, Holloway sighed.

"I brought her into the Bureau myself."

"You brought me into the Bureau," Shay put in. "But this feels different. Cut to the chase. You two have an affair?"

"She's my goddaughter." The impatience in his tone said it wasn't the first time he'd fielded such a question. He tamped it down, got on with it. "You and Harris are like night and day. You never let your private life get in the way of your work, even when your work invaded your private life."

True. Shay Cooper had been called the Bureau's perfect recipe, handling the collision of her worlds with a trained sense of removal that was nothing short of miraculous. Shay didn't like to be reminded of the past, especially what Holloway was referring to. She rifled her fingers through her dark, jagged-cut hair and was suddenly nervous. She shifted, kept her sour feelings about Bureau-grade professionalism in check. She was only too glad to be educating agents these days instead of working alongside them.

"So she's a wild child? A slacker? You don't want your ass in a sling over it?" She was losing patience. "Rog, am I approaching warm on any of this?"

Holloway's mood swings surrounding the subject bordered bipolar. "She's a damned good agent, don't you forget that." He softened his posture again, and again looked troubled. "I think she was involved with Williams."

"Wouldn't be the first time a partnership made its way outside these hallowed halls."

"I didn't think he was her type, if you know what I mean."

She didn't. "Why am I meeting her?"

"I don't know what to do with her." His expression suggested he might have meant only to think the statement, not say it. He self-corrected. "I want your take on her."

"My take," she echoed suspiciously.

"Just meet her. Then we'll get lunch and you go back to ⸰r cushy Academy office with your outrageous pay grade." He ⸰r shoulder, smiled. "That's all."

Coop didn't like his tone and liked the mention of her salary even less. What she liked least of all was that whenever Holloway said "that's all" about anything, it was always only the beginning.

CHAPTER TWO

Shay could have sworn she saw AD Holloway sign the cross over himself before they entered Harris's office. The interior was chock-full of filing cabinets and bathed in drab yellow light and was about as homey as a janitor's closet—in fact, it could very well have been one at some point. The centerpiece of the office was an oversized antique library table, probably leftover from the John Dillinger days.

In the midst of it all, at the side of her desk, sat Agent Kate Harris, with her delicate facial features, blond hair cascading carelessly about her shoulders, and legs that went on forever before ending in a perfect pedicure. Her legs were crossed daintily at the ankle, bare feet several inches away from casually discarded two inch open-toed pumps. Agent Harris looked more like a mermaid than any fairytale drawing Shay could recall from childhood. If mermaids wore open-toed pumps, pinstriped straight skirts and satin blouses with billowing fronts...

Suddenly Shay could see how Agent Harris inspired complications of a variety of natures.

Because Agent Harris didn't regard them right away, the pair had time to take in the view and both did, though for entirely different reasons, Shay was certain. She was struck with discomfort, wished she weren't standing in a strange doorway wearing a ridiculously surprised expression, watching a mermaid wriggle her toes. At very least she wished Agent Harris would slip her shoes back on. She swallowed hard and bowed her head prompting her bangs to swing forward enough to shield eyes wide with curiosity. Shay smoothed her slacks, shifted nervously and cleared her throat with as little commotion as possible.

The sound cued an obligatory greeting from Agent Harris, though she didn't so much as raise her eyes to her guests.

"AD Holloway has brought me another new partner." The simple announcement was delivered with careless disregard. To further substantiate her lack of enthusiasm, Agent Harris added a bored-sounding, "Goody."

Holloway dodged her chill. The corners of his lips turned up into a terse smile and he nudged Shay forward, intending to draw her into the conversation. Shay, not keen to be touched, shot him a look, anchored her feet firmly in place, and then subtly as possible, shrugged off his hand.

"I thought you'd like to meet Special Agent Shay Cooper, an old buddy of mine." Holloway stepped aside, his wits obviously dangling every which way. Shay wondered why he was nervous as he performed the introductions. "Agent Cooper, Agent Harris."

"How do you do." Shay extended her hand, a gesture that went ignored. It struck something cold and hard inside her. She jammed her hand back into her slacks pocket.

"Why?"

Confused by the woman's question, Shay leaned slightly forward. "Pardon?"

"I was speaking to AD Holloway." Kate Harris employed great theatrics in capping her pen and closing her notebook. She easily located one shoe while her bare foot rooted around for the other. To Shay's relief, she found it and slipped it on. She primly clasped her hands together and rested them on the book before her. Only then did she aim her turquoise-green eyes at the pair. "Why did you think I'd like to meet an old *buddy* of yours?"

Her question caught Holloway off guard and Shay shot him a sheepish little grin. She rocked back on her heels, watched and waited. In truth, Shay was every bit as befuddled about the meeting as Agent Harris. Almost.

"You don't remember me mentioning her before?" He seemed to be talking to himself.

Those blue-green eyes flicked to Shay for a quick head-to-toe assessment. "You don't look like you're from Miami," was all she said.

Shay knew her pale skin practically repelled sunshine. Add that to her lean, lanky form, dark clothing and deep-set brown eyes, and she looked the furthest thing from anyone rolling out of a beach town.

Harris continued her summary. "I'd have guessed New York."

Shay nodded once. "I was in New York before Miami."

The blonde furrowed her brow, reconsidered it. "But not originally, the accent is vague."

Shay gave another nod, made a small full-circle motion with her hand. "Born and raised in Chicago."

And like that, Harris's interest in speaking to her guest evaporated. She turned her attention back to her boss. "That's right. The New York hotshot who busted all the mob guys. Now, why would Special Agent Cooper want to be my partner? What promises did you make her?" Agent Harris's gaze shifted again toward Shay, but she continued to address Holloway. "You make her feel sorry for the agent stashed in the basement whose career is on death row?"

"Kate..." Holloway's demeanor hardened somewhat and it was clear that despite any familial feelings he might have had for the agent, he was exasperated with her antics.

Harris's gaze flitted between the pair before landing on Shay again. "You must be some kind of sucker."

As was her nature when confronted with arrogance, Shay was

suddenly drawing unusual strength from the younger woman's insulting behavior. It was the same brand of overconfidence she'd endured from fellow fresh-faced agents years ago. Even from the start, she herself had never dallied with arrogance, choosing action over the empty intimidation of words. As a result, she'd quickly and quietly earned the respect of even her highest ranked colleagues. Nowadays, the only true arrogance she encountered came from legal eagles representing criminals circling the societal drain.

Having shifted into her typical cool defense, Shay could almost forget that this same low-level attitude was not being perpetrated by neither rookie, nor criminal, nor scum-sucking lawyer. The arrogance hardly differentiated despite the fact that it was spewed from two such beautiful lips.

"Thanks, but I already have a job wrangling new hires with a false sense of entitlement because they honestly believe they can save the world. They have an excuse, they're rookies." Shay tipped her head ever so slightly, didn't surrender an ounce of control. "What's yours?"

A smug smile tugged at Agent Harris's sweet lips. "You've been conned, Agent Cooper. AD Holloway brought you here under the pretense of lunch, made you wait, then caught you unawares and whisked you straight down to the Bureau's bat cave. Am I on track so far?" She paused but Shay didn't even flinch. "In a moment you'll shake my hand and leave this office and he'll guilt you into trying on the position of my partner. Then within weeks you'll transfer out to a quieter office in, say...Wyoming."

Figuring the ball was safely back in her court, Shay gave the woman several moments to fester in the cool silence. But Agent Kate Harris only seemed to savor the quiet she'd inspired. The women's chilly gazes remained locked on each other and in truth, only Holloway appeared to be suffering from their silent standoff. He broke into a sweat. Shay noted this and felt compelled to end it, if only to cure his obvious pathetic agony.

"It's clear that you like to make things hard for yourself," she said, her tone low and controlled. "That's a shame."

Agent Harris, apparently tired of their game, averted her glare from Shay to AD Holloway. "Wouldn't it be easier to just give me the damned transfer and save everybody the hassle of reassignment?"

"We've talked about this before, Kate."

"Then why not assign Agent Buchner? He's familiar with the inner workings of this office."

"He's too green." Holloway shook his head. "James Buchner is a Tony Williams wannabe."

The two began their quiet argument which had the same impact on Shay as the low hum of a dentist's drill. She recognized the mutual emotional drain between agent and boss. It was a vacuum she didn't wish to get sucked into again. Her thoughts drifted to her own closet-size office at the makeshift Academy with its malfunctioning thermostat that made warm days hot and cold days frigid. She thought about the mile high stack of requisitions on her desk and the rubbery cafeteria food she was missing that complemented lukewarm coffee peppered with enough grounds it required a sieve just to drink it.

At the moment, nothing could have been more appealing.

She didn't at all envy this pair. She checked her watch and turned her thoughts toward a class that started in two hours and the lesson she still needed to prepare. She'd have to fight city traffic just to get back there.

"I'd give her the transfer," Shay announced. She clapped her hands together indicating an insanity cease-fire. "But that's just me. Look, I'm going to grab a bite on my way back to campus. Goodbye, Agent Harris." She then looked at her old boss. "Holloway, call me sometime when you want to do lunch for real."

Harris wore a small knowing grin for having correctly figured him. "So it was the lunch routine."

"You were right about that." Shay nodded, forced a stiff grin. "But you were wrong about my shaking your hand, or about my responding to guilt. Not even his puppy-eyed mug could make me consider being your partner." She looked at Holloway like he should be ashamed for even having tried, and then back to Agent Harris for her parting remark. "Nice to meet you. Sort of."

CHAPTER THREE

An Olympic runner would have had met her challenge keeping up with Shay's exit. Utilizing long strides, she made the winding turns of the cement corridor guided by memory and the red glow of exit signs. Holloway finally caught up with her in the stairwell.

"That was good and tricky," Shay told him, keeping her swift pace. "Lead me to the poisoned poppy field, will you? Boy, you must think I'm some kind of stupid."

To her surprise, Holloway grabbed her sleeve and practically spun her around on the stairwell landing.

"Trick you?" He practically spat desperation. "You see what I'm working with here? I'm asking you to help me."

"Help you with what?" She shook his hand off her elbow but didn't otherwise move. "You've got a real treasure trove down here, you know that? What else you hiding? Capone? I'm out of here. Christ, Holloway—give her the frigging transfer and leave me alone."

He started to grab her sleeve again but was stopped by the warning glare she issued. They stood staring at each other. In moments, Holloway's shoulders softly slumped, his voice bled with exhaustion.

"This is a dire situation."

"For you or for her?"

"Both, actually." He scrubbed his hands through his thick hair. "Look, this is her last stop, there's no transfer. Nobody wants her. It doesn't take long for word to get around that she's poison."

"What makes me immune?"

Holloway had plucked Shay out of the Academy years ago, taught her everything, watched her grow and thrive, then suffer and nearly break. And yet here she was, standing before him, a testament to her sheer strength and determination. Neither of them moved nor spoke for several seconds. At last he answered her in a confidential tone.

"You and I both know you're wasting your time playing teacher."

Shay smirked. "Yeah, because anyone can see my time's much better spent babysitting *that*." She glanced in the direction of the office they'd just raced away from. "Where do you work into this puzzle?"

"I've got Internal Affairs breathing so far down my neck they're fogging up my ass crack. They're putting the squeeze on me because they think Kate could have information about Williams' abductor. Her Bureau-wide freeze-out is not helping her case, and IA thinks I'm covering for her because of—"

"Blatant nepotism?" Shay finished for him. "Jesus, Rog, you had to get her on at your own division? How stupid can you be? Most people keep their godfather gifting to flowers—a puppy, tops."

"If Kate knows something about Williams' disappearance, I need to know about it too. And if she doesn't, I need her to move on and reestablish her career here with the Bureau before

it's too late for her. And if it is, then she just needs to get out."
His voice dropped a notch. "She's a good agent, Coop. I promise
you that. One month, that's all I'm asking. Consider it agent
rehabilitation."

"What if she can't be rehabilitated?"

"What makes you think I'm only talking about her?" He
paused and watched as Shay digested this before giving him the
worst possible glare. She turned with the intention of charging
downstairs, but his words stopped her. "I can think of a time
when you felt like everyone had given up on you, Coop."

She spun on her heels and in an instant was beneath his nose,
jamming an index finger into his chest. "People did give up on
me. I lost everything for this damned job—and for what? And
what the hell makes you think I owe you *anything?*"

"You don't. But don't you wish someone had done the same for
you?" In the ductwork above more messaging capsules fired up
and began crisscrossing overhead, thoroughly rattling the tubes
as they rocketed along. Holloway yelled to be heard. "And look
what happens when you go it alone—you have a motherfucking
aneurysm? We're damned lucky to be *having* this argument right
now!"

"No thanks to you!" She started up again and Holloway
let her yell. Enumerating everything that had happened to her
in the last few years, the painful details were muffled against
the noisy background. Though safely insulated by the echoing
clatter, she let him have it and looked utterly depleted when
she'd finished.

"Done?" He took another glare from her and shrugged.
Appropriately timed, the basement was momentarily silent again.
He sighed, turned almost fatherly. "Look, try it. If it doesn't work
out you go back to the Academy and I'll buy Kate a puppy."

They remained staring at each other for several more
seconds. Shay's brain cranked out a slideshow featuring a barefoot
woman with mermaid hair and blue-green eyes that burned right
through her. She couldn't imagine she could help—or that she'd
even *want* to. But it wasn't like things could get worse than they
already had in recent years.

She clenched her eyes shut sounded drained when she said,

"I don't know if I can get a teaching replacement on such short notice."

"I've already taken care of it. You don't even have to go back there this afternoon. Just take the day, blow the suds off a few root beers and show up tomorrow. I'll have your lanyard waiting at security."

She spewed a string of curses that went largely unheard thanks to the vent system loudly rattling and choking its way back to life. A lot of nerve he had—replacing her at the Academy without even knowing that Shay would take his offer.

What was she thinking? Of course he knew she would accept it. Once again she'd fallen victim to the Old Holloway Maneuver.

CHAPTER FOUR

Holloway must really have the goods on Agent Cooper. That or she was a glutton for punishment. Those were the only conclusions Kate Harris could arrive at. Of course agreeing to take her on as her partner and actually honoring that commitment were two different things. Sadly, Kate would bet the agent was high on honoring commitments, and that would surely make things difficult.

Not only had Shay Cooper decided to become her partner, but she'd marched right back into the office only minutes after they'd been introduced and announced that they were vacating the crypt-like premises at once. Holloway, on her like a shadow, had made short order of commandeering a bigger, brighter and, most importantly, *higher* quarters, a chore made difficult by the fact that Holloway couldn't get service on his cell in the Bureau's concrete belly. After he'd resorted to the office line, it all was carried out in minutes.

It was aggravating for many reasons, starting with the fact that Kate's own requests for an above-ground office had been falling on deaf ears for years. By now, she felt safe in her little tomb; its deep darkness seemed to fit her somber mood as of late.

She sighed, rolled her neck from side to side, and looked around her swank, yet very empty apartment. An easy chair and a mattress were the two pieces of furniture she'd bothered to acquire after the split, and only because she could order them and have them delivered without setting foot into a store. The remaining two-thousand squares of apartment would require some actual shopping to furnish. Kate figured she should probably make that effort before everything in her world changed yet again. She tiredly dropped into the chair, at once realizing every painful muscle as a consequence of the action.

The afternoon-long office move had required transferring the contents of her present office to an upstairs room. Feeling double-teamed, Kate had spent the balance of the day angry at her boss and her new partner. She'd slung her fair share of digs in Shay's direction but they were deflected with a coolness that made her want to pull her hair out. Shay had refused to engage her, only issued an occasional zinger through her sweet smile. Like the remark she made regarding Kate's apparent struggle in pushing a wheeled file cabinet to the elevator.

"My guess is it's the shoes. If I was going to rebel against Bureau rules, I'd sure as hell make it something better than wearing open-toed pumps." And then Kate could have sworn she heard the woman mutter, "Suck it up, buttercup."

Agent Cooper had handled her by alternating patience reserved for a spoiled child and thinly veiled sarcasm. It was the same basic psychology employed in suspect interrogation designed to push individuals to the boiling point and get on with it. Kate should know—it was her specialty. She quickly realized that she hated having it used right back on her.

She wondered if it was the physicality of the move or the emotional drain of the day that had her feeling exhausted. The toll of it forced her to regard her condition, and that caused her to cringe.

"Well, if the FBI decides to fire me I've got a great future moving furniture." She aimed the comment in the general direction of her belly. "Sorry about the M&M dinner. Those guys are idiots." But she knew it wasn't anyone else's fault. No one knew she was pregnant, so how could they possibly be to blame?

Roger Holloway would sooner lay his life down than to let harm come to her, she knew that. In truth, she herself was the irresponsible one for not having informed the Bureau of her pregnancy. But telling them would lead to questions—if only from Uncle Roger. Inevitably the child's paternity would come into question and she wasn't prepared to speak about it yet. She wondered if she would be a disaster of a parent.

A single parent.

Of the two of them, her former lover was definitely the most family oriented. Now here she was, alone with a baby on the way. It was truly the last thing she could have imagined.

Sighing, she rested a hand on the world's tiniest belly, felt her mood sink even deeper. "I am really sorry."

Kate closed her eyes. Her head was a congestion of her partner's disappearance, an irreversibly broken romance and a baby room without so much as a crib. Now today, she had Special Agent Shay Cooper to worry about. It seemed that her personal and professional lives were racing neck and neck toward chaos.

Tony's disappearance had done strange things to her, markedly detaching her from everyone around her. Even Roger, her only remaining "in" at the Bureau, seemed to have tired of her bad attitude. He'd encouraged her to move forward, get over her heartbreak.

"Heartbreak," she echoed the memory and tiredly laughed. "If only he knew."

Kate shifted in her chair, tried to get comfortable, considered moving into her bedroom, but it wasn't even eight o'clock yet. She wouldn't sleep even if she took herself to bed. Her gaze settled over a mound of boxes still containing books and dishes even though she'd moved into the place more than four months ago. She'd spent an interim month at a hotel before that.

One of the boxes served as a table and was strewn with files she'd brought home for review. Sitting atop the heap was a picture; a years-earlier version of Kate with her arm around Elise. She sighed, forced it out of her head and instead focused on her newest research project.

After spending the day playing hide-and-seek with furniture, she'd logged an additional two hours at the Bureau Library trying to find out everything she could about her new partner. She knew Roger's old stories had been painted with a brush of friendship. But Kate wanted to know all the hard facts about Agent Shay Cooper; she wanted to know the stories that never made it to the dinner table.

Her search capabilities were limited or else she risked leaving behind a mile-wide trail of virtual breadcrumbs. Without entering her access code and with no managerial protocol to back it up, so far she'd discovered a bunch of nothing.

Agent Shay Cooper had attended University of Illinois, Chicago, specialized in criminal justice, and was recruited by Roger Holloway for the Chicago Bureau. She transferred to New York, then to Miami. Then there was a strange hole in the agent's information timeline. It was as if the woman had dropped off the radar for months before making her reappearance in Pleasant, Illinois.

How perfectly boring.

Kate sighed, caught another glimpse of the picture of her with Elise and in a childish move, reached over and turned it face down on the box. It disturbed her that she no longer felt emotionally attached to the picture; in fact, to anything at all. She wondered if she was cured or mortally wounded.

But now there were bigger things to worry about than sentiment, or lack thereof. She had to find Tony, despite the fact that the case had turned colder than she herself had. Having a partner underfoot wouldn't be helpful. Though she'd managed to chase the others away, somehow she didn't think getting rid of Agent Cooper would be quite as easy. The two of them were already firmly planted on opposite sides of a prideful standoff.

To Kate, Shay seemed relentless, seemed to have nothing to lose, and that was the worst kind of person to engage in battle.

If only Roger Holloway knew what was truly at stake here.

As if on cue, although it seemed too early to be real, Kate felt a flutter in her belly and she was worried all over again. More than being in danger of simply losing her job, she carried the secret piece to a deranged puzzle that could bust the whole case wide open. And that put her in even greater danger than she cared to think about.

Forty-two miles away, Shay Cooper was hauling a garbage container to the curb for early morning pickup. The evening was colder than her memories of April in the north and the wind off Shore Lake blew through her like she was made of Swiss cheese. But the sky was cloudless and crowded with stars and she hated to leave it so soon to go back indoors. Shay crammed her hands into the front pockets of her hooded sweatshirt and started for the backyard by way of a crumbling, overgrown cobblestone path.

It was probably only the third time she'd been in the backyard. The first time was when she'd toured the house with a real estate agent a month ago. The second time, she tried out the first and only lawn mower she'd ever purchased. The slow growing grass had been damp and brown, and likely wouldn't need to be mowed again until the end of May. She was actually anxious to tend to it and wondered why the prospect of doing mundane house chores now seemed to delight her so much. Perhaps because it gave her a sense of purpose in her control-driven life. Or at least that's what the Bureau-mandated shrink suggested to her.

Getting counseling when one was injured on the job or lost someone in the line of duty was standard. That she'd endured both made the weekly sessions a necessary part of her life for as long as she hoped to keep her job and "cushy pay grade," as Holloway called it.

Shay sighed, wandered over to a decrepit wooden swing dangling from the low branch of a monstrously large oak tree.

She leaned her knee on the seat to test its strength and decided it was okay. The ropes scratched and creaked against the branch when she lowered herself onto it, and she dared not have too much faith in the old contraption. She wondered about the swing's last riders and figured the two-story cottage-style house was large enough to have held at least a few kids.

Shay's thoughts inevitably turned to Kate Harris, a woman seemingly hell-bent on being crowned Bitch of the Bureau. She'd been second-guessing her chosen task all day long, wondering why she'd ever agreed to be Harris's partner. If she'd actually *had* lunch with Holloway, Shay could have at least accused him of slipping something into her drink. But this had been done of her own free will, sort of, blame it on her inescapable love of a good challenge.

"You've lost your mind," she muttered aloud, momentarily silencing nature's night sounds. Her words echoed off the rickety fence, trees and gardening shed and returned to her ears, as if nature were seconding the notion. Shay froze, waited for the night sounds to resume, and then gradually her swing began to sway again.

Roger Holloway was nothing if not utterly convincing. A con man, some would say. But she'd made the choice to act as Kate Harris's partner, and it was time to get over all the whys of that decision-making process because it was a done deal.

After hauling every file and folder from the basement quarters to a more livable office on an actual floor, Shay had bid her new colleague an exaggerated saccharine-sweet goodbye before driving all the way back home to begin a different mission. She wanted to know Kate Harris's story.

A friend from the New York Bureau's personnel office actually executed the check, lest Shay should appear obvious. Checking out your partner without proper credentials or reason displayed like digital Dumpster diving. She risked looking sneaky and iffy. Under the guise of performing a standard employee audit, Special Agent Beth Hausley pulled it off in a matter of an hour and faxed the information to Shay's home.

Special Agent Kate Harris was the daughter of a highly acclaimed holistic doctor who'd nannied her up good while he and his socialite wife flew around promoting his books and vitamins. In 1977 he was worth six million dollars. By 1980 they were bankrupt, owed the government two million thanks to his partying lifestyle and overuse of a private jet, a debt that would never be paid because of a plane crash that had orphaned Kate, a toddler by then. Probably afraid of acquiring her attached debt, the child went unclaimed by family and wound up on the doorstep of an old Harris family friend, Roger Holloway. The remaining history read uneventfully—public schools, university, Quantico and then the Bureau. She'd partnered with Anthony Williams eight years ago.

As for her personal life, Kate didn't appear to have one. A thorough background check revealed that she'd never been married, never been placed on administrative leave, never even had a parking ticket. Yet here she was, full of obvious unadulterated hate for the system that employed her. Was it because everyone had abandoned all searches for her missing...*lover*? Only to Shay, it didn't feel like the former partners had been lovers. Perhaps it was her wishful subconscious.

The brisk wind kicked up and whistled past her ears, jolting her fully alert. Yes, probably she'd made a dumb move in agreeing to partner with the mermaid-haired woman with nice toes. Shay rolled her eyes, told herself that if it all went belly up, she could transfer to a quieter office in, say, Wyoming.

But Shay was the proud owner of her first piece of real estate in lovely Pleasant, Illinois. Transferring anywhere was not an option; neither was running away, no matter how appealing either choice sounded at the moment. Not anymore. She would get to the bottom of whatever was going on in Kate's world, find the woman's missing partner, and get back to her teaching job, nice and simple.

Shay's eyes stung and watered in the cold breeze and she clutched her hooded sweatshirt tightly around her. Somehow she doubted that anything about Kate Harris would be nice *or* simple.

CHAPTER FIVE

"Sorry about this, again, Agent Cooper."

The guard at the Bureau's parking garage apologized for the ninth time. Shay drummed her fingers against the steering wheel of her Jeep and kept her impatience in check, even though the delay would have her sliding into the morning meeting by the skin of her teeth. The guard shot her an occasional nervous smile as she hammered away at the computer keyboard.

"You'd think that after being here for almost a month they'd have you in the system. I know a guy—took him a year before he was in the parking computer."

"Yeah?" Shay glanced at her watch from behind darkly tinted glasses. Shifting her gaze, she studied the early-twenties woman with a slight, boyish figure and enough keys attached to her belt to sink the Titanic without need of an iceberg. From time to time, wild cerulean eyes flickered Shay's direction, and each time the senior agent would smile, politely acknowledging the guard's flirtatious behavior. It had become a standard between them since Shay's arrival and she'd already been forced to recite to herself her strict no-interoffice-dating policy speech.

Everyone called the attendant Lou, but Shay was pretty sure her name was Louise or something more feminine. Beneath Lou's uniform cap and coveralls was also something decidedly more feminine—namely an ultra thin tank shirt and G-string and wild-ass three-color hair. Shay knew this because she'd been fully exposed to Lou's alter ego one late night while attempting to exit the lot. Insert repeat lecture about no-interoffice-dating. Lou's cheeks had pinked and she'd quickly re-dressed, apologizing all the way. Shay promised not to mention the incident to anyone on the condition that she not do such an awkward thing again. Then, of course, she'd reassured her that the package was indeed highly tempting and that she was flattered by the attention. In truth, the tiny tomboy wasn't her type and she was far too young for her taste.

Shay had been alone for a long time since her breakup. Before that, she'd had a penchant for the willowy and seductive femme fatales, the colder, the better. It seemed to be her cross to bear; as if by selecting heartless beauties, Shay could punish herself before anyone had a chance to punish her first. After her split, and usually after drinks, an occasional friend would tell her she'd followed the same pattern, chosen the same qualities in her domestic partner. Maybe.

Shay looked at the pixie inside the booth and absently considered that she'd actually stand to get treated better by the this eager, sweet tomboy than the harsh women she'd selected in her previous life. But not anymore; not since she'd sworn off love—or anything remotely close to it—including all its sexy preliminaries.

Shay snorted aloud regarding the situation, but poor Lou took it to mean she was dallying. She quickly looked at the agent with wide, apologetic eyes.

"I'm so sorry, Agent Cooper," Lou repeated for the tenth time.

"No worries. Keep at it."

"So…you getting used to this place yet?" Lou made nervous chat as she clacked away at the keys.

"Yeah, you know. Except the weather."

Actually, Shay could care less about the change of weather, but the subject seemed to be on the lips of everyone she'd encountered at the Chicago Bureau so far. She'd become suspicious of even benign inquiries about the weather figuring folks to be poking around for an "in" to find out why Shay had agreed to sign on as Harris's partner. She'd felt staring eyes on her back in the hallway and heard voices drop to whispers in the cafeteria when she passed certain tables. Shay avoided them all, determined to steer clear of water cooler gossip. She wanted to make her own assessment of Harris. If Shay was anything, she was fair.

And now she was starting to get antsy.

"Lou, I've got a meeting in fifteen minutes. Do you think we could somehow—"

"Wait!" Lou cut her off, looked slightly panicked. She snatched up the twenty-pound ring of keys and sorted through them quickly as she exited the booth, calling over her shoulder as she went. "Let me scoot my bike over and you can park in my space."

"That's really not necessary." Shay doubted Lou was listening. She watched the adorable little butch girl jump onto a dangerous-looking green motorcycle. "I'll move your car when I get it straightened out. How's that?"

"Sounds good." But the throaty roar of the bike firing up swallowed her reply. She watched as Lou rearranged her bike then she pulled her Jeep into a narrow leftover space next to it. She got out, grinned and tossed her keys to Lou as she passed by her. "Don't go joyriding, you hear?"

"Thanks, but I've got my own joyride," Lou said through a smile so big Shay could see the young woman's tongue piercing. The agent winced, felt slightly weak as she considered the possibilities. She shrugged it off and laughed.

"You are a handful, kid."

"You have no idea," Lou answered teasingly. She chucked her hands in her back pockets and rocked back on her heels. Her smiling eyes followed the agent all the way out of the parking ramp.

April in Chicago still meant winds that felt like small arctic blasts and Shay began to wonder if she'd turned pansy after just a handful of years in tropical weather. She pulled her jacket tightly around her and considered the day ahead, which gave her even more of a chill. Not only had she been suckered into a hellish partnership, but the Bureau valued her return so much they couldn't even remember to register her car with the parking attendant. So far the score appeared to be two-zip, the Bureau.

If anyone had told her a month ago she would be where she was now, she would have had them drug tested. She'd gone from days spent pursuing drug leads and lining up busts to days spent dodging evil looks and combating sarcastic replies from her partner to even the simplest inquiries, like, "Nice weather, huh?"

Shay hustled up the front steps and flashed her badge at security posted beyond the heavy glass doors of the employee entrance. It was the same guy every morning, perkier than anyone had a right to be at eight a.m.

"How's it going, Agent Cooper?"

"Good, thanks."

"The north treating you fair after that year-round summer?"

"Not too bad." She smiled politely as she scooted through the metal detector. She unwound her lanyard, looped it around her neck and adjusted it below her collar before making her way toward the first bank of elevators.

Of her first week, she'd spent three days just getting them resituated in their new office space, organizing, and, frankly, laying down the law with her partner. She figured if Agent Harris insisted upon acting like a child she'd give her childish boundaries. As for the punishment of not staying within the boundaries, Holloway had taken that matter into his own hands: if Kate Harris chased Shay out of the place, she was to tender her resignation at the Bureau. Period.

That was a little tough, Shay figured. Still, his announcement of punishment gave her plenty of leeway to establish new guidelines for working together, a system that had earned her even scarier glares from her new partner.

The first set of elevator doors parted to reveal a dozen starry-eyed interns on a tour. Coop smiled, gave a polite wave of dismissal, and waited for the next car. She was in no mood to field questions from wannabes on this day, ironic since that's exactly the mood she'd been in this time last month working at the Academy. How quickly everything had changed. Now she had to reserve her patience and wise tactics for her partner.

Shay had wanted to find out about Agent Harris's former partner, Tony Williams, but details about him were still heavily guarded since he was the target of an investigation, albeit a closed one. Anyone caught even peeking into his file would surely be brought in for questioning by Internal Affairs, and Shay wasn't in a hurry to reacquaint herself with that department. Instead, she'd been forced to eavesdrop on a bit of office gossip to help her paint a picture of the missing agent.

It seemed Agent Williams was a stubborn egomaniac who, like Harris, had chased away one partner after another during his first year at the Bureau. Why Kate "stuck" was anybody's guess. The only legitimate information Shay could access was his original application, which consisted of normal pre-hire screens and references. It wasn't much.

Another door opened revealing an elevator car crammed full of suits, all men. Coop pressed her body into the mix and stared at the mirrored doors as they closed. Tall and lean and also in a suit, she could have very well been mistaken for one of them at first blush. But her facial features had an unmistakable softness to them and her jagged haircut had a tendency to curl into soft, wispy ends by the day's end. She studied their reflections, noted the ones whose gaze lingered on her the longest, summarily formed and dismissed notions of connections they may have to Tony Williams's disappearance. Yes, it could have been an inside job. And yes, she was becoming paranoid.

Shay had pondered the dynamics of the Harris-Williams partnership and their extremely low solve rate. True, cold cases were tough, but Shay wondered how, as a tenured agent, Williams could remain employed without delivering any numbers to speak of. It didn't feel right.

It felt even more wrong that Williams name was mentioned

in several criminology textbooks for his ability to crawl inside the criminal mind. Because of this talent, he'd become somewhat legendary at the Academy. She herself had used some of his papers in preparing her lectures. But honestly, to Shay it seemed as if he was all talk, no walk. So, what was the threat? Who wanted him gone?

When Williams vanished clean off the face of the earth, his status had been elevated into that of a ghostly hero, and all talk about his virtually non-existent solve rate vanished right along with him. Shay was sure that Kate was more to him than just his work partner, though she'd yet to determine the exact nature of their relationship. Moreover, she suspected Kate was still working his disappearance on the sly.

The elevator doors parted and Shay hustled through the throngs of agents on their way to morning meetings. She pretended to study something on her phone to politely avoid making eye contact with anyone. People were really far too curious about her. With some relief, she reached their office and made her entrance, unnoticed by her partner. Kate was quietly sitting at her desk, a curtain of blond hair obstructing Shay's direct view of her face. She stole a few moments to study the woman before clearing her throat to initiate morning niceties.

"Good morning, Agent Harris." Shay forced a small smile, even a slight trill into her voice.

Momentarily startled by the greeting, Kate recovered and issued an obligatory reply. "Agent Cooper."

Shay sauntered over to her own desk, casting occasional glances in her partner's direction. Kate's hair had been purposely blown straight that morning, which nicely complemented her rigid posture, completing a nice back-the-hell-off package. Kate felt her stare. When their eyes met, Kate rolled hers.

Shay grinned. "Good. We got that out of the way."

Harris glared at her. "Excuse me?"

"The eye-roll thing." Shay wagged her finger. "I usually don't get that until around noon." Shay hefted her briefcase onto her desktop and unsnapped it. She continued as she arranged paperwork onto her desktop. "Maybe we can expedite the insults and nasty looks and actually get something done today, hmm?"

"I suppose you think you're funny."

"Do I think it's funny that you spend so much time winging arrows my direction and I spend so much time deflecting them that we don't get a thing done?" Shay finished organizing, took a seat behind her desk and clasped her hands in front of her. "I don't find that funny. I find it a waste of time."

Kate turned her attention back to the work spread out before her. Shay's eyes roved over the spread, but Kate quickly drew it around her like a tiny fort. Shay tried to ignore the childish reaction.

"I'll just assume that's not the file on our guy, right?" Shay was referring to the paperwork they'd been waiting on for a newly assigned case.

"No, it's not," came her quiet answer without even a glance in Shay's direction. Though the new office had been significantly upgraded from the windowless crypt, the dead quiet and dark atmosphere had miraculously remained. Kate Harris harbored so much pain, it could be felt from across the room. Four weeks ago, her apparent anguish was mildly touching; now it was borderline annoying and downright pathetic at times. Shay was tired of the woman's secrecy and self-imposed exile.

Perhaps she could let it go, let her heal—do whatever she needed to do. But she'd caught Kate reviewing long-retired leads from her former partnership without even the courtesy of consulting with her new partner. Each time this happened, Shay was again forced to define what a partnership was. In turn, this would prompt Kate to remind her they wouldn't be partners for much longer. And what the hell was that supposed to mean?

It made Shay so angry, she found it necessary to take little mental escapades just to remove herself from the seemingly hopeless situation. Like now. In her mind, she wandered back to Miami, made it a weekend morning, sitting on the wooden deck of her little houseboat which was permanently docked in Cray's Marina on the cusp of Key Biscayne. She was sipping coffee, having a smoke.

The image wasn't serving her very well this morning, and now she was craving a cigarette. Anyway, she'd given it all up—the boat, the Floridian sunrises, even cigarettes, thanks to her doctor's strict orders. She'd taken it a step further and had resigned herself to the freezing north, enduring an even crueler brand of cold being dealt by her frigid partner.

"Yeah, things have really worked out well," she absently mumbled aloud. Kate shot her a puzzled look, but Shay only shrugged and changed the subject. "What are you working on there? Anything you want me to take a look at?"

"It's nothing."

Being that it was Friday, Shay decided to press her luck. "The same nothing you were working on Monday? I believe it was the missing child case in Peoria? Or Tuesday's look at the body washed up last year in Rock Ridge? Those kinds of nothings?"

Kate seemed annoyed that she knew any of these things. "Doing some extracurricular detective work, Agent Cooper?"

"No more than you are," she immediately answered.

Kate closed the file folders, stacked them together and laid them neatly upon her desk. "I believe there might be more rats aboveground than there were in the basement."

Having already heard a similar remark from Holloway, Shay was increasingly uncomfortable with the obscure insinuations.

"I'm not a rat," she quietly put in.

"So you say," Kate muttered.

"I'm not asking you to trust me. I'm asking you to let me in." Shay kept a low, reserved tone. "Tell me what you're working on and why, and maybe I can be of some help."

"Or maybe you could file a report about it with Uncle Roger." Kate issued her a tight smile. "You do know he's my uncle, right? I'm sure you know too much about me already."

Shay shifted slightly in the hard wooden chair. "The only information I'm interested in is what you tell me yourself, but you're not talking. Now, there's always water cooler gossip, but is that what you want me to know about you?" When there came no answer, Shay shrugged. "And for the record, tattletale reporting to Holloway isn't my style."

Kate's interest was hardly piqued. Her follow-up inquiry sounded bored as hell. "And what is your style?"

"I just ask." Shay leaned forward onto the desk. "So, what's on your mind, Agent Harris? What are you working on? What do you want me to know about you?"

For once, Shay had her partner's brief, but full attention. With that curtain of hair parted and the sun softly coming in from the window behind her, she was able to see Kate's face for the first time in days. She looked tired, sad, dark half-moons under her eyes; she looked like hell. Shay's insides turned to gelatin as her guilty conscience kicked in, though she tried to fight it every inch of the way. Damsels in distress were not her specialty. In fact, she preferred an adversary in the office, it kept her competitive, sharp, tough...

What would she do with this wide-eyed, seemingly hateful, yet sad woman? Shay felt simultaneous softness and anger brewing within her. The unidentifiable emotion made her feel queasy, downright lightheaded. She glanced at her watch and quickly stood up, faked a stretch, mindful of her suddenly unsteady stance.

"Morning meeting," Shay practically grunted. She crossed the small office floor and pushed through the door and held it open expectantly for Agent Harris to join her. "Come on, we'll talk about this later." And when Shay realized her tone had gone as soft as her insides, she summoned a terse sound, added, "And we will talk about it."

Though Kate's anger had been momentarily deferred, it flared again upon hearing Shay's order. She rose from her seat, drew her sweater more tightly around her, and glared at her partner all the way to the door. Shay drew in a breath and tightly held it. That same subtle scent assaulted her senses as she passed. *Baby powder? Lavender?...Vanilla?* She craved an insult from those sweet lips—a curse, slur—*anything* to get her libido back in check. Shay was so desperate to regain her rigid self-control, she was willing to spearhead the effort and lob the first jab. She prepared herself to do as much, but thankfully, didn't have to.

"I have no interest in telling you anything about me now or later, Agent Cooper."

Shay expelled such a deep breath of relief her head bobbed toward her chest. *That's right, mermaid girl, keep 'em coming.*

She heard the stern sound of Kate's clicking heels grow

fainter as she walked down the hall toward the elevator. Shay proceeded to take her sweet time locking the door behind them, then double-checked it. Hello paranoia. She turned to see her partner in the distance, still waiting for the elevator. She studied the woman's slight form, lean, muscular calves emerging from pointed toed, two-inch heels, and nice figure, evident despite the sweater draped over her fashionable dress. Suddenly a strange notion occurred to Shay about the league of "former partners" Roger had mentioned.

It was quite possible that those countless departures had less to do with Harris's meanness, and more to do with wounded male pride. Kate had obvious....*assets*, and she'd taken "hard to get" to an impossible level, probably slaughtering fragile egos all over the place. It made Shay angry just thinking about it, and that was a good thing. That anger coupled with Kate's razor sharp tongue was crucial for this partnership to survive.

Discontent was Shay's secret weapon. It propelled her forward, got things done. She wasn't proud that she knew this about herself. She walked toward the elevator, her eyes trained on her partner, drawing strength from each step she took toward her. She recognized that Kate had discontent, too, but her partner was too inexperienced to do more than to simply suffer hurt from it and retaliate with puny blows.

Shay considered her "mission of rehabilitation"—as Roger had phrased it. She wondered if teaching Kate to use her hostility to their benefit was what the AD had in mind. She could do that, all right. The Bureau would surely love it if she cured the woman by turning her into a similarly broken, heartless robotic agent. Like herself.

The thought of it gave Shay enough anger to fuel the whole day.

CHAPTER SIX

It was the kind of week that made tolerating rookie stunts at the Academy look like a cakewalk. Friday, nearly six o'clock, and Shay cruised back down the hallway on her way to the office. She jiggled the doorknob, but found it locked. She sighed and rummaged through her pockets until she found her key and jammed it in the deadbolt. Inside the place was dark, and her partner's desk was empty. Of course. She'd probably been gone since five, if not earlier.

Instead of fleeing the office for the hard-earned weekend, Shay took a moment to enjoy the rare peaceful mood in the office. Generally, despite the quiet, the terse atmosphere was anything but peaceful. It was almost effective in keeping Shay's bizarre dreams of late at bay. These were disturbing scenarios, weaved by her newly reemerged Eros, and of course they starred

Kate Harris. At first she found the fantasies mildly amusing; that was before they'd evolved into a full-fledged-self-destructive sleep pattern she couldn't seem to cure. If her guard was low, the dreams would sneakily follow Shay to the office, and wait with bated breath until she could catch Kate unaware for her increasingly creative study. In her mind's eyes, she could see messy, morning-after mermaid hair falling across pillows...

Shay roughly rubbed her forehead, tried to purge the insanity. She turned her thoughts toward reviewing her day, particularly the last hour she'd spent in Holloway's office. They'd been discussing a tip left on the Bureau hotline pertaining to an old case about a former senator's daughter. She'd disappeared back in the early eighties, at a time when Shay's career was focused less on crime fighting and more on passing a grade school math quiz. For Shay, the crime sparked a more personal memory of her own mother's reaction to the crime. It had shocked her that a prominent citizen's daughter had been swiped right out of her own college dorm room, in broad daylight, never to be seen, or heard from, again.

Her mother's fascination with the case bordered on morbid. She'd combed the TV channels every morning and evening and bought every newspaper with a headline about the missing young woman. Perhaps she was obsessed. Or perhaps, like Shay, injustice made her edgy. In a sickening, ironic twist, Shay's mother presumably met her own violent demise only a handful of months after the young woman's disappearance. The memory of it now inspired only anger within Shay. She hated it that her mother had spent so much of their precious remaining time together glued to the damned TV news. She supposed it was a hard-earned lesson containing all the clichés about not knowing what the future holds and enjoying each moment while you can.

Her mother's alleged death was newsworthy for a few minutes, news that paled in comparison to the continuing coverage of the senator's daughter. Soon enough folks stopped talking about the little girl from Lincoln Park whose only family vanished while she was at school. Her mother's body was never recovered. Incidentally, neither was the senator's daughter, and Shay supposed that with the socioeconomic and societal differences between the women, there was probably no real connection other than timing.

Shay vividly recalled the details of her house that afternoon, a young cop puking his guts out, blood all over the wall and floor of the foyer. She remembered overhearing detectives saying there was too much blood for any human to have survived. They were satisfied with their assumption that a mysterious intruder had killed her mother. As nothing was missing, the subject of robbery was taken off the table. Whispered words kept her from hearing the accompanying details of their suspicions about a sex crime possibly gone horribly wrong. Even to this day, it made no sense to Shay. The only thing she knew was that her mother was gone.

As for Shay herself, her father had bailed on her before she was born and there was no "Uncle Roger" to be a pinch-hit parent. There was certainly no inheritance to lure any gun-shy relatives out of the woodwork. In the end she was shuffled through the dreaded Child Services system, a process she wouldn't wish on any kid.

She wondered what she was doing back in her home state, an hour from where the grisly crime had happened all those years ago. Worse yet, why was she laboring over missing persons cold cases? It was a perfect recipe for flashbacks from hell. She wondered if the Bureau knew about her childhood. If not, she'd been successful in keeping at least one secret from them. There was a file on her mother, she knew that; however, she'd never dared even a glimpse at it for fear of setting off all the bells and whistles that come with having contact with personal cases. If the Bureau knew, they would strictly forbid her from reviewing the case. She knew this from a different, more recent, brush with tragedy.

She felt compelled to check into the anonymous tip about the senator's daughter, if for no other reason than as a strange ode to her lost mother. But there was protocol to be followed, and Shay's days of forging ahead, gung-ho for any case, were over. These days she did everything by the book, utilizing complete transparency. No matter the personal ties, even this case would wait for the proper go-ahead papers.

She was secretly glad the papers hadn't come across today anyway. On this day she was prepared to go home, go for a run, hit the shower and chill out. She was contemplating breaking in her new barbecue grill as she headed for the door. She grabbed her jacket and cruised past Harris's desk where she caught a glimpse of a large red envelope. She stopped in her tracks, snatched it up. It had both their names on it. She unwound the clasp and dumped its contents onto the desktop.

There it all was, in black and white. The case was officially theirs. She quickly checked the time stamp on the front of the envelope. It had been delivered three hours earlier and she recognized the wide, looping acceptance signature as that belonging to her partner. Kate was fully aware that they'd gotten their paperwork. Surely she had not gone home for the weekend?

Volcanic fury plumed up inside Shay as she picked up her cell phone and hit autodial. She figured she should have counted to three, taken a few deep breaths—anything to get her rising temper back in check. As it was, there was real risk that her anger might erupt at the precise moment Harris answered the phone. Four rings later, Shay skipped all introductions and burst into inquiry.

"Agent Harris, did you forget anything this afternoon?"

Her partner sounded genuinely caught off guard. "Pardon?"

Shay employed the count-to-three tactic—better late than never. She swallowed down everything she wanted to unload on the woman, considered that things might not be as they so clearly appeared to be. Plus, Kate sounded terrible. Shay softened her tone, selected her words carefully, and reframed her attack.

"I see that you signed for the Lanterman case file. So knowing that we've been waiting on it all week, and that we'd like to get started on it as soon as that paperwork came through, I imagine you are on your way back here having gotten…coffee…?"

A sigh could be heard down the line. Kate cleared her throat a little. "Sure."

"Very good. I'll get things going on this end." Then, so she didn't sound like she'd gone terribly soft, Shay added, "See you back here with that coffee, sunshine."

It was her new sarcastic nickname for her partner. She could practically hear Harris seething down the line, and hearing that bit of anger gave her some consolation about kissing her own peaceful weekend goodbye. She hung up, peeled off her jacket, rolled up her sleeves and waited.

When the line went dead, Kate glanced at the clock on the bedroom floor. She'd been asleep only half an hour. She felt dizzy and disgusted with herself, the flip-flops going on in her belly had nothing to do with the baby's typical squirmy movement. She was sick.

She drew back the covers and looked down at her remaining half-business ensemble. She'd left a trail of her heels and skirt all through the house on her way to lay down. She hefted her aching legs off the side of the low mattress and breathed in a whiff of bathroom cleanser that was too strong. Weekly apartment cleaning came with the place, and though she had no furniture to dust or dishes to wash, she was happy to know that she had probably the cleanest toilet in the building. The chlorinated smell of it was nauseating.

She sat a moment, caught her breath and willed her head to quit spinning. She figured whoever coined the phrase first trimester morning sickness should be hunted down and flogged. Well toward the end of her second trimester, her nausea ebbed and flowed all day long.

She grabbed a metal bottle off the floor, popped the cap and took a long swig. She swiped tiny beads of sweat off her forehead. A pounding headache hammered out accompaniment to her noisy stomach. As the mattress was lying on the floor, it wasn't a far reach as she toed her skirt and dragged it toward her. Begrudgingly, she slipped it back on and with some teetering, slowly stood up. She stared at the heels from hell carelessly discarded near the doorway. Not one to adhere to dress code anyhow, she abandoned them in lieu of a pair of flat sandals. She grabbed her bag and headed for the door, silently cursing all the way to the parking garage.

CHAPTER SEVEN

Kate Harris emerged from her apartment building more casually dressed then he was used to seeing her look. Her businesslike white blouse wasn't up to its usual crisp standard, and the creased tails dangled on the outside of her characteristically fashionable short skirt. She wore sandals, had ditched her jacket, and had a bag slung over her shoulder. Sunglasses protected her eyes, but he guessed she'd look as tired as she had all week. Strange. Despite everything he knew about her by now, he wondered if she was truly mourning her lost partner.

She'd been sleeping, as she did so much of lately. He knew from the tiny bird's-eye view he'd established for himself more than a month ago. The device under her car would track her every move and report it to his cell phone navigation system. But the office, that was another story. He'd had no way of knowing she'd be exhumed from her deep quarters. Agent Shay Cooper had insisted upon it, and worse, she didn't allow anyone into their new office. She was fanatical about keeping the place locked up tight, even for a simple trip to the bathroom. Paranoia. Must be a side effect of having lived in New York all those years.

He dropped his binoculars and they thudded a hollow sound against his chest. He leaned back on the balcony of the apartment he had rented across the courtyard from Agent Harris's place, under a different name, of course.

"Boring bitch," he muttered to himself. He was itching to move on, get something else going. He had a whole new life ahead of him. He felt like he'd been given wings and he was anxious to try them out. But it was Harris's partner who had him nervous. From his careful study of her life, and his newly emerging refined instincts, he figured he knew Agent Cooper too well. And because of this, his gut instinct told him to take no chances. It told him to wait and see.

CHAPTER EIGHT

"I take it this is not a typical hot-rocking Friday night for you."

Shay's words were the first to penetrate the silence that hung between them. They were commencing hour two of their stakeout in the west quadrant of Glen Park. Shay spat a sunflower shell out the window, took another peek through the binoculars and then set them back on the console between them. A piece of shell stuck to her shirt and she flicked it off, her eyes fixed on the same antiquated phone booth at the end of the parking lot.

Kate maintained her end of the silence from the passenger's side of the forest green Jeep. Night sounds infiltrated the open vehicle—spring peepers and an occasional evening elderly walker shuffling past. The only other noise was the steady cracking and discarding of sunflower seeds. By now there was a good-sized pile of shells below the driver's side door.

Shay had effectively ignored her partner's evil stares about the repetitive shelling, but figured it preferable to smoking, her former vice during stressful times. A look from Kate said a thousand words, which was good, because she herself did not. But Shay had tired of their mutual bout of silence.

She made a second attempt at initiating conversation. "Not much of a talker, huh?"

"Not when I don't have anything to say."

"Fair enough." Shay nodded. "Is it that you don't have anything to say, or that you don't have anything to say to me?"

Kate paused a beat. "Can't it be both?"

Shay thrust her empty hands out the window and brushed them together until the shell pieces and salt were gone. She wadded up the empty sack and crammed it in the cup holder next to her. She could swear she saw Kate breathe a sigh of relief.

"I suppose it can be whatever you want it to be." She shrugged, added, "It's your game."

Shay turned slightly in the driver's seat and leaned around to reach the back floorboard. She snagged a fresh bag of seeds from a knapsack situated there.

"Jesus." Kate rolled her eyes. "What are you—a squirrel?"

Shay grinned, and made a big play of tearing the new bag open and plucking out the perfect seed. She popped it into her mouth. "Cut me some slack—I'm a former pack a day. It soothes my nerves."

"Well, it's getting on mine."

Shay shoved the bag directly beneath Kate's nose. "Want some?"

Kate's nose shriveled, she looked repulsed. "No."

Shay shrugged, pulled the bag back. She tossed a look behind them. "There's other stuff too." She leaned around again, examined the contents in a shopping bag on the back floorboard of the Jeep. "Got granola, pumpkin seeds…dried fruit."

"No." Not no thank you, or thanks anyway.

Shay popped the lid off a tiny cooler. "Iced tea? Lemonade?" But Kate shook her head. "Come on, now. I've got everything in here but the kitchen sink."

Silence festered between them once again until Shay gave

up. She let the cooler lid drop and turned back around in her seat to face forward. Kate quietly picked up the binoculars and aimed them carefully at the old phone booth where the same nothing was still happening.

"Too bad. If you actually had the kitchen sink in there, I could get a drink of water," she mumbled. There was movement in the Jeep and in a split second, an ice-chunked bottle of water was dangling directly in front of the binoculars. Startled, Kate lowered them and timidly accepted the bottle. Shay presented it to her like it was a trophy. Then finally, "Thanks."

Shay, feeling some measure of accomplishment, nodded and shifted to face forward.

"Tell me again why we didn't get a Bureau vehicle," Kate quietly asked.

"Because it would look like a Bureau vehicle." Shay spat another shell out the window. "Besides, might as well be comfortable. Who knows how long we'll be here."

Kate's tired expression said she hoped it wasn't too long. She took a careful swig of water and recapped it, speaking in an absent-sounding, low monotone as she did so, "Plastic ruins the environment. I use polycarbonate BPA-free containers and my own reverse osmosis filter for drinking water. Purchasing bottled water makes no sense whatsoever."

Shay's expression showed evident shock which spiked Kate's annoyance. "What?"

"That's the most you've shared with me about yourself in our entire time together so far."

"I wasn't sharing anything about myself."

"No. You were ass-chewing by way of accidentally sharing something about yourself. I'll take it." Shay arched an eyebrow. "Anything else you want to talk about?"

"No." But Kate quickly seemed to change her mind. "Yes—why do you care about this case so much?"

Shifting gears, Shay felt her normally protective cover slip into place. Always guarded, always careful, she feigned absolute disinterest. "I don't care about it any more than the others."

"Yes you do," Kate prodded. "I can see it in your eyes."

Shay blinked, momentarily blindsided by the fact that Kate

even realized Shay *had* eyes. She tamped down a questionable bit of rising panic and shrugged nonchalantly. "I remember it from when I was a kid, I guess. I grew up around here."

But Kate wasn't satisfied. "I grew up around here, and I barely remember it at all."

Shay found herself stammering when she said, "My mom had sort of…a fascination with the case. I guess maybe that's why."

"Who's that?" Kate suddenly sat up straight, alert to movement around their target. Two figures appeared in the distance. "Two guys, right there."

Shay snatched the binoculars away from her for a better look. She made a quick assessment of the pair—mid-teens, mere boys, wearing dark clothes and low drawers that exposed more underwear than jeans. Her posture relaxed as she lowered the binoculars and passed them back to Kate.

"Just a couple of vandals."

They watched as the boys emptied their satchels of multiple cans of paint, and like artists, lined them up carefully on the sidewalk. They went straight to work spraying down the side of an elaborate wooden play structure situated feet away from their phone booth. Kate's jaw gaped slightly.

"Aren't we going to stop them?"

"Not our jurisdiction, sunshine." Shay shrugged and added, "Besides, they're not taggers. They're just expressing themselves."

"They're defacing public property," Kate went on. "Lots of society ladies spent time and energy raising the money and labor to build that play yard. It was in the newspaper."

"And I'm sure those same little society ladies will delight in doing it all over again in the name of corruptible youth."

Kate stared at her. "That is a terrible, cynical thing to say."

"No. What's terrible is how much folks with money spend on dresses and social extravaganzas to raise cash to build a measly play yard." Shay waved her hand toward the structure which was becoming more colorful by the moment. "If they just cut the caviar and wardrobe budget, they could do ten times their do-good projects. Of course, then they couldn't sprain an elbow patting themselves on the back or see themselves smiling from the society pages." Shay wound down her fierce lecture, but not before adding, "And *that*, my friend, is mocking the commoners, which is far worse than any cynicism I can conjure up."

The silence between them was thick and when Shay turned to see Kate, she was staring at her, wide-eyed at her unexpected monologue. And she looked…troubled. Shay wondered how her partner could act like she cared about nothing at all, yet be so obviously bothered by vandals defacing a play structure.

"Christ…" Shay mumbled. She rolled her eyes and patted her waistband to indicate her concealed sidearm, leaned forward slightly. "You want I should go shoot them?"

Kate rolled her eyes and turned away. "Don't be ridiculous."

"Shall I arrest them for being punks?" She settled back in her seat when her question went unanswered.

They watched as the boys worked under the dim park light across the lot. As a finale, they blazed an oversized rainbow across a dark, crying sky and Shay figured they probably considered it a political statement of some sort. She tipped her head slightly to one side as she considered it. "Not bad, really. Kind of artistic."

"It's vandalism."

Shay's hand went to the car's door handle. "Fine. I'll go over and chase them off."

"Would you just forget I said anything?"

She would not. "But I have to warn you, that one there—" Shay pointed out the one with the lowest riding jeans ever, "—he's going to lose his britches inside a five foot getaway. He'll probably trip and fall and then sue everyone—including your society ladies. Ask yourself if the government can afford that kind of negative publicity."

"Forget about it, I said." The second protest was delivered with a shaky undertone that said she was stifling a laugh, and Shay knew she'd made the smallest possible achievement with her partner. She softened somewhat, felt something brewing inside her akin to delight. Shay had to turn away to avoid getting caught smiling.

They watched as the boys carefully sorted their newly emptied paint cans into nearby recycling receptacles. Shay nodded. "Hmph. Considerate juvenile delinquents."

Under the safe cover of darkness they shared a chuckle and watched as the vandals collected their bags and scrambled up the hill, the low-rider boy clutching tight to both sides of his jeans. "Bye-bye," Shay whispered.

"So, do you see them often?"

Kate's question momentarily bewildered Shay until she moved to clarify herself. "Your parents? Do you see them often now that you're back?"

Suddenly Shay didn't feel like sharing despite whatever information or trust she might gain for doing so. She thought of her mother. Because no body was ever recovered, there wasn't so much as a marker to lay flowers upon. Even the house they'd lived in had eventually been torn down in lieu of hastily assembled, cookie-cutter condos. There was nothing to memorialize the existence of her mother except for her own very early memories. Sometimes even that felt like a dream.

"No, not much," was all she said.

Silence threatened to consume them once again and it took everything Shay had to forge ahead, keep the conversation alive. She heard Roger's voice in her head prompting her with his talk of "agent rehabilitation." Shay knew better than to make similar inquiry about Kate's long-dead parents. She struggled with casual conversation.

"So….what do you do with your time?" Shay scrubbed her forehead, as if she could manually relieve the tension wrinkles that had cropped up there. She had to keep on because Kate had come so far. *What am I—an on-site psychologist?* She rolled her eyes at own internal ramblings and pushed onward. "You know, when you're not working."

"Not much."

"Surely you have something or someone to occupy your time." She was aware that she was dancing along that line that demarcated personal space—and maybe to satisfy her own curiosity. She wanted to know if Kate had been involved with her former partner, but her methodology seemed terribly obvious and she felt obligated to soften her query. "Dog or cat…something like that? Something to look forward to at the end of the day?"

Kate's admission was unrehearsed, quiet. "I actually don't have a lot to look forward to these days."

"That's morbid." It was out of Shay's mouth before she could stop herself. She drummed her thumbs on the steering wheel. The park was dark and the chill night air had chased all the evening walkers back to their cars. Their target was quiet. Shay turned the key in the ignition and the Jeep roared to a start. "Let's call it a night."

Kate's relief was abundantly evident. She adjusted her seat and refastened her belt as they backed out of the parking lot. Shay veered the Jeep down the frontage road to the park's exit, then steered them into two lanes headed for the freeway.

"Torturing me," Shay said at last, breaking the spell of silence that had settled around them. She merged the Jeep into the main stream of traffic.

"Pardon?" Kate was caught off guard by the odd statement.

"You can always look forward to torturing me." Shay shrugged in the semidarkness. "I can see that it brings you such pleasure. That's got to be good for something."

Streaks of moonlight and sporadic highway lighting filtered in through the open roof, casting blue shadows across mermaid hair and a poorly concealed, slow-growing smile. It was through these sly glimpses at her partner that Shay discovered Kate was beautiful when she laughed.

The glorious sound would provide Shay's dream-weaving subconscious fodder for nights to come.

CHAPTER NINE

Kate Harris remained in bed an hour longer than usual. Plagued with nausea, she wondered if she could possibly overcome it long enough to make the fifteen-minute drive into work. If so, could she possibly manage the rest of the day in her condition?

Her bag was just where she'd pitched it after the previous night's stakeout. She leaned out for a hard reach, snagged it, and dragged it toward the mattress. She fished out her cell and stared at it. Kate had never called off work before.

On a weekday, she figured she would have called Roger's secretary to inform her. But this was the weekend. She sighed, punched the autodial button for her office extension with plans to leave a brief voice mail. She was pondering her message when the line suddenly picked up.

"Cooper, here."

The sound of her partner's voice dismantled every lie she was mentally concocting. Suddenly, Kate's voice was gone.

"Hello?" Cooper repeated with less patience. Kate was used to inspiring annoyance out of her partner by now. She sat up in bed and lightly cleared her throat.

"Agent Cooper?"

"Harris?" Cooper said down the line. They sounded like they were taking roll. "You sound like hell, sunshine."

Shay Cooper's true concern relayed itself loud and clear, something that made Kate feel uncomfortable and comforted at the same time. An emotional oxymoron, she figured, and she moved the necessary conversation forward with an unqualified lie.

"I'm fine." Kate forced a confident tone. "But I'm afraid I can't say the same for my car. There seems to be no starting it today."

Normally Shay would have volunteered to pick her partner up—anything to get on with the job. But something about Kate's tone was forced, downright flimsy. She found herself nodding, then heard her shrink's voice reminding her to use words.

"Take care of your car, by all means."

"How will my absence effect your stakeout?" Kate couldn't believe she was disappointed about her partner's willingness to work without her that day. She wondered if her presence was required at all.

Shay eclipsed that suspicion. "You mean *our* stakeout? No worries, it will be fine."

Kate hesitated, then asked, "Why are you in the office so early?"

"Catching the worm, reviewing some files," Shay casually reported.

Kate was struck with a bevy of paranoid notions. "For the purpose of...?"

"You've got the jump on me, Harris. You know your way around these cases. Thought maybe if I gave them a look, you'd let me in on some of your adventures."

Kate didn't like sharing files. Her cheeks grew suddenly flushed and she wondered if it was her fever or her fear. "They're hardly adventures."

Shay guiltily relished the fact that she'd be working alone for the day. Agent Harris inspired something inside her that she couldn't pinpoint; and that uncertainty made her uncomfortable. Shay's relief felt more obvious by the moment. So was her unexpected compassion.

"I've been thinking about that. You're heavily invested in these cases and I come along and crash your party." Shay chuckled. "Look, I'm former Narcos and we only operate on two settings—hot and boil. Might not be the best approach for Missing Persons. You're different, Harris. You let things simmer before you do anything about them."

Suddenly Kate heard herself defending her new partner's work habits. "I don't think there's anything wrong with your investigative tactics, Agent Cooper."

"Look, both our tactics are solid. They're just different, that's all." Again, Shay heard her shrink's southern drawl in her brain prattling on about the art of compromise. She blinked it away, put it in her own terms. "Maybe if I get myself up to speed on these cases you won't consider me dead weight to drag around."

Kate was momentarily stunned into silence. It was true that she wanted her partner to feel so left out that she just *left*. To her dismay, the vindictive groundwork she'd laid to make this happen wasn't serving up the anticipated rewarding payoff. Agent Cooper was annoying, but she was staying, and now she was even trying. Kate had never been regarded as anyone's equal before. She sighed and her voice was heavy with unexpected contrition. "I apologize for having made you feel that way."

"No worries." Shay could be heard shuffling paperwork and Kate wondered what new knowledge the woman would be armed with by the next time they were face to face. The anxiety surrounding it worsened her already lousy condition. Shay seemed to detect this. "So, you get some rest and I'll see you tomorrow, deal?"

"Right," Kate absently agreed before realizing that her partner had called her ill-disguised bluff. Kate perked up, and healthily reinforced her earlier lie. "I'll see if I can get my car into the shop."

"Of course." Shay carefully selected her words. "Maybe get

some qualified person to check things out. And Harris, don't try to drive it until you're sure everything's in working order, got it?"

Kate closed her eyes and felt too horrible to itemize and debate the double meanings. She simply said, "Goodbye, Agent Cooper."

Shay hung up and stared at the phone a bit longer. Harris sounded funny to her, but then again, she usually did. She selected four thick files, grabbed her jacket and left the office.

In her Chicago apartment, Kate nestled more deeply into the blankets and shifted positions again. She punched a pillow into shape, adjusted it until it padded her barely-there belly. She thought about the ridiculous car conversation, but figured Shay was right. She should go to the doctor, but she was starting to feel like she was crying wolf to the OBGYN every week. Each time they gave her an IV and warned her against dehydration. Her doctor had quietly, sweetly implied self-sabotage due to what was obviously depression. Try as she may, Kate couldn't sound convincing enough when she told the woman she was eating and drinking enough. The pain continued and was, at times, unbearable.

All this had Kate preoccupied with karma and she wondered if her troubled pregnancy was payback for the only indiscretion she'd ever committed. Of course when it was a doozy, of that magnitude, she figured one was sufficient to inspire such backlash. Kate had considered herself to be a pretty good person prior to that event—even generous to a fault. Now, she was linked to what could possibly be the scandal of the decade. She'd been forced to alienate everyone around her—including her beloved Uncle Roger—just to keep her and her baby safe. This was best achieved through off-putting behavior previously uncharacteristic of her. It was tiring as hell. Being bad took too much energy.

She was in too deep, thanks to her idiotic logic and a baby she wasn't even sure she ever really wanted. For this, she figured she deserved to be alone.

Kate laid a hand on her painful, fluttering belly. Funny, but for all the turmoil that tiny baby had created for her, she suddenly wanted him or her more than she could have imagined.

CHAPTER TEN

It was hard to believe she actually missed her partner's foul mood and incessant nagging, but she did. Shay sat alone in the Jeep, Sunday, day three of the park stakeout. Her partner had been a no-show that morning, just like the morning before. It didn't make Shay angry, only curious.

She shelled her umpteenth sunflower seed and popped it into her mouth. She considered that she simply missed the company, but she was a professional loner if ever there was one. Besides, she preferred aloneness to the company that had been offered to her, repeatedly. Another agent, a young guy named James Buchner, had placed half a dozen calls to her already, asking to tag along on her mission. She understood from Holloway that Buchner had true hero worship for Agent Williams. He drank in Williams's theories and served as a scribe of sorts for the missing agent. Apparently now, Buchner was looking for a new hero to fill the void in his work-centered life. Shay had no interest in being the young agent's new mentor.

She brushed the salt off her hands, got out of the car and stretched. The sun was fading, but the day had been warmer than usual. She peeled out of her jacket and tossed it through the Jeep window.

All this "simmering," as she'd earlier referred to it, had her thoroughly restless. Maybe she wasn't cut out for patient chores like people watching or profiling or even forming loose associations. It was true that she liked hard and fast rules just as much as she liked quick action and absolute closure.

Shay dusted the salt off her black jeans and straightened her sweater over her holster. She grabbed her bag of seeds and walked to the park bench near the Jeep, still within scope of the phone booth. She wondered if the whole tip about the senator's daughter had been a hoax. Her mother hadn't been the only one consumed with the case, after all. She plopped down on the bench and breathed in spring air. After today it was back to the drawing board. She popped another seed into her mouth and tossed the shell behind her.

"Face forward, Agent Cooper. Don't turn around."

At the quietly issued command she froze mid-shell, tried her best to utilize her peripheral vision to see who was leaning terribly close behind her left ear. She felt the breath below her short-cropped hair, and wondered if she'd soon feel the muzzle of a gun between her shoulder blades. She coolly selected another sunflower seed and waited for further instruction. The park before her was virtually empty. No witnesses. Great.

"You're the boss," she muttered as calmly as one can with a stranger looming over them.

"Lovely evening, isn't it?"

And her insides sank. In a heartbeat she recognized Len Ortelli's prim, controlled Italian-American accent. The same voice had haunted her dreams for at least five years. The smooth rolling tone was uncharacteristically pristine considering the source: a scumbag, drug-dealing dock master. However, he was far less accustomed to rubbing elbows with the underlings who worked the docks he controlled, and more used to hobnobbing with the society types for whom he supplied designer, highfalutin drugs. Like most individuals sprung from fortunate families, he was properly attired, held himself just so and had been formally and expensively educated. Where on that path to greatness he'd taken a turn toward the underworld was anybody's guess.

Shay dropped the bag of seeds on the ground before her. Fury coursed through her veins with the unexpected feeling of ice water. She prepared to swivel toward him.

"If you turn around, I'll disappear and take my valuable information with me. Do we have an understanding?"

She forcibly pressed her shoulder blades against the seat back, and quietly enunciated each word. "What. The. Fuck."

It wasn't necessary to see Ortelli to feel his seemingly disappointed grimace. She had it memorized by now. He made a clicking sound with his tongue. "Filthy, vile sounds coming from such a nice mouth."

"What gives, Ortelli? Find another kid to snatch? Another life to ruin?" Her pulse quickened as she envisioned his deep olive complexion, dark hair and bushy eyebrows. If he hadn't been such a scumbag, she would have only thought him to be a sensational Dean Martin doppelganger. In his ever-present crisp white shirt and tie, he reminded her of a foreign music conductor who didn't quite know how to dress to fit in with the common audience. She heard herself hiss, "Let me see you. I want to see what it looks like when you answer that question, you son of a bitch."

His tone was stern inside his hasty response. "Kidnapping is not a business practice of mine. I have standards. You and I have had this conversation before."

"You mean you've told me these same lies before," she sneered. "Still diving into rabbit holes, I see. Which one led you here?"

"I came to see you, Agent Cooper. I wanted to make sure you were well after Miami."

"You mean when you left me for dead?"

"The hospital said you'd had an aneurysm."

"So much for medical privacy," she muttered.

"I was quite concerned," he said, ignoring her. "You looked dreadful."

"How'd I look in New York when you snatched my kid away from me?"

"For the last time, Agent, I had nothing to do with Christopher's disappearance." He sounded funny. Breathless. He gasped, seemed to catch his breath, and quickly answered the next question before Shay could ask it. "Nor did I order anyone else to touch the child."

She rested her hand on the sidearm riding her hip beneath the hem of her sweater. "I could kill you right now and wipe my ass on your obituary."

"Everyone knows your history of pursuing me. If ever a car hits me, they'd first check to be sure you weren't behind the wheel." His voice rang with a smile. "You'd lose everything."

She felt she already had. She flipped back the snap of her holster, ran her fingers along cool metal.

"I take it you're the one who dragged my ass out here. You come to tell me where you put my son as a punishment for my putting the whammy on your lucrative 'business collaboration'?" It was the quote made famous in the newspapers during his years' earlier trial.

"Everyone eventually gets the answers they want."

She smirked. "What'd you ever get besides a get outta jail free card and all the cash you could stash away?"

"You ruined me. I had no choice but to make a fresh start."

A pair of arms appeared beside her, rested on the back of the bench. Shay stared at the impeccable camel hair coat sleeves and black leather gloves despite the fact that the day was warmer than usual. He was making a show that he had nothing with which to harm her. If she trusted even that truth, she would have grabbed him and hurled him ass over ears, flat onto the concrete slab in front of her. She forced her glare forward and fully concentrated on not killing him.

He droned on. "Now, years later, you've left it all behind for a fresh start. We're quite a bit alike in that regard. That we're our own worst enemy is just another thing we have in common."

She moved her weapon to a slightly better angle beneath her sweater, tapped her fingertip on the trigger. "I have my gun pointed at you as we speak Ortelli. Get to the point."

"Would you like for me to assault you first? It may hold up better for you in a court of law if things go badly. Again."

"Why are you here? You want me dead?"

"If I wanted you dead, I could have killed you in Miami. I had opportunity. I could have looked you in the eye and completed the job, like a man of honor."

"Honor?" Shay spun around and glared at him, nose to nose. Her voice was a ragged whisper. "Don't you speak to me about honor, you son of a bitch."

He looked momentarily alarmed that she'd broken the only rule he'd laid down. Deep-set brown eyes stared into her own and neither he nor she blinked for several seconds. Shay finally couldn't resist looking him over. His usual sun-kissed complexion was now faded and marred by liver spots. He was pinched and gaunt and his thin, papery lips stretched to their limits when he at last smiled at her.

"Does my appearance startle you, Agent Cooper?"

She stared at him a little longer, contemplating all that she could do with the mere shell of a gangster who'd ruined so many lives before he'd narked out his crew to stay out of prison. It wouldn't take much to kill him. She could toss his worn-out body into the lake where time, tide and whatever hungry thing beneath the murky water destroyed all DNA evidence. But in his present condition he was no challenge to her whatsoever. He'd managed even to rob her of that perverse joy.

"You should be dead." Was all she said.

"I'm a survivalist. Do you know that, Agent Cooper?"

She smirked. "You don't look like you're going to survive much longer."

He grinned at her. "Do you know the difference between a survivalist and a predator?" And when she didn't answer, he continued. "The survivalist never kills more than he requires to live. The predator will kill for that same reason, but he will also kill if his authority or loyalty is challenged. It's more of a sport,
lly."

"So which one did you kill that guy for in Miami? Survival or sport?"

"He stole from me which compromised my income thereby threatening my existence." His tired eyes thoughtfully flitted upward. "I would say survival. Once upon a time, the same motivation drove me to find you. You also compromised my existence by destroying my 'business collaborations'."

He emphasized the phrase as she had, as if they'd shared a joke. Shay didn't twitch.

"And that was my son's price to pay?"

"No. Off limits. And risky, too. With all the criminology advancements today, the average criminal is hardly a fair match."

She lowered her voice. "I never said you were average, Ortelli."

The old man seemed suddenly more anxious and his dark eyes conjured a dull sparkle. "Can you imagine an individual armed with the benefits of science and the instincts of a predator?" And then, "What do you know about the absent Agent Williams?"

She glared at him. Throngs of questions clumsily assembled themselves in her brain, which she hoped to mask with her curt response. "I'll find him."

His eyes hardened. "Agent Williams is not to be found."

"You snatch him too?" She feigned surprise.

"He was a dangerous man," he stated matter-of-factly. "Know what you're up against. Sometimes it's necessary to behave more like a predator than a survivalist if you want to catch one."

"Such valuable advice from you, Ortelli." She forced a sarcastic laugh. "First you want me dead, now you're having a come-to-Jesus moment? You trying to square up with the Big Guy before you die?"

"Find Williams and you'll find your answers." Ortelli's patience had vanished with his grin. "Find Williams and you'll see it's just the beginning."

"Sure," she muttered.

"If you don't, the answers will find you anyway." He whispered, "Don't repeat sins of the past."

"Words, words, words..." she nattered, annoyance in her

voice. She put her back to him, a clear message that she wasn't afraid of him, nor was she taking his warning seriously. She raised her eyes, directed her words at the clouds. "God? Why can't I just kill this son of a bitch?"

"You could but you wouldn't be doing Agent Harris any favors," he said.

In a flash, Shay's hand shot out and clutched Ortelli's coat sleeve.

He could be heard chuckling. "So I do have your interest?"

"Any more of my interest would land you in the morgue."

"Let go," Ortelli demanded. She did so and then watched as he brushed the wrinkles from his sleeve. "It was never about your son. It wasn't about Agent Harris, either. But people and circumstances get in the way."

"Tell. Me."

"Agent Harris and her baby are in danger."

Shay shook her head, started to protest the statement. Harris had no children—in fact she had no one at all. The words had come straight from her partner's lips only days earlier. Shay soaked in Ortelli's meaningless statement. Harris was too angry for kids and moody as hell. She wasn't built for parenthood—the woman was constantly tired appearing, frail and on this day, she was home, sick...

"Oh, no way," Shay muttered to herself. She raked her hands through her hair. "No, fucking, way."

Her eyelids sprang open like window shades. She leapt off the bench and spun around but he was gone. She scanned the grounds, beat her hands through the shrubs and then her eyes returned to the bench where she'd sat only moments earlier with a dried-up mobster leering over her shoulder.

Gone.

CHAPTER ELEVEN

The Critical Incident Response Group had invited them to their latest powwow. The behavior analysts and CIRG functioned under a larger umbrella, the National Center for Analysis of Violent Crime. On occasion, CIRG would invite the profilers into their realm to study the perps CIRG tracked down in order to formulate better profiles for future use. In the end it was considered a big win for everyone.

Coming from what she considered to be the academic side of the program, Shay had never attended such a meeting and she wasn't sure how beneficial she'd be to the team. Especially not on this day when her head was otherwise preoccupied with notions of a baby à la Kate Harris. Was Tony Williams the father? Did someone want Kate dead because she was his partner? Perhaps

Kate was closer to knowing who'd snatched him than anyone knew. Perhaps Holloway was right.

The meeting droned on in the background as she considered her assumptions. If there actually existed a baby, and if Williams was the father, then Holloway was right again—there was a very definite "thing" between Williams and Kate Harris. So many ifs. Shay wasn't used to her gut instinct failing her.

She'd spent the previous night lying awake, counting the months and weeks since the agent's disappearance, calculating how far along Kate's alleged pregnancy would be, and none of it made sense. Kate looked like she could step out of a swimwear advertisement—Shay would be blind not to notice this. There was no way she was hiding at least five months' worth of baby inside her. After running the calculations through her brain a million or so times, she would then fall into troubled sleep only to wake with Ortelli's wretched image in her head. Equally tortuous, but on an entirely different level, were the times she'd awaken with the aforementioned swimwear body in her tired, Kate-addled brain. Wracked with startling desire that bordered painful, Shay would drop back onto the couch, drenched in perspiration.

Altogether, these things conspired to keep her awake for hours. For that reason she was edgy and desperately in need of caffeine this Monday morning.

That Kate was not present at the CIRG meeting shifted Shay's concerns away from the possible Williams-Harris relationship, or baby, and toward Kate's health. The personnel records Shay had accessed said that her new partner hadn't missed a single day in four years. Go figure.

Shay stretched her back and arms with as little commotion as possible. She stifled a yawn and saw that Agent Buchner was eagerly grinning at her from across the crowded room. She issued him a brief acknowledging smile and tried to focus on the speaker of the group in a half-hearted attempted to glean any pertinent information.

CIRG was planning a major drug bust. A months' long sting operation in the worst part of the city had led up to this event. The committee reiterated how fortunate they were to have Shay on their team given her extraordinary history. She was promptly enlisted to lead the operation, something that thrilled the committee much more than it thrilled her.

The CIRG meeting consumed the entire morning which bought Shay a few more hours to fabricate something believable about closing the Lanterman case. Obviously there was no new lead concerning Senator Lanterman's daughter. Shay wondered how Ortelli guessed she'd jump at the chance to take the stakeout.

She'd found it necessary to create a report alluding to a prank or hoax for the Assistant Director, which in reality it had been. Still, she couldn't very well have them know she'd seen Ortelli. She would have to weave a grand, believable lie to have the phone tap and stakeout forgiven, as both were expensive and elaborate efforts. In short, the park rendezvous had her lying to protect her job, which was making her hate Ortelli even more than she thought possible. He'd wasted their time; however, if he was at all right about her partner, Kate's protection would be worth it. So much lying and protecting.

After the meeting, safely back in her office, she was still thinking about it. Shay bounced her pen on the desk blotter, felt the gears cranking in her brain as she fabricated the lie. Even if she could get her boss to buy it, she still had to explain why she'd closed the case to her partner without Kate's input or signature. It was an arrogant move that discounted Kate's participation and Shay would likely take some abuse for it later. For now, Shay wanted to keep Kate as far away from it as possible. She'd figure out how to deal with repercussions when the time came. Her partner's anger about it would be a mere bump in the road compared to what could possibly lie ahead.

If discovered, Shay's visit with Ortelli would still set off all sorts of alarms inside the Bureau. She'd be off the job for sure, and without that job, she might never find out what happened to her own son. Yes, she was thinking about Christopher again. So much for years of therapy. She was chasing too many ghosts.

Shay took a deep breath and blew it out. Fabricating a report wouldn't be much different from altering Bureau records— illegal, but not impossible. She would know, from years of fiercely protecting the memory of her son. It was nobody's business.

Shay scribbled her signature on the last form, stacked the paperwork together, and sealed it inside an interoffice folder for AD Holloway. Next up, another undercover operation probably more risky than the one she'd just signed off on: Shay needed to discover if there was indeed a "product" of the alleged Williams-Harris merger. She needed to know what her partner knew about Williams disappearance and how dangerous it was to have such information.

But not tonight. She was so tired, she hoped she could stay awake for the forty minute drive home.

Agent Kate Harris pulled into the Bureau parking garage shortly after seven. The day had been a total loss and she'd missed the all-important CIRG meeting that morning. Now, well into the evening, she'd come by the office to check for the notes she knew Shay had left for her.

Lou was still in the parking garage booth. The young woman stood a little straighter and issued Kate a polite smile upon seeing her.

"Evening, Agent Harris," she quietly greeted her.

"Don't you ever go home?" Kate handed her a security card.

"The night guy, Kato, is out sick."

"Extra money for you then, I hope."

"That's one way to look at things." Lou scanned the barcode three times, looked frustrated. She went to the keyboard and pecked away.

"The system still giving you trouble?"

Lou made an exasperated sigh. "I keep telling them it's all screwed up, but nobody listens to the parking girl, you know?" She realized she'd lapsed into casual conversation with the agent, a first between them. She wondered if the hard-nosed woman was finally chilling out a little bit. Her attention turned back to her task at hand. She groaned, looked tired. "Nobody's clearing these days. Park in my space again over there, would you? Next to the bike?"

"Sure." Kate gave her a little wave when the gate lifted.

The building was quiet save for the buzzing of vacuum cleaners and the noise of a few late-stayers. Inside her office, Kate quickly found photocopied notes from the meeting in Shay's lefty scrawl. She put them in her bag then checked for telephone messages. She gathered her bag and keys and started to leave when she saw it. A red envelope had been shoved through their mail slot and had drifted to the side of the door. She knelt to retrieve it, and dumped the contents onto her desktop.

AD Holloway had officially closed the Lanterman case. The time stamp said it had been delivered literally minutes earlier. She figured Holloway must be working later than her own partner, which was a rare occasion.

She skimmed it and sighed. The case had been pulled from their office, no surprise. She doubted Shay would take the news well. Shay hadn't worked in this particular division long enough to realize it was commonplace for Holloway to yank a case from beneath them without explanation. She had a feeling Shay was at home, yet probably still hard at work on the details of the now-defunct case.

She admired her new partner's dedication. That, and she seemed reliable. Like leaving the meeting notes for Kate. She quickly retrieved Shay's address from the computer. She owed it to her partner to break the news to her in person.

"Olive branch," she mumbled to herself. Kate stuck the scribbled address into her bag before locking the office door.

The pounding on her front door rousted Shay from her poor sleep. She aimed her fuzzy vision at her watch. Eight thirty. For a moment she wondered if it was still Monday. She stretched and stood to the rhythm of the second round of door-pounding. She wiped sleep from her eyes and inventoried her wrinkled pajama pants and old T-shirt, decided it was suitable attire enough to answer the door. Besides, from the sound of it, the annoyance wasn't going away anytime soon.

"Coming..." she called as she flicked on the small hallway

table lamp and unchained the door. Two locks later and she was staring at Agent Kate Harris. The subject of her late-night musings was standing on her doorstep in the flesh. She tried not to think about the flesh part.

Shay quickly tamped down all extracurricular thoughts and hoped her expression wasn't conveying anything beyond general surprise and mild confusion. She let her in, then briefly stepped onto the stoop to see if hell had frozen over. Shay followed the woman back into the foyer and closed the door behind them.

"I was beginning to wonder if I had the right place." Then, taking her first good look at her partner, Kate was suddenly embarrassed. "I'm sorry, did I wake you?"

"No…" Shay rifled her fingers through her unkempt hair, slightly nodded. "Maybe."

"I should have just called." Kate started for the door, but Shay stepped in front of her before she could make her exit.

"No. Stay." She then took her hand off the doorknob, lest she should come across as controlling. She straightened her posture, folded her arms across her front to hide the vintage pub logo on her sleep shirt. "What's on your mind, Agent Harris?"

Kate was caught off guard by the note of formality. She also stood a little straighter, even cleared her throat to indicate that only business was at hand. But no words came right away, leading Shay to wonder if her partner had something to get off her chest. A confession, perhaps? Eager to give her every chance to make one, Shay motioned toward the hallway.

"I was just about to make some coffee. Want some?"

"Sure," Kate timidly agreed. She allowed herself to be steered through the living room, past a muted television flickering in the dark. A pillow and blanket had been hastily discarded on the couch that faced it.

Shay saw her notice this and continued to nudge her ahead, through the swinging doors, and into the kitchen.

Kate saw that the house was sparsely, yet tastefully, furnished. She stammered, "Nice place."

"Nice and empty," Shay laughed, suddenly nervous. She measured two level spoonfuls of coffee into a filter, and then thought better of it. Was she going to caffeinate a woman who could be pregnant? She went to the refrigerator instead, casting little side glances at her partner on the way. Per her usual, Kate had a long sweater wrapped around her effectively masking her waistline. She turned back to the refrigerator, looked past the beer. "Juice or water?"

Kate smiled. "I thought you said coffee?"

Shay quickly covered for her own error. "It's too late for coffee. We'd be up all night." Then repeated, "Juice or water?"

"Water is fine, thank you."

"Sit down." Shay retrieved the water and headed toward the kitchen table where Kate was standing. "Can I take your sweater?"

"I'm fine." Kate eyed her warily, but took a seat anyway. She accepted the bottle of water. "Thank you."

"No worries."

Shay was pondering her next line of baby inquiry when Kate said, "I wanted to tell you myself before you found out at the office."

Shay felt her pulse quicken. Baby confession?

"I'm all ears, Agent Harris," she encouraged her.

"AD Holloway took the Lanterman case away from us."

Shay stared at her a moment and felt her insides collapse a little. She blinked, waited, nothing. "And...that's what you came here to tell me?"

Kate nodded. "I didn't want you to waste any more time on it. I figured you'd be hard at it still tonight." She glanced at her partner's attire again. "Of course, I didn't figure I'd wake you."

"I said you didn't wake me." Her voice was flat. Shay pulled out a facing chair, plopped into it and stared right through her partner. "Anything else?"

Kate had mastered innocent. "No."

Shay's perpetually neutral expression sometimes worked for her, sometimes against her. For the moment she was grateful for it. How she wished she'd paid closer attention to Kate's waistline before. Truth was, she had spent so much time *not* looking at Kate, she'd gone almost the opposite direction.

"I just wanted to tell you myself before you went back to the office."

"For real? That's it?"

Kate mistakenly took her partner's disbelief to be directed at Holloway and the yanked case. She nodded.

"That's the way these boys work. You'll get used to it." But Shay only stared at her. Kate dipped her head, squinted. "Agent Cooper, is something wrong?"

"I just expected more," she finally said. And it was true.

"Well, you can't fight that system. God knows I've tried." Kate shifted under her partner's intense stare.

"I suppose you only get what people want you to have."

"I suppose."

Silence settled around them in the aftermath of their tricky dance with words. Kate seemed oblivious to it.

Kate grew uncomfortable under her partner's scrutiny. She wondered why she'd intruded in the first place. "I should get home."

"Sure." They both rose, and Shay handed her the bottle of water. "Take this."

Shay followed her to the foyer, ashamed of herself for basking in the wake of the woman's sweet scent. She unlocked the door and stood back to allow her exit.

There was something about Kate, something different from the other women she worked with. Perhaps it was the way she didn't care what men thought of her. She dosed Shay with the same attitude, but Shay wasn't buying it. In fact, she believed that despite her aloof attitude, Kate cared very much what her partner thought of her.

Shay followed her outside. Her bare feet curled slightly beneath her, guarding her from the cold cement step. Her eyes quickly adjusted to the black night and she habitually scanned the street once, twice. She watched as Kate carefully navigated the steps. Her partner turned around once she was on the lower sidewalk.

"Did I do something wrong, Agent Cooper?"

The question caught her off guard as much as the entire visit had. Though Kate hadn't arrived on her doorstep bearing any great truths, Shay got the distinct impression that when she felt safe enough to tell the truth, she would. She wondered if Kate would ever feel safe with her.

Shay shrugged. "Well, Agent Harris, only you know that answer."

Kate stared at her a little longer. "I'll see you tomorrow."

Shay felt her insides sink a little. Despite their progress, it was clear that Kate didn't trust her one little bit. Holloway was probably right.

Kate Harris's trust belonged solely to one person. As did her heart. And more than likely, so did her baby.

CHAPTER TWELVE

There was no falling to sleep after Kate had gone and by midnight, Shay was back at the office. She fired up the computer and sorted through every superficial file on Ortelli to try and discover why he was in Chicago. More importantly, she wanted to find any connection he may have to Agents Williams or Harris. Without deeper diving, requiring passwords and authorization, she found precisely nothing. No surprise.

Ortelli liked to play games. But dragging Kate Harris into the picture and teasing Shay with questions pertaining to the woman's safety—even a baby—certainly changed the dynamics of his usual game. She should know, she'd been studying him for years.

Who wanted Williams gone? Once again, Shay pulled up the very limited file on Agent Tony Williams. She stared at it.

Education. Qualifications. References. She selected the topmost name, Vonda Young, and followed the line to the phone number. California area code. It would be about ten o'clock there. In moments she was listening to an automated disconnect message. She hung up and pondered her next move.

As she knew it would, her gaze floated over to Kate's perfectly organized desk. A calendar, a notebook, a pen that was lying perfectly parallel to the base of her desk lamp.

Shay rolled her chair around her desk and toward Kate's, as if not actually getting out of her chair would make her any less of a snoop. She zeroed in on the side drawers, opened them and rummaged through each before her conscience could kick in. Her treasure hunt yielded paperclips, more pens, a staple remover, a telephone book and a small stack of envelopes. The bottom drawer was locked.

Shay stared at it for several minutes. With some reluctance, she pulled a lock-pick out of her pocket and shoved it into the lock. Yes, she'd brought it with her. The whole night reeked of premeditation. It was too late now. She opened the drawer.

A coffee mug, spare pair of pantyhose, deodorant—the kind of innocent things that make snoopers feel guilty. Not exactly the key to the universe Shay had in mind.

She expelled the breath she'd been holding and scrubbed her hands through her hair until it stood on end. It was cool in the office, but she'd managed to work up a nervous sweat. She thought about Ortelli. It wouldn't be the first time that rat had lied to her. But her instincts told her there was more to the picture than what she was looking at. Of course, her instincts had clued her into other things about her partner—things she couldn't emotionally afford to consider for even a second. Shay wondered if she even trusted herself anymore.

She considered Kate, smart and beautiful, and tried to imagine how she ever got together with Williams in the first place. What made him the perfect match for her? They had had a relationship of some sort that lasted nearly four years. How much of that time had Williams spent earning her absolute trust? Thinking about it had Shay's stomach in knots.

She sighed loudly and drummed her fingertips on the desktop.

If Kate was in some kind of danger, she didn't have four years to gain the woman's trust. God help Ortelli if he was frigging with her. She would kill him for it, if he didn't die sooner of natural causes.

She stared at the drawer, which had produced shallow results and hardly seemed worth locking. *Shallow results.* She removed the coffee cup and thunked the drawer bottom with her knuckle. It sounded hollow. She quickly removed the remaining items and carefully lifted out the false bottom. Well of course. The desk formerly belonged to Agent Williams, notoriously the most narcissistic, paranoid man on the planet. He'd bequeathed the paranoia to Kate, along with his desk, along with God knew what else. She leaned close to the drawer to take a look.

Jackpot. It was a sort of memorial to Tony Williams.

Shay mentally etched the position of each object in her brain for careful replacement afterward. She then went to work carefully removing the items—nameplate, gold monogrammed pens, postcards and a few letters. Then she hit pay dirt: a detailed copy of Williams case file.

"Ho-lee shit," she muttered. Shay moved it to the desktop and carefully laid it out.

It was a complete report with feminine handwriting in the margins, and pictures and notes throughout. Kate had gone all out, spared no detail. While the actual typewritten report was peppered with words like "inconclusive" and "yet to be determined," Kate had handwritten one hypothesis after another. No real leads, an abundance of shaky evidence, a crime scene contaminated by the local PD, and not one eyewitness on record. So much for any hope at gaining additional insight. No wonder Kate was frustrated as hell.

A man had simply vanished one sunny afternoon leaving behind a burned out car. The end.

Included in the file was a phone log dotted with sticky notes. Every detail had been highlighted by Kate. Habit had Shay comparing this Missing Persons case to her son's. There were no similarities beyond the fact that both were gone, and probably both were dead.

Shay put the paperwork back in order. She stared at the

envelopes containing what appeared to be personal letters. She snatched one up, started to open it, but stopped. Kate Harris was a smart woman. If there was even a fraction of evidence in those notes, she trusted the woman had already paid it due diligence. Besides, Kate had an advantage no other investigator did. It appeared she'd been in love with Williams, and love could drive one to extract the most impossibly weak clue out of a perfect patch of camouflage. Shay knew this too well.

She replaced the letters in the drawer along with the other items, just as she'd found them, and secured the false bottom back into place.

Shay's temples throbbed and she rested her forehead in the palms of her hands, breathing deeply. Just what she needed, aneurysm round two. When she reopened her eyes, Ortelli's claim was unexpectedly verified. The proof had accidentally slipped out of the file she'd just replaced and now stared up at her from the floor. She reached down to retrieve it.

She held the four-inch picture against the dim lamp to get a better look. It resembled a three dimensional peach-colored paisley. Shay knew exactly what it was.

As if the ultrasound printout wasn't confirmation enough, small typewritten letters on the bottom edge of the picture spelled it out as plain as the moon in the sky: HARRIS.

Baby Harris.

Something physically shifted inside Shay. A familiar sadness swept through her followed by a powerful sense of protectiveness. A third phase moved in, overwhelming the first two: she was angry.

Chanting the case number to herself, Shay left the office and marched to Evidence Lockup. It was manned around the clock. A guy named Rocco was in charge and he was happy for the few minutes of company. So happy, he talked the entire time she wielded her pen over his clipboard and neglected to notice that she hadn't left a single mark on it. Shay handed it back, thanked him and entered the storage room.

Tracking the case number, she found a small box of Williams' personal effects—a watch, business cards, everything but the man's pocket lint. Shay replaced the lid and read the scribble on the front panel. She cross-referenced it to a different part of storage on a quest for something that was apparently too bulky to fit in the simple ten-by ten-inch box.

Her mind relived the first actual conversation she'd had with Kate. She'd asked Shay point blank if she'd been sent to spy on her or if she had anything to do with the raid on their basement office. Impossible, Shay had assured her, particularly since she'd only been re-employed by the Bureau for a total of six hours at that point. Kate had initially accused her of helping to dust the case. She said they'd taken his briefcase, they'd taken his computer...

Suddenly Shay knew what she was looking for. She tracked the number, found Williams' laptop, and in a well-rehearsed move, popped the back off with the lock-pick. She shoved the hard drive into her jacket pocket. On the way out she made polite conversation with Rocco, careful to make a show of hands, a subtle verification that she'd apparently not taken nothing out of storage.

She drove quickly, but safely home, figuring it would be awfully hard to explain the hard drive and the ultrasound picture she had on her should she be involved in a traffic accident. The Bureau wouldn't study the Evidence Lockup cams unless there was a reason to. She swallowed hard, felt nervous, figured if she was in an accident, it better be good enough to destroy evidence of her theft. That or she should try to die to avoid having to answer for it. Sneaking around made her as paranoid as they said was true of Williams. And though she was willing to try just about anything, Shay was certain that it was the worst possible way to go about gaining Kate's trust.

The night's findings had shed new light on things. For one, she now understood and almost could forgive Kate's wide-swinging moods. The woman was surely a splendid combination of grief and hormones. It also explained unexpected tearfulness she'd witnessed from Kate weeks earlier at a grisly crime scene. She'd excused herself and Shay had quietly followed her into the backyard prepared to chide her for having a weak stomach. But she'd stopped short when she heard the woman's soft cries.

Though Kate was never aware of her presence, Shay had

stayed behind her. She'd felt compelled to indirectly share a sadness that had nothing to do with a dead man at a crime scene, and everything to do with losing someone dear to you.

Safely back in Pleasant, she pulled into her driveway and scanned around her the whole way to the door. All in all, getting the guts to take the computer had been easy. Now she hoped her old talents would return with sufficiency enough to make the theft worth possibly getting fired for. She took her time getting out of the car.

Ortelli's words rolled through her mind for the millionth time.

"Find Williams and you'll find your answers."

She would. If it meant saving her partner—and her baby— from meeting the same fate, she'd find out exactly what happened to Agent Tony Williams.

CHAPTER THIRTEEN

The Watcher made careful study of Agent Shay Cooper's home. He had her pegged as a big-city girl, yet this home was located in a town called Pleasant, home to dog parks and elementary school carpools. How perfectly boring. He didn't know what new information he expected to learn about the agent. He already knew her so well.

He made a quick analysis of her place. A sparse collection of homey furniture said she desired the look of comfort but never made time to enjoy it. Her refrigerator contained a handful of imported beers, which, on an agent's salary, told him she wasn't much of a drinker. A quart of juice and one percent milk said she was at least attempting to be healthy. A second check confirmed the milk had expired the previous week, and he concluded her healthy lifestyle was a work in progress. An empty salad container in the garbage bin—not much of a recycler—and a few frozen single-serving dinners in the freezer said Shay Cooper didn't like to cook. The energy tag still dangling inside the oven confirmed it.

There were two empty but freshly painted bedrooms on the second floor. A larger furnished bedroom was on the main floor. Tags on the mattress, slight dusty sheen on the new headboard. She never slept there. She slept on the couch, the single piece of furniture to show even a miniscule cushion indention. Plus he'd found a folded blanket on a shelf in the laundry room that smelled like her bath soap, so she'd used it recently. There were no photographs, of course, damn the reminders of her past life.

The only room of interest to him was the basement, which must have been another eight hundred squares in itself. Dry and carpeted, it was also freshly painted and could have easily been used for two more rooms had it not been for the network of wires and cables, blinking and flashing above him. The ceiling looked like electronic spaghetti that ran for miles.

Techno clutter littered every square inch of flat space of the electronic haven—keyboards, drives, routers and outdated mainframes. It was clear that Shay Cooper had more than a passing interest in computers. That was probably how she'd so efficiently erased every juicy personal detail from the Bureau's network. Maybe she just wanted to play it close to the vest. Or maybe her ego wouldn't allow anyone else to know how thoroughly she'd been ruined.

The Watcher figured she was out for the night, probably to some lesbian bar in the city. He knew she'd had a fetching domestic partner in New York, a pretty, albeit quirky-acting thing, lean and tall with coppery hair and green eyes. His thoughts inevitably went to the couple's child, a case he had also become familiar with.

The sound of a car pulling into the driveway snapped him back to present. He didn't panic, but calmly assessed his surroundings for the best exit. He selected his window. In a well-rehearsed move, he deftly snipped the wires and twisted tinfoil around each end effectively fooling the security network into thinking it was still a full circuit. The Watcher popped the narrow window out and shimmied through it. Outside, he replaced the glass and then the screen, made it look like it had never happened.

He'd taken his time inside the home, but not enough time to plant his electronic eyeball. There was probably no need for ongoing monitoring, but just to be safe, he'd return again. The Watcher thought about the basement and that got him thinking about a way to get back "in" without ever actually setting foot back onto the premises. He formed the thought in thirty seconds, could execute the plan in less than ten minutes, and this time tomorrow night, he would be having some good fun with the agent all while keeping tabs on her. Just in case.

It was ridiculously easy.

CHAPTER FOURTEEN

Shay found her partner just as she did each morning, hunched over her desk, nose buried in paperwork. But the air in the office was different. Shay gave the place a once-over, saw that it looked fine, and that it did not appear obvious she'd been nosing through Kate's personal belongings the previous midnight. Maybe the difference in the air was her own guilt. She dropped her briefcase on her desktop and shrugged out of her jacket.

Kate was still suffering strange feelings from having shown up at her partner's home the night before. She took Shay's odd glances in her direction as verification that yes, it had been awkward. So much for the olive branch.

"I've been thinking about your case," Shay started, breaking the smothering silence.

Kate closed the folder she'd been studying, tipped her head slightly. "It's closed. I told you."

"Not the Lanterman case," Shay explained. She made a motion in Kate's general direction. "The case you really care about. Your missing partner. I had time to review some similar files during the stakeout and I thought we might work on it together."

Kate was suspicious. "For the purpose of...?"

"Closure. Peace." Shay shrugged, utilized a voice she hoped wouldn't tell her just how much she understood the need for such things. Nor would tell her that there might be more at stake than mere closure and peace. "I imagine it's terrible—the never knowing part."

"In case you don't recall, Agent Cooper, that case has also been closed." Kate softened. "But I appreciate your concern. Anyway, it won't matter for much longer."

Shay leaned against her desk, folded her arms, curious. Maybe the woman had her own leads. "How do you figure?"

"I've put in for a transfer to Dallas," she told her. "I should hear about it any day."

"You're leaving?" Shay's voice pitched slightly. She shook her head as if to dislodge anything that might be making her ears hear funny things. Things like her partner wanting to bail on the case—or on *her*. She tried to focus. "Does Holloway know about this?"

"I'm sure he does." Kate shrugged. "Anyway, I appreciate your efforts. It's more than anyone else around here ever tried to do."

Shay only stared at her.

"Look, I know I'm not...easy. I hope they get you someone better."

Kate looked uncomfortable. It was the largest admission she'd made about herself in their time together so far. Shay recalled her conversation with Holloway and now contemplated his sneaky tactics. She wondered if Roger really thought he was doing Kate a service by neglecting to inform her that no other office wanted her.

At last Shay nodded. "If you wouldn't mind, Agent Harris, I'd like to continue to look at the case on the side anyway." She softly chuckled, added. "I'm told I have a bit of a hard head. Maybe I'll get somewhere on it."

Kate started to protest but looked too tired for it. She only nodded. "It's your office and your time, Agent Cooper."

"I didn't want to do it behind your back, is all." It would be the first thing Shay hadn't done behind her partner's back in the last twenty-four hours. Her monologue was obviously guilt-driven. She clapped her hands together, a signal that she was changing the subject. "Don't forget about the CIRG meeting this afternoon."

"I won't." Kate watched as Shay grabbed her jacket and headed for the office door. "Where are you going?"

"Dentist appointment," was all she said. It was the same thing she'd tell Holloway if he asked her about her absence. In reality she was headed for the park for an hour-long snooze in her car. She had two hours of sleep under her belt, tops. And that she was getting so good at lying, why not?

Kate took a longer than normal lunch at her apartment. Physically, she was feeling much better, but didn't trust her perpetually queasy stomach to anything beyond saltines and water with lemon. She vowed to her unborn child that she'd make up the missing nutrition with some nice, soothing soup that evening. For now, she had important work to do.

Without her partner looking over her shoulder, Kate went no-holds-barred Internet fishing for information about her partner. On the surface, Shay appeared to be too good to be true, something that always red-flagged Kate's intuition. Even Shay's Bureau records read squeaky clean. It seemed impossible that Shay could expunge personal details from the Bureau database, but Kate knew old headlines would not be so easily hidden. She contacted each major newspaper in New York and Miami, and within hours her printer was cranking out every possible piece of public information about Shay Cooper.

She sipped water, and waited. The whirring of the printer was comforting. She was drowsy coming off her adrenaline rush.

Of course Kate was a no-show at the CIRG meeting. Shay herself bounced her pen on her folder for the last, long ten minutes of it. She went back to the office to find it locked and dark. Angry, she looked up Kate's address on the computer, grabbed her jacket and briefcase and mentally formed her new mission.

Kate awoke hours later to the alarm of the printer. A hundred pages gone, and it was hungry for more paper. She started to sit up in bed but was struck with a pain so radical she dropped back against her pillow to muffle her own scream. Utilizing every deep breathing exercise, Kate forced herself upright. She'd temporarily changed into pajama pants to avoid wrinkling her skirt for what was intended to be only a short nap. She glanced at the clock; it was almost six.

Pain shot down both legs momentarily paralyzing her. She struggled to stand, slid her feet into the nearest pair of sandals, grabbed her coat and her phone. Moving slowly, painfully, she called her doctor on the way to the emergency room.

Shay found the apartment with little trouble, but much surprise. It was in a far better neighborhood than any agent should be able to afford. She'd bluffed her way around a uniformed doorman, but there was no breaking and entering into these suites, not with their laser key card receptors and security on each floor. She'd been hammering away on Kate's door for several minutes when a woman emerged from the next apartment door.

She was easily in her eighties with white hair, a plump middle that she attempted to conceal beneath her pink rhinestone-studded track suit. She looked sweet enough, but her tone was nothing short of sour. "Well, she's not home, obviously."

Shay sighed, took a step toward her. "I'm sorry, ma'am. Do you know Ms. Harris?"

"She doesn't have any friends around here. She doesn't want them," she said in a know-it-all voice. "Always running in and out of here, talking on that little phone of hers. She's going to get brain cancer, you know."

Shay struggled to remain calm. She had an ass-chewing prepared for her partner, and now it was being deterred by this odd conversation. "Have you seen her today?"

"She ran out of here earlier, didn't say so much as a hello or excuse me. In her skivvies, no less, like one of those young pop stars you see in the trash papers." She clicked her tongue admonishingly. "Offensive, if you ask me."

Puzzled, Shay tipped her head slightly. "Skivvies?"

"Yes. Her nightclothes."

Shay's anger slipped, replaced by a lump of panic rising in her throat. She turned to go. "Thank you, ma'am."

From behind her, the woman snidely remarked, "I *knew* she was a lesbian."

Confused, she blinked but didn't turn around to question the old bat's logic. Trying to ignore the woman's accusatory tone as she proceeded to ramble, condemning everything from Kate's attire to her questionable lifestyle, Shay reached the elevator but waited only seconds before the old woman's babbling and her own impatience got the best of her. She headed for the stairwell.

A call to Kate's mobile phone got her voice mail. Shay dropped the phone in her pocket and headed for the parking lot. There, she sat in her Jeep, thinking, remapping Chicago in her brain, reassembling buildings and streets from years ago, information that was probably outdated by now. There was only one place Kate Harris would be going in her pajamas in broad daylight.

She started the Jeep and pulled into traffic. Four blocks later she turned into the parking lot of St. Anne's Hospital. She found Kate's BMW five rows from the entrance.

"Can I get you anything, Ms. Harris?" the young nurse said as she dropped her chart back into the door holder. "Dr. Michaels is on her way in."

Comfortably fuzzy, thanks to whatever they'd put into her IV bag, Kate shook her head. "Just dim the lights on your way out, please?"

"Sure thing." The woman smiled and in moments she was gone with a final, "Hit the button if you need anything."

Once she was alone, tears sprang to Kate's eyes. She rolled onto her side and tried to block out the blips of monitors and distant buzz of the emergency room. She tried not to think about anything at all.

The emergency waiting room was noisy and crowded. Shay Cooper went to the front desk where a large African-American woman peered at her from over the tops of tiny bifocal ovals. She couldn't have looked more uninterested in Shay's concern if she tried.

"Kate Harris? Which room?"

"Have a seat and they'll find you." It was a well-rehearsed answer.

"Not necessary, I just need a room number."

The woman glowered at her and waved her pen toward the patient privacy chart posted behind the desk. Her voice was slow and deep. "Let me introduce you to my friend, HIPAA."

"Just point. I'll take it from there."

The woman pointed toward the waiting room.

Shay rolled her eyes and turned away from the Queen of Reception. She made toward the waiting room to pacify her, but quickly ducked alongside a rolling gurney next to an ambulance crew. She sailed alongside them unnoticed, through the double doors of the emergency wing.

It was quieter there and she poked along the dimly lit hallway, casually glancing at each chart name for her partner's name. She found Kate in room twelve. Her footsteps slowed and she held her breath as she peered through the door's tiny window. Though the patient faced away from her, a mane of blonde hair spilled across the pillows. She'd know it anywhere.

Kate looked considerably smaller lying there in the hospital bed connected to all those tubes and wires. Shay had dealt with loss, but she didn't have any experience with sickness. Seeing her partner looking that way made her uneasy.

She lingered a moment longer until she heard the approaching smart click-clicking of high heels. That the doctor was dressed in off-duty clothes said she'd been summoned to the hospital especially for her patient, and that certainly didn't allay Shay's anxiety. Kate was in trouble. She hurried down the hallway before the doctor could inquire about her presence in the off limits wing.

"You're fine," Dr. Michaels told Kate almost immediately upon entering her room. Kate's shoulders sank with obvious relief. The doctor elaborated. "There was a minor fluctuation in your glucose level and your blood pressure is a little on the low side. But all told, you're good."

"I don't understand. I was in so much pain."

"You did the right thing by coming in. Kate, these things seem to generally clear up by the time I get to you, so it's hard to say." She looked thoughtful. "If you're experiencing early contractions, that's a problem."

"And if I'm not, I'm just crazy," Kate rubbed her eyes, added, "That's a problem, too, right?"

Dr. Michaels sat on the edge of her bed. "You're not crazy. But stress does funny things to the body, especially when you're pregnant. Don't fool yourself into thinking you can talk yourself out of true pain." The doctor's voice was sympathetic. "Slow down. Take it easy."

Kate sighed. "Now that is easier said than done."

"Have you told the Bureau yet?" And when Kate shook her head, Dr. Michaels looked concerned. "I'll help you as much as I can, but the longer you wait, the worse they'll take it."

Kate knew that.

"Meanwhile, work from home as much as you can. Get some help, too. You'll need a nanny or nurse once the baby's here. Don't think it's a sign of weakness to get somebody now."

"I'll think about it."

"Do it." The woman's voice turned stern. "You're growing a life inside you, Kate."

"I'll think about it," she repeated.

Dr. Michaels patted Kate's leg through the covers. "Rest for another hour or so, then we'll see about getting you out of this godforsaken place."

When she was gone, Kate nestled back against the pillows and watched the blips on the screen of the fetal heartbeat monitor. She was alone, but there was a presence she couldn't account for. Something dark. She felt exposed. Kate pulled the blankets more tightly around her in the chilly room and willed herself to remain alert and keep watch. But for what, she had no clue.

In the wake of the biggest bust in New York history, a crime journalist had asked Shay Cooper if she believed profiling could benefit her in tracking and capturing drug dealers. She answered no, and her explanation was simple: profiling was the ability to get inside a perpetrator's brain; drug dealers had no brains.

She thought about this and other things as she rolled the upcoming CIRG drug bust around her brain. She fished through a cardboard box of old laptop computers, discarding one after another, searching for a make and model similar to Williams' laptop. She came upon an ancient Fujitsu. Jackpot. She placed it face down on the basement table and unscrewed the back. With a little work, she re-fitted the hard drive and fired up the system. It was old and took a while.

Thinking about the drug bust she'd agreed to head up had her feeling a little less guilty for not actually studying the case files. It could go down any moment. It was certainly risky, and she wondered if they could successfully pull it off. Shay couldn't afford to think such negative thoughts. Nor could she emotionally afford thinking about Kate in the hospital, surrounded by all those beeping monitors. She'd have to trust the woman was being well cared for because she couldn't help with such things. Instead, she focused on what she could do.

The screen flickered and sprang to slow life making an awful lot of noise for such a small thing, as if it were begrudging having been brought back from the brink of death. With rising anticipation, she watched the icons arrange themselves on the desktop and in moments she was accessing the general files on the hard drive. Minutes later, Shay concluded that it was the most boring computer she'd ever seen. It crossed her mind that perhaps the Bureau really had dusted the thing. Not even a virtual bread crumb remained. A general e-mail account was easily accessed, but failed to excite her. Spam mail, mostly.

Then she found Z-CyberShare, a virtual parking space where one could park information on the web for access anywhere, anytime, providing they had the correct password. Though placing important information in cyberspace was not secure by any means, Shay considered the possibility that Williams might utilize such an account when he traveled. She wished she could access better password-busting software without leaving behind a trail. The Bureau's version of the program was top-notch. Shay loaded her own low-level software into the computer.

She recalled the code of four. A password, lowercase, all letters would take four seconds to crack. Uppers and lowers, four minutes. Add in numbers, four days. Punctuation increased those figures to four weeks. A combo platter of uppers, lowers, numbers and punctuation could theoretically take as long as four hundred years. She really hoped it didn't.

Her eyes grew heavy as she watched the numbers and letters spin their combinations. Eventually the soothing electronic buzz lulled her to sleep.

CHAPTER FIFTEEN

Thursday's damp chill added dreary dimension to the gray sky. Shay took a late dinner after the last meeting—a gyro sandwich—and headed back to the building under the constant threat of rain. Kate hadn't made an appearance that day, no surprise considering the previous night's trip to the ER. Holloway had pulled Shay aside, asked her to bring him up to speed on her "progress" and explain Kate's absences from the meetings. Shay had covered for her partner, and convinced Holloway that she and Kate were in constant communication about the CIRG meetings. Naturally, she did not mention her partner's apparent health issues.

The elevator doors parted on their floor and Shay was surprised to see their office light on. Her heart hammered against her ribs as she made quiet approach. She pushed through the door and breathed a sigh of relief. Kate was there, sleeping at her cluttered desk. Shay had to give her credit for showing up, better late than never. She went over to wake her.

Her relief at seeing the woman dissolved with each step, and her concern rapidly transcended every emotion into full-on anger. Newspaper articles covered every square inch of her desktop—the *Post*, the *Times*—heralding familiar headlines: Biggest Mob Bust In NYC History; Hero Takes a Fall; FBI Agent's Son Goes Missing...The print wound through her brain with a dizzying effect. She reached out to steady herself against Kate's desk, nearly missed, and slammed her fist hard.

Startled, Kate sat upright at the noise, absently swiped the hair out of her eyes. The women stared at each other for a long time before Shay finally whispered, "Working late?"

"I thought you were gone."

Shay nodded, her lips formed a thin line. "Obviously."

Kate made a worthless attempt to gather the newspapers together. She squinted at her watch. "What time is it?"

"Time to go home, Agent Harris."

"This looks bad—"

"It does." Shay's harsh words cut her off. "I have spent days in meetings taking notes for you because I have your back, Harris." Shay snatched the closest newspaper article, wadded it into a ball and pitched it across the room. It bounced off the wall and silently landed. "I've got your back while you're stabbing me in mine."

"Agent Cooper—"

"First things first." Kate's condition was long forgotten as was Shay's previously gentle approach regarding such things. Shay shoved the newspapers and sent them feathering to the floor. She braced her hands on the desk, leaned over to Kate and made her intentions very clear. "These meetings you can't bring yourself to attend? There's a reason for them. To get in, make a clean bust, and stay alive."

Kate broke eye contact with her, focused instead on her clasped hands.

"For days I've been covering for you to keep you out of hot water. We're supposed to be heading this thing up—how are you going to keep me out of trouble if this bust goes bad?" Shay's voice rose. "I'm not talking about the kind of trouble that gets you suspended or fired—I'm talking about the kind that lands you in the morgue."

"I understand." Kate's voice was a monotone. "I'll be at tomorrow's meeting."

"Great," she responded with sarcasm. "I pray we don't get word tonight."

"I said I understand."

They stared at each other for several moments. Shay's eyes briefly flicked toward the newspapers then back to her again. "You investigating me now, Agent? Do you waste *all* your time chasing ghosts?"

"I had some questions," she stammered.

"And you thought sneaking around behind my back was the way to get the answers?"

Kate mustered every ounce of courage within her. "Why are you so interested in Agent Williams' disappearance?"

"You can't accept that someone might be interested in finding him for your sake?"

"Not the people I know."

"Then you're hanging out with the wrong friends, Harris," she remarked with disgust.

"If we're *friends*, as you say, why didn't you tell me about your son?"

Shay leaned close to her partner, narrowed her eyes, whispered, "Because that is none of your business."

In seconds, Shay had her jacket and briefcase and was headed down the hallway. She heard the office phone ringing in her wake but didn't bother with it. She counted every step to the elevator and jammed her finger multiple times against the button. Her head ached. The doors dinged and finally parted.

"Agent Cooper." Kate's voice echoing down the empty hallway stopped her from leaving. The blond agent hurried toward her. The doors shut again with Shay still standing in the hallway.

Kate looked paler than her new usual and the timing of her message couldn't have been worse. "Things have fallen apart with CIRG. We're moving in."

In the worst neighborhood in Chicago, CIRG's tactical unit awaited the pair who would lead them in their rendezvous. They arrived on scene, and were receiving a walking briefing by the team leader. Agent Shay Cooper had her heart in her throat as she half-listened. Someone had tipped off their target house and it had escalated into a hostage situation.

"Agent Cooper." Tim Vander addressed her with full respect. "Who's leading the team in? You or Agent Harris?"

Now, that was a peculiar question. Shay utilized the pressure of the situation to put some of her own on Kate. She turned to her partner, played it cool. "Your call, Agent. You want communications or lead?"

"I'm ready for either assignment, Agent Cooper."

It was a stunningly brave performance from the waif-like agent. Shay grinned, pushed it a bit further. "Well, suit up then, Agent Harris."

Kate's eyes went momentarily wide, but not so much that anyone else would notice it. She nodded and stepped off to the side where the team leader was waiting to suit her up in a bulletproof vest. Shay watched this, blown away by her partner's stupidity at going through with it just to show her. She could barely comprehend the balance of the plan that Vander was verbally outlining. She nodded and made small talk before heading over to Kate. She pulled her aside.

"You good with this, Agent Harris?" Her voice dropped to a whisper, lest she should appear to the others to be condescending, or worse, lacking faith in her partner. "You did miss the meetings."

"I have the same tactical training as the others."

If Shay hadn't known the woman was pregnant, if she hadn't known she'd missed every last damned meeting, Kate's courageous front would have actually fooled her into believing that indeed she was ready. She heard Vander calling them, then radio his men. The plans were set. Kate didn't appear to be panicking; Shay was a wreck. She tried one last time.

"Is there any reason you believe you shouldn't go in there, Agent?" She shook her head. "Any reason at all?"

"Any reason you think I shouldn't?" Kate put the question right back on her.

Shay's head buzzed. She reached over, roughly gave Kate an attaboy smack on her shoulder. She expected the woman would break down, give up, spill her secret, but that was just another thing she'd misread about her partner to this point. She pretended to not know or care.

"Then you're the superstar. I'll take directives." Shay took the headset from Vander, feigned full confidence in her partner. "Watch yourself in there."

"Will do."

She watched as Kate attempted to fasten the last strap on the heavy vest. Shay went to her with the intention of securing it, but their game had gone into overtime. There were hostages in a drug house and dozens of tactical team members scattered in its radius. She couldn't believe Kate was screwing around with her—taking such a potentially fatal chance.

In a fit of sudden anger, Shay grabbed the straps and yanked them apart.

"Give me this," she said in such a low growl that only Kate would hear it. "Are you out of your mind? I swear to God..."

A few others looked on with surprise as she all but tore the vest off Kate. Shay practically threw the headset at her partner and quickly suited herself up in the bulletproof vest, making short work of the straps, cinching them tightly around her. She glared at Kate, crazed with her partner's stupidity, then turned and called to her team, leaving Kate behind in her wake of absolute fury.

Kate trembled out of near-fear as she put the headphones on, and ignored all the odd looks being dealt her way by the other members. In moments she heard her partner's voice in her headset. "We're in position."

A tiny camera on Shay's helmet provided Kate and the others at the command post with a bird's-eye view of what was in front of them. Other screens and other angles made it feel like they were all inside. Kate felt something tug in her chest.

She swallowed hard, blinked back tears she could suddenly feel behind her eyes.

"Just give me the word," she quietly said.

In moments she heard Shay's command. "Word."

At once, Agent Cooper and her team converged upon the house, through every opening. The front door splintered off its hinges and landed inside the dilapidated residence.

"FBI! Get down! Get down! Antonio Las Palmas—come out!"

In her tiny camera view, Kate watched Shay lead the ambush, wielding her gun in every direction, shouting orders. "Get down! Get these kids out of here."

There were a few children inside, scampering about in the chaos, being gathered by the tactical team for immediate removal. Women cowered in corners of the dingy room, some crying, and a few men simply raised their hands in surrender. Shay spat a string of Spanish commands at the women. They got up and also exited with the children, escorted by the tactical members. Kate watched as Shay slowly approached a hallway.

"Las Palmas! Come out! You are surrounded!"

She lightly kicked open the door of the first room she came to. It was a pure filth hole much as the rest of the place.

"Stinks in here, Christ," she heard Shay mutter. The camera showed her poking into a closet full of pizza boxes and beer bottles. She taunted Las Palmas. "This is the high life, huh? This all the drug money buys?"

She called clear before leaving each area which made Kate very nervous. An outside undercover had already positively ID'd Las Palmas when he'd entered the house an hour earlier. Each shout of "clear" only meant her partner was closing in on the man. Kate felt her pulse quicken.

"Antonio Las Palmas! Come out!" Her voice bellowed across the airwaves. And then much to Kate's horror, she heard Shay whisper, "Somebody's here."

The crackling of garbage underfoot was all that was heard. Kate strained to see on the monitor. She grabbed a pair of infrared binoculars and trained them on window after window until she saw red figures. She pushed the button on her two-way.

"You've got company, west side, no more than twenty feet in

front of you," Kate told her. She watched the slow-moving red blotch as it approached her. "Headed your way, definitely not one of ours. Maybe ten feet now."

Then the radio turned to static.

"Agent Cooper? Respond." She asked again, more alarmed by the second, "Agent Cooper!"

Kate aimed her binoculars at the same window. The figures stood dangerously close to each other. She hit the button again. "The SAC is not responding. We need backup in the rear of the house, west side, now! I've got two figures in the rear west room. Repeat, rear west room."

"Roger that."

She recognized James Buchner's voice and felt a small measure of relief. The young guy was a good agent, if a little gung-ho. She followed his bold approach through the view of her infrared binoculars.

Shay had lost all radio contact in the rear quarters of the house and she quickly assumed it must be scrambled. She was seemingly off the radar, but knew she wasn't alone. She blinked to adjust to the near blackness of the last bedroom. The house bore the stench of rotting food and stale cigarette smoke. But now there was a different smell, like body odor. A presence was verified when she heard someone take a breath. She tightened her grip on her service pistol and took a careful step forward.

Just then the door swung open and Buchner stepped in. The agent aimed the lighted scope of his rifle at Las Palmas, giving the dealer a crystal clear illumination of Shay Cooper standing directly in front of him. Las Palmas fired two shots in rapid succession.

From outside, three flashes lit up the back bedroom. Kate tore off her headset and ran for the house, but was tackled by a member of the tactical team. She fought him, gave him a run for his money, but he held tight, ultimately sweeping her feet off the ground, and holding her tight against him.

"My partner is in there!" she yelled, but no one heard her cries in midst of the chaos.

"Agent down!" was all she heard.

CHAPTER SIXTEEN

Agent Shay Cooper was a rotten patient. She hated hospitals, hated the fuss, and made enough of a ruckus that the nurse told her not only was she not going to be admitted, they would refuse her admission even if she wanted it.

She had a sum total of two bruised ribs and one nasty gash where a bullet entered the side of her vest and grazed her good. Nobody needed to tell her how lucky she'd been. Las Palmas hadn't been as fortunate. Buchner had taken him down in a single-kill shot. Any information that could have been gained through his capture was now also dead. Truthfully, a dead drug dealer didn't break Shay's heart.

Her clothes was spattered with the perp's blood and had been long since collected by the lab for analysis. Utilizing spastic, painful moves, she pulled a borrowed FBI T-shirt over her head, then attempted to slip on her jacket. She was struggling with the second sleeve when the door of the emergency suite flew open and Kate burst in.

Their mutual relief at seeing each other was evident. They started for each other and stopped a few times before awkwardly blinking and mumbling. Exactly what was the protocol one exercises to say "Glad you didn't die"? Shay chuckled, took the pressure off.

"It's okay, I can't hug anyway." She motioned toward her ribs.

"Right," Kate mumbled. When she snapped out of her strange reverie, she realized Shay was suiting up to leave. "Cooper, you can't go home. You just got shot."

"Actually, the doc says I can."

Realizing there was no changing her partner's mind, Kate caught the other jacket sleeve and helped her. "How do you feel?"

"Like I was just shot at point-blank range. Twice." She grimaced. "Love that Kevlar."

Kate started to help button her jacket, but was sidetracked when she noticed the bulging bandage beneath Shay's thin shirt. She'd never known anyone who'd been shot. Fascinated, her hand automatically went to it, traced along a lower rib.

The movement sent a chill through Shay, caused her stomach to feel light and tingly. She clenched her eyes shut, a response Kate would interpret to mean she had caused her pain. That part was true, but Shay suspected the nature of her pain was rapidly becoming far different than what Kate believed it to be. In truth it was deep, hot and tortuous, and getting harder to ignore.

Embarrassed, Kate drew back her hand. "I'm sorry."

"It's all good." Shay went to work buttoning her jacket before Kate could help her again. If helping meant touching, it wasn't such a great idea. Shay hadn't been touched in years. Add that to those nightly dreams starring a woman with mermaid hair…

She swallowed hard, put it out of her head. Thinking about it might destroy her.

Kate's eyes went to the floor and her voice grew quiet. "I feel responsible for this."

"Don't be ridiculous." But Shay knew she'd failed to convince her. Kate's eyes were blue pools. There was no way Shay could handle any more unexpected emotion on this day. She reached out and lightly cupped Kate's chin, startling her. Conveying more desperation than she intended to, Shay said, "Please don't cry. I'm begging you." She let go of her.

Kate nodded, stood straighter, swiped a hand across her moist eyes. "We need to talk."

"We do," Shay agreed. "Me first. I can't protect you if you're not honest with me. It doesn't work."

"I'm pregnant," Kate blurted, saving Shay further careful inquest. Shay's eyes flashed wide, but she didn't otherwise waver.

It wasn't the shock or horror Kate had envisioned when she'd run the practice scenario through her mind.

"I see." Shay didn't lower her gaze. "Does Holloway know?"

"No." Kate looked uncertain. "Only you."

And though she'd already done the math a dozen times, she asked, "How far along?"

"Six months." Her voice was whisper soft.

At last, Shay felt it was permissible to openly look at the woman's midsection. She took a step back to put some space between them. Kate slowly unwrapped her sweater, but it wasn't much of a big reveal. She was alarmingly small, causing an altogether different worry to tug at Shay.

"You should tell Holloway. You'll need time off before long anyway."

"I suppose so."

In a brave move, Shay stepped close to her and hovered with her lips just above Kate's ear. She whispered, "Thank you for trusting me with it."

Kate didn't answer and Shay wondered again if she would cry. She didn't, but still she looked utterly miserable.

Shay nodded toward the door and Kate started to pick up her plastic patient bag. Shay stopped her by gracefully swiping it from beneath her grip. "I've got it."

"You just got shot."

"I've got it," she repeated.

Kate's attitude edged toward defensive. "Don't treat me differently because of what I've told you. I'm as capable as ever."

Shay started for the door, but her partner's tone caused her to stop. She turned abruptly, and made her point crystal clear. "Don't try to prove any points with me, okay? What you almost did today was dumb. It could have cost you your life or your baby's. Not worth it."

They remained locked in a mutual gaze for several long seconds.

"Message received." Kate softened at last. "Don't mention this to anyone, okay?"

Shay's eyes looked uncertain as if she were questioning the intelligence of making such a promise. At last she nodded.

On the way home, the relief she felt was almost enough to offset her physical pain. She knew it was difficult for Kate to confide in anyone, let alone the woman who had come along and taken Agent Williams' place.

But a different feeling loomed and troubled her down to her core. Given that Ortelli had been right about the baby, he could very well be right about Kate being in grave danger.

Shay couldn't afford to discount his claim. She'd done that once before, years ago, and she'd carry that missed warning with her for the rest of her days. Knowing this, it took everything in her power to let Kate go home alone.

CHAPTER SEVENTEEN

As she knew she would be, Shay was sore in the morning. It made getting showered and dressed difficult enough, forget about making a cup of coffee. She arrived at the office slightly late and feeling extremely tired. She smiled cordially at her partner when she pushed through the door and avoided looking at her too closely.

"Good morning, superhero," Kate softly chided. "How are you feeling?"

"Better." Shay set her briefcase on her desktop. "How are you feeling today? You good?"

Kate made an eye roll, but it lacked its usual meanness. "I'm fine, Agent Cooper. But please remember what I asked you about not talking about it?"

"But you asked me how I was." She painfully shrugged. "It's fair."

"Because you just got shot." Kate added an uncharacteristic, "Duh."

"Seriously, how can I not think about...*it*?"

"Try your best."

"Okay, fine." Shay smiled. "But truthfully it's going to be hard not to think about. I mean when I can't get around your belly to get into the file cabinet, I'm going to think about it."

Kate looked at her, smiled and politely whispered, "You're still talking about it."

Shay yawned, too tired to argue with her. Besides, it didn't feel right calling Kate's baby "it."

She studied her partner, wondered why Kate looked different. Maybe her relief at sharing the secret was expressing itself through eyes that were brighter, features that were softer.

Somewhat familiar with the life that lay ahead of her, Shay didn't envy what she was going through. Raising a child with a partner and a good support network was tough enough, let alone going it all alone. For a split second, Shay was dizzy with the notion that she seemed to be Kate's only support network. The responsibility of it felt suddenly overwhelming.

She swallowed hard, wondered if it was for lack of caffeine. She excused herself to get some coffee and returned ten minutes later armed with a Styrofoam cup, a carton of milk and a banana. She set the latter two on Kate's desk, earning a puzzled look.

"When did they start putting coffee in milk cartons?" Kate grinned. "Or are you going to tell me it's inside the banana peel?"

"Don't ask me about it, Agent, or you'll be making me break a promise." Shay sauntered over to her partner's desk. "What are you working on?"

She already knew it was Kate's extracurricular composite, but she wanted to change the subject, reduce the limelight unexpectedly cast on her for inflicting a little nutrition on her partner.

"Files from other cases of what I believe are abductions."

"You say what you believe are...?"

"They were never before considered to be connected." She set four files on the desktop, and pointed to each as she explained, "These people are media, law enforcement, people in power, or connected to them."

"That's a mixed bag." Shay leaned in for a closer look. "None from Agent Williams, though. Correct?"

She looked sheepish as she nodded. "The single thing they have in common is that their bodies were never recovered."

"Still, it's a strong factor. I can't believe nobody looked into this." She flipped through the folders, glanced at evidence photos.

"They're pretty strung out over the course of a decade, and there's no consistency in location."

"Any hits on CODIS?"

She shook her head. "No bodies, no secondary blood. These were exceptionally clean and careful acts."

"So the lack of evidence is the evidence." Shay considered this, winced in minor pain as she leaned against her partner's desk. "Show me the others."

"Seriously?" She arched an eyebrow. "All of them?"

And within fifteen minutes Kate had plied her with at least a dozen case files. Shay sighed, wondered what she'd gotten herself into.

After a two-hour overview, Shay was achy again and badly in need of Tylenol. She excused herself to get a bottle of water from the commissary.

Once she'd gone, Kate flipped through the one file she'd been holding onto. The case of Christopher Cooper, a five-year-old boy who'd vanished in New York City one sunny afternoon. She considered that she'd cast her net in too big a circle, and wondered if she might be subconsciously attempting to draw Shay in on a personal level to guarantee her help. But it didn't feel like it.

Christopher was the only child in her loose composite, but no matter how she tried to eliminate him, the circumstances of his disappearance kept dragging his name back onto her roster. And if it was true that the boy had fallen to the same perp, he may very well have had the misfortune of being the first victim.

It was Agent Williams who had originally plotted the cases on a timeline. He'd been able to determine the interval of time and relative location to make calculations about the perp's next victim. He'd even allowed a percentage of acceleration based upon the cognitive profile of the criminal mind. They had been really onto something big before his disappearance. Then, using the same parameters, she'd been able to plot Williams' abduction on his own timeline. Creepy. Even creepier was the reason she suspected Williams was so good at it.

But Williams had never included Christopher Cooper in his version of events. It was a leap, but according to the time and location statistics he'd reported, the boy worked into the picture quite nicely.

Perhaps she'd eventually share this information with her partner. First she had to bring herself to share a very different, even more bizarre theory with her. Shay would think Kate had lost her mind for sure. Maybe she really had.

CHAPTER EIGHTEEN

Shay Cooper took a seat on the backyard bench left behind by the former owners of her house. In the moonlight, she studied what had once been flower beds and nicely trimmed hedges. They'd long since turned into a weed patch surrounded by misshapen hedges. She sipped decaf coffee for warmth against the chill night air and relaxed as much as she could with her painful ribs. As usual, her mind was on work, and, more than it should be, Kate Harris.

Her partner was easier to work with, more trusting of her than ever before. The downside of this was that Shay's workload had literally doubled in the past week. Kate had burdened her with dozens of closed cases she felt could be connected to her missing partner. Add that to her normal duties and Shay felt she barely had time to breathe.

Case upon case differing in classification, race, origin, affiliation, everything, nothing. Yet Kate had managed to string them together in a fashion that made the barest sense. She knew that Kate had been the brains while Williams had tended to the field work. Perhaps Kate was trying to make up for lost time with so much hands-on work. Or perhaps she'd lost her mind.

But each time Shay felt she'd reached the end of her rope, she had to acknowledge that perhaps her partner was actually onto something.

Shay watched the blinking lights of an airplane soaring overhead, which reminded her of another case that had made its way onto her desk. The disappearance of a young airport security worker in Champaign, Illinois. A tox report cleared him of drugs, save for caffeine. He had friends, no apparent enemies. The guy wasn't a clubber or a girlfriend-stealer, and it didn't appear to be robbery, his apartment was intact.

Motiveless crimes intrigued her. After all, there should be a good reason to want a person dead, right? Could have been that the poor guy was in the wrong place at the wrong time. The case would probably remain unsolved unless someone stepped forward and took credit for it. Shay wondered if the lack of motive and evidence made the case a candidate for the never-ending series of murders they were investigating on the side.

Shay sighed. Aside from all the increasing physical effect Kate was having on her, the woman's paranoia also seemed to be contagious.

She glanced at her watch; it was after eleven. She stood and carefully stretched, surveyed her surroundings. The place had real potential—privacy fence, lush lawns that were a bit on the shaggy side at the moment, and raggedy foliage that could be trimmed into something more pristine. She looked at the swing dangling there, and as usual, felt an incredible heaviness settle in her chest. Yes, the place had all sorts of potential.

Too bad it was wasted on her alone.

The game was becoming as tiresome as its players were stupid. The Watcher warmed himself by the campfire outside the pup tent he'd pitched in Rock Bluff. He enjoyed being close to nature and familiar places. Far from the public campgrounds, he had situated himself in the thick of the forest where he could be alone to think. Under a sky dotted with stars, he stirred the dying fire.

It was a plan he liked and he'd made it his. He followed it to the letter leaving behind no significant evidence. He'd done such a good job, he'd almost robbed it of challenge. A match of wits with dimwitted fools was hardly a match at all. His opponents were thoroughly stymied and his own ego swelled by the day. He was so much better a monster than his predecessor in a ritual that seemed destined to go on indefinitely.

The meeting in the park had been designed to shake things up if only temporarily. He'd yet to determine the weight of its impact. For now, there were more pressing things on his mind.

He'd never fancied himself a child killer. He could still clearly see the wide, dark eyes on a small boy's face staring at him from a picture. Thinking about the possibility of bringing harm to a child didn't stir fear within him and he wondered if fear was actually a part of him anymore. Instead, it had done something unexpected; it had given him strength.

He'd taken corrective steps, verified by Kate Harris's puny appearance and recent late night hospital visit. But still he'd not prevailed. He remembered the day he'd first learned of this error. He'd tossed his head back, even laughed at the carelessness of it all. It wasn't the first mistake he'd discovered, but the grandest by far. Given Harris's history, he'd foolishly not previously considered this to be a possibility. Clearly he wasn't the only one to make that mistake. Reckless thinking for sure. Kate Harris was a lying, conniving, baby-bagging slut.

The master profiler might say this error screamed of a secret desire to be caught, even stopped. Either way, it didn't matter now. Besides, there was an unexpected thrill that came from the long-term torture he'd inflicted upon her without yet ending her life. The feeling was akin to being on the perpetual verge of orgasm. But as all good things do, this too would end.

He'd draw upon the same strength that had been used years ago with the Cooper boy—anything it took to see that the child was never born. It simply couldn't happen. It had been an unexpected and interesting part of the game, but nonetheless the game must prevail.

Stirring the last of the glowing embers he succumbed to letting them burn out on their own. It had turned into a chilly night and the sky was damp. He was itching to leave the town for a bit. He craved a little sunshine and a change of scenery. He had in mind someplace warm. It would be good to shake the doldrums if only for a day or two. A little vacation to tide him over until he could move freely about once again. He had business to attend to. Soon this chapter would be a memory. He'd studied every aspect of the game and now he was in charge of it.

The Watcher unzipped the canvas tent, crawled inside and bedded down for the night.

CHAPTER NINETEEN

"Good, you're here."

It was an unexpected way to be greeted when Shay entered their office that morning. She juggled a cardboard drink holder atop her briefcase and set it down on her desk. She raised an eyebrow in playful suspicion. "Such an improvement over our previous morning rituals."

Kate ignored her remark, forged ahead. "I think I've found another connection with the cases—you know, something firmer."

"First things first." Shay pried loose her own coffee cup, then placed a bagel and a carton of milk on Kate's desk along with napkins and a tiny container of peanut butter. Kate looked bewildered. "Slather some on that bagel, would you?"

"I'm being serious," Kate admonished her.

"Me too. You could use some protein."

Kate dipped her head, gave her one of her famous glares, but it only lasted a second before she smiled helplessly. She wasn't used to anyone looking after her. Annoying, she thought, but admittedly somewhat nice. She shook her head, turned toward the map spread out on the back table. Shay followed her, peeling the lid off her coffee. She took a sip and since her partner was operating without caffeine these days, grimaced as if it wasn't delicious.

"What if we run the plot points on all the vics?" She tapped the map. "All the places where the last evidence was discovered. See if it means anything. See if there's a pattern."

Shay studied her. "That's what you've got?"

"Well, it's just a theory."

"You want to hear my theory?" Shay didn't miss a beat. "My theory is that you're trying to make me forget what day this is."

Kate's shoulders slumped slightly. She'd already promised Shay she'd tell Holloway today. It was a long overdue conversation—about six months overdue, to be exact.

Kate sighed. "Fine. I'll get it over with." She started for the door. She stopped short, almost causing Shay to smack into her back. Kate turned around, chastised her, "I can get there by myself, Agent Cooper. I'm a big girl."

"Oh, I'm sure you can get there. The question is, will you go inside once you do?" She held their office door open, made a sweeping gesture with her hand. "After you, I insist."

Forty minutes later, Shay was still waiting for her partner on a bench outside Holloway's office. She had claimed to be there for moral support, but the longer her partner remained in the meeting, the more nervous she was becoming. Shay played with her phone, pretended to check e-mail and text messages. When at last Kate quietly appeared beside her, she looked paler than usual. Shay hurriedly stood up, dropped the phone into her pocket. Surely Holloway hadn't fired her.

"What is it?"

"Roger just informed me they've recovered a body in Dekalb..." Her voice trailed off in her obvious shock. Shay stepped closer, but offering any measure of comfort wasn't exactly her strong suit. She guarded her words from passersby, whispering, "Is it Agent Williams?"

Kate's clear devastation confirmed rumors of a Harris-Williams relationship. Shay gently nudged her shoulder. "Kate?"

"They're doing an autopsy this afternoon." Her eyes flickered back to life, her voice pitched some when she said, "I need to go there."

Shay gave her the once-over. "That's not a good idea."

"I have to see for myself." Kate stared at her. In moments she was off. "I'm going."

Shay watched her for only a moment before catching up to her, falling in step beside her. "You'll need someone to drive you."

It rained for the entire hour-long drive to Dekalb. They rode in silence to the background of rain beating softly against the windshield and wipers swishing it away. Shay easily found the facility, but could barely believe it was a hospital. She pulled into the lot of the tired, industrial-looking building.

The Jeep had barely rolled to a stop when Kate jumped out. She hurried along the crumbling cement path toward the double doors. Inside they were greeted by musty and antiseptic smells and a white-haired gentleman who looked as old as the building. He identified himself as the assistant coroner and led them into the place.

"Sorry about the mess. Central Hospital's under construction. This is temporary housing for our dead." He pushed through another set of double doors. The pair followed him down steeply sloping floors, deep into the building. "But our new John Doe was sure a case. Talk of the town. We don't get too many murders here in Dekalb." He shot them a look, hiked his bushy eyebrows and lowered his voice. "Especially not this grisly. Cut his head almost clean off."

Shay glanced in Kate's direction, but the woman stared straight ahead, focused solely on their destination. The assistant coroner seemed kind enough, Shay was certain, but she was concerned about the brashness of his words. After all, he believed them only to be representing the Bureau. How was he to know they were also on a personal quest?

"Any luck with ID?" Shay said, trying to keep the conversation on a professional level.

"I thought that's why you folks are here?" The odd fellow shot her a look and slowed as they approached a row of bodies lined up in the cool hallway. He gave a low whistle. "Banner week for us. Lots of old folks. Sepsis in a nursing home. Bad stuff."

Her checked one chart after another, then drew the sheet back on one, grimaced and nodded. "Here's our guy."

Shay stopped her partner from lunging forward. "When was he brought in?"

"Last night, I reckon." He flashed a grin but it quickly faded. Under the bright fluorescents he got his first good full-body look at Agent Harris. "Ma'am, you sure you want to see this in your condition? It's not a pretty picture."

Without the cover of her sweater, Kate's small, rounded belly slightly protruded in her snug-fitting dress. She nodded. Shay pulled her aside. "Look, I can do this for you."

Kate mustered steely determination. "No, I have to."

Shay hesitated a moment, then gave the coroner a nod. He drew the sheet back and three sets of eyes studied a corpse.

People look different in death, mere shells of their living selves, drawn, dry and gray. This face bore a particularly gruesome expression, immortalizing the final pain the poor man had obviously endured when his throat was slit so deeply, it had nearly decapitated him. Even a seasoned pro would have a tough time with this one, let alone an emotional pregnant woman who spent the majority of her days in an office.

Shay tipped her head, furrowed her brow. The corpse did have similar features to Williams. Given that rigor had fully set in, somewhat distorting the man's facial features, it was more difficult to make a positive pronouncement than she thought it would be.

But Kate touched her lips, gasped, took a quick step backward, and bumped into Shay, then spun around, buried her face into Shay's shoulder. So it *was* Tony Williams on that slab.

"I'm here." Shay had no time to ponder her hang-ups about touching or being touched, even less time to analyze her seemingly robotic reaction. She was startled at the feeling of her partner's emergent belly against her own flat one. But the tears she felt through her sleeve drew her mind toward more pressing matters of comfort. She swallowed hard. "I'm right here."

"It's not him," Kate mumbled against her shirt. "That's not Tony."

Shay breathed a sigh of relief.

"She says no," she told the assistant coroner, and then motioned for him to give them a second. When the door shut behind him, she whispered sweet reassurance. "That's good. That's really good news."

"No, no…" Kate wept into her shoulder.

But nobody understood the equally miserable pain of not knowing the fate of a loved one better than Shay. She changed her approach. "You have to find a way to hang onto hope."

"You don't understand," Kate said, limply striking her hand against Shay's shoulder. Her body trembled and she seemed inconsolable. "You don't understand at all!"

Shay wondered if the woman was having a breakdown. Confused, she gently clamped her partner's shoulders and leaned her back slightly to get a better bead on her emotions. Her words were low, calm. "Tell me, then. Make me understand."

"He has to be dead," Kate sobbed. "If he's not dead, he'll kill me!"

Shay locked eyes with her emotional wreck of a partner. Utterly perplexed, she enveloped her in her arms, stroked her hair, and contemplated this strange turn of events.

What did Kate know? Just who *was* Tony Williams? And what had Shay gotten herself into?

CHAPTER TWENTY

Brilliance did not equal fame.

Some of the smartest people on the planet were severely underappreciated by the masses; remained a mere freckle on the face of existence. Ignored by everyone.

Almost everyone.

A long, sleek goddess of a woman lay basking in the glorious Arizona sunshine beside her pool. Baking her skin was an afternoon ritual, and on this afternoon she was nothing short of a matter of pure pleasure for The Watcher.

Janice Tremmel was attorney to the big stars and politicians and any other hotshot who wanted things done quickly, quietly, and efficiently. She was one of the most gifted attorneys he'd ever had the privilege of seeing in action. Of course, she didn't win them all. He recalled his own juvenile case, years ago, when

Attorney Tremmel was nothing more than a fresh branch on her family's law firm tree. He smirked. She certainly hadn't won that one.

His admiration for her came with equal parts abhorrence.

She was a knockout in that barely there designer bikini as she slathered oil on her arms and legs until she was sufficiently shining. Leaning back in her chaise lounge, she closed her eyes while he fumbled with his zipper and prepared to enjoy the view. He'd discovered the scenery in Scottsdale to be better than the brochure.

True, she'd made a substantial mark in the legal world, and she would be sorely missed by her colleagues and tight-knit family, but she'd be a virtual no-namer to the general public. Brilliant and likable, but as it was her job to keep big names out of the papers, she'd enjoyed no fame.

Tomorrow, Janice would make the paper.

CHAPTER TWENTY-ONE

Now that the corpse wasn't Tony Williams', the partners spent the balance of their workday and late into the evening holed up in a nameless dingy roadside café off East Lincoln Highway. The curtain of rain added to the anonymity of the place with grease in the air and warm beer on tap. Shay would know, she had promptly ordered her first one as soon as they'd slid into the corner booth.

She downed half the glass in one long drink, swiped the suds off her upper lip, and motioned toward the waitress for another.

"Do you mind?" she inquired out of courtesy.

"No." Kate pushed a wavy section of drenched hair away from her wide eyes. "Under the circumstances, I only wish I could join you."

"Me too." She turned to the waitress. "Another beer and...?"

"Water."

"Water with a juice back." Shay hadn't completely taken leave of her senses. "And some menus, please?"

They settled in. Over grilled cheese and pie, Kate unraveled tales of the Missing Persons unit, namely, that she was convinced that her former partner might have helped to create his own caseload. Shay listened intently, nodded occasionally, and when her partner finished, she closed her eyes for several long seconds to process the deluge of information.

"You think Agent Williams is the serial abductor?"

"I know it sounds crazy." Kate glanced over her shoulder for the hundredth time in an hour. "Look, you said it yourself, the only MO for these abductions is no MO. Tony's the single person who could string these together, and I found out after he'd vanished that he'd never filed a single report on his findings."

"Didn't he work the profiles?"

She nodded. "To a T. Which means he either knew them all too well—"

"Or he kept mixing up the details to keep everyone at bay so his true identity would never be discovered." Shay thumbed her chin, watched as Kate nodded in agreement. "Jesus, we're teaching rookies how to form composites based on his potentially bogus work. This could have a far-reaching impact."

"It seems the only true connection between any of these cases is Tony himself." Her voice grew quiet, her eyes looked into the distance. "Otherwise there's nothing more than a timeline he created and filled in periodically."

Shay watched her partner whirl around in her seat to check the front of the diner each time the door bell jingled.

"You're going to get a sore neck doing that. I've got your back, okay?" Then when Kate looked at her funny, she added, "You're going to have to trust someone. It might as well be me."

She admitted, "I'm not good with trust."

"No shit?" Shay blurted before she could stop herself. She dipped her head apologetically. "All right. Supposing this was all true, tell me how such a person could work for the FBI? He'd never pass a background check or mental health screen."

"He's got a genius level IQ," was her answer. "Anyone

who's studied psychology can swing the screen. It's not rocket science."

Shay admitted, "I guess if I can pass it, it's anyone's game."

"Your words, not mine." Kate hiked an eyebrow. Neither of them laughed. She took a sip of warm juice and made a face, then quickly recovered. "Tony was obsessed with these cases. Toward the end, he was even making predictions about when and where the next bodies would turn up. He was calling them spot on, I'm telling you."

Then came the million dollar question. "Why would he want you dead?"

"I suspect Tony's falsified his DNA on file at the FBI. Replaced it or something," she whispered. "He's bound to get sloppy. All psychopaths eventually do. And if someone links his DNA to secondary blood found at a scene, the killer's suddenly got an identity."

Shay studied her frazzled partner. "If what you say is true and he has falsified his DNA—which would be nearly impossible, by the way—nobody would connect him to the cases."

She unwrapped her sweater revealing bare, goose-bumped arms. Shay followed Kate's gaze down to her baby belly. "I could."

Shay blinked, let the information trickle through her, tried her best at not looking as shocked as she was. The rumors were true. Holloway was right. Repetitions of *holy shit* rolled through her mind.

"That's a hell of a tale, pal," she croaked at last.

"I'm telling you the truth."

"I don't doubt that you think you are, no offense."

Kate didn't look fazed. "I realize it's a lot of information to digest."

Shay put aside emotion and focused on the science. It rarely failed her. "How did he falsify his DNA information?"

"I don't know how he did it." Kate leaned forward again, chose her words carefully. "I was having some...problems with this pregnancy. As you know, a little bit of the baby's blood mixes with your own. I'm type O, the doctor found B in my blood. Tony's composite on file specifically says he's type O."

"Slip of the finger?" Shay offered, but it was more wishful thinking than a legitimate question. Kate shook her head. "So it's likely he's actually B."

"Or AB, but that's rarer."

"I'm AB," Shay absently remarked. She rolled it around until a different notion occurred to her. She abruptly changed the subject. "You never went to any of those crime scenes?"

"No. Tony was a control freak. He didn't want anyone to contaminate the crime scene."

"Son of a bitch wanted to contaminate them himself," Shay half-whispered. Her eyes flitted to her partner when she realized what she'd said. "Pardon me."

To her surprise, Kate said, "He is a son of a bitch."

A grab bag of thoughts swirled through her mind. She selected an odd one. "I can't believe doing his secretarial work didn't bother you."

"It wasn't the career I dreamed it would be. The FBI's still a man's land." Kate contemplated their recent bust and whispered, "Of course, to his credit he never dragged me to a crack house."

Shay flashed her a quick grin. "Hey, it's not a real partnership until everybody gets shot."

"In this case, I hope you're wrong."

They both went quiet again.

Shay lowered her voice, leaned across the table to get as close to her as possible. "Does anyone else know this baby belongs to Tony Williams?"

Kate shook her head.

"Good," Shay whispered. "Let's keep it that way."

"Who knows where he's at," Kate said, casting little glances out the window into the dark, dreary night. "He could be in the parking lot. Does he know I'm pregnant? Has he figured out that this baby's his?"

"Don't do that to yourself. You'll never sleep at night."

"I already don't," she admitted before lapsing into a quiet paranoid rant. "He'll surely want me and the baby dead—it's too risky for him to let us live. I sit around thinking the house is bugged, our office, my car...who the hell knows? I feel like I'm losing my mind."

"Stop," Shay firmly commanded. She reached across the table and clasped her partner's clammy hands, rousting her from the self-flagellating abyss she'd fallen into. "Keep quiet. Lay low. Let me figure some things out."

"You're going to exclude me, just like he did," she said, her tone suddenly defensive.

"Calm down. I guarantee that's not going to happen. I just need some time to think it through." Shay stared at her as she pulled her wallet out, dumped two twenties on the old Formica tabletop. "Meanwhile, no talking about this in the office. Guard your phone conversations at home. Let's try to prove you're wrong about…all this. Right now, your safety is job one for both of us."

"And if I'm right about all this?" Kate asked her.

"No offense intended…" Shay's shoulders fell slightly and she suddenly looked exhausted. "But nothing would make me happier than to prove you wrong."

CHAPTER TWENTY-TWO

The haunted tone of Kate's voice rolled through her head. *"Has he figured out that this baby's his…?"*

It had become the question of the night. Shay considered that it wasn't the type of inquiry someone involved in a serious relationship would make. She concluded that contrary to water cooler gossip or Holloway's initial allusion, Kate and Tony Williams were not long-term lovers. Was it a new relationship? A fling?

She steered into her neighborhood and slowly coasted down the lane. She wondered why the prospect of Kate having a mere fling with the guy provided her a small measure of comfort. Perhaps it was because she didn't think much of Agent Williams and couldn't stand the idea of Kate with him. A different, truer notion niggled in the deep recesses of her overwrought brain: perhaps she couldn't stand the idea of Kate with anyone else at all.

She quickly put it out of her mind, parked her Jeep, and scanned the quiet neighborhood for anything unusual. All was quiet at nearly midnight. She jammed her key into the front door lock, quickly entered and relocked. She heard the digital beeps that meant she had ten seconds to get to the security box and enter her code. She punched it in, looked around. Safe and secure. In the dark, she trundled to an overstuffed chair and plopped into it, sighed.

The phone rang, inciting a full body spasm-jump. It was late and nobody ever called her at home; there was really only one person it could be. With a pounding heart, she snatched the handset out of the cradle before it could ring a second time.

"Kate?" she breathlessly asked.

A chuckle could be heard down the line. "My, how comfortable we've gotten with Agent Williams' partner."

"Ortelli." Her entire tone changed.

"Have you thought more about the conversation we had in the park?" The old man's tone was bright, as if two old friends were merely having a chat. "I trust you've learned all you can about Agent Williams and the baby by now."

"Cut to the chase."

"I came to see you tonight, Agent Cooper. I suppose you were busy crime fighting with your pretty partner."

"Well, you know how it goes." She slumped back into the seat, assumed a forced casual tone that matched his. "Just another day at work, keeping scumbag assholes like you off the street. That sort of thing."

"It's a lovely house. Are you renting or did you go all in?" His words caused Shay to tense for a moment, then she relaxed. Bluffing was a trademark Ortelli move. But then he unexpectedly added, "Are those the Degas prints from your New York place?"

Shay's anger surged to the surface. She quickly rose out of her seat, padded in sock feet to the window to check both sides of the street in front of the house. Empty.

"I'm calling bullshit." She made a slow circle around the living room, glanced at the Degas prints that lined the hallway walls and told herself they could be seen from the sidewalk. She forced her voice to remain calm. "What do you want from me?"

"Walk into the kitchen." And when he could tell she hadn't moved, he kindly repeated his request as if he were speaking to a child. "Come now, Agent Cooper. Walk into your kitchen."

Her feet moved slowly, as quietly as possible, down the hallway toward the kitchen. He narrated her journey. "Have you ever considered taking up the linoleum in the hallway and putting down some real tile? Sure, it looks similar, but knowing it's authentic, you'll appreciate it more. It feels better. Trust me on this."

She rounded the corner, paused in the kitchen doorway, eyeballed every corner of the room.

"Don't touch the wallpaper, it's a classic. But I would consider granite countertops."

She glanced toward the knife block, counted every handle, felt some minor relief that none were missing.

"On the center butcher block. I left you my housewarming gift."

Her eyes went to the center island. She tried to make out the outline of something lying in the middle of it.

"Come on now. It's not a horse's head. Silly, silly woman."

She cautiously scooted to the center of the room where a single yellow rose lay atop the butcher block. After checking to be sure that it wasn't attached to trip wire or some other ridiculous thing, she picked it up, inspected it. She felt the petals, checking to see if it was bugged. When it was limp from her thorough prodding, she blew out the breath she didn't realize she'd been holding.

"Okay, what gives—this a friendship flower or something? Some kind of bullshit symbol?" She dropped it back on the island, smirked. "What is proper flower etiquette after you destroy someone's life?"

"It's not a symbol, it's a security warning."

She leaned against the counter, watched for any mov

in the nighttime shadows outside the kitchen windows. "Yeah, I'm obviously paying ADT too much."

"Entering your home is hardly a challenge. This one operates under the radar, moving in and out of shadows as automatically as some people breathe." His voice was suddenly stern. "If he catches you unawares, you won't live through it. I promise you that much."

The line went dead.

Shay held the buzzing handset for a few seconds before pressing the off button. She listened to every night sound. She snatched the flower off the center block and tossed it into the garbage. The same time it hit, the phone rang, causing her heart to leap to her throat. She angrily punched the on button.

"Listen, asshole. If you know what's—"

"Coop?" AD Holloway's voice cut off her intended rant. She breathed a sigh of relief, but her anxiety peaked again when she looked at the kitchen clock.

"Rog? It's nearly one."

"I apologize for calling you so late." He sounded tired. "Who did you think was calling you?"

She considered who she could trust, played it safe. "Damn telemarketers."

He moved past it to his reason for calling. "I just got a call from Dan Tremmel."

"Governor Tremmel? I know the one." Shay's heart was still pounding. She clutched her hand over her chest, leaned against the island once again, and breathed deeply. "Arizona, right?"

"Yes. He's asked me for a personal favor. Apparently his niece went missing this afternoon and he's a mess."

"How old?"

"Thirty."

Shay shook her head to no one. "Thirty years old, missing for less than twelve hours? She could be at a day spa."

"I know it and you know it." He paused, sighed. "But Governor Tremmel says he has a bad gut feeling about this. And since I owe him a favor, he's calling me on it."

"How does this involve me?" It was time to put on a united front. She amended her statement. "How does this involve *us*."

"I need you to fly out there first thing tomorrow, walk him through the Missing Persons steps. Then don't bust my balls when she shows up fresh from Vegas or someplace."

Shay rolled her eyes, but a new thought occurred to her. It might be good to get her paranoid partner out of the office. And frankly, the time away might give her a chance to digest everything she'd learned over the past twenty-four hours—figure out what to do with it.

"We'd be happy to do it."

"It's hardly a two-man operation," he told her. "You've been good to work with Kate for this long, and don't think I don't appreciate it. I do."

"It's not a problem." In truth it had become much less of a problem only recently.

He was quiet for a moment and Shay felt the subject shifting. "I've been thinking about letting her transfer go through. Let Texas do what they want with her. Maybe it would teach her a thing or two. We'd get you a real partner—somebody you don't have to babysit."

Shay tipped her head to the side, considered it. "Sure have changed your tune, Rog."

"I think I was too close to the situation before. I had to put things into perspective." He laughed lightly. "I know how she can get to people, Coop. I see she's got you looking into cold cases, wasting Bureau resources, casting a hell of an expensive dragnet. I see every file you check out—we both know that's not you."

Shay blinked, swallowed hard. "That many disappearances across several states? Not only does it qualify for our attention, it could be the crime of the century, if it's legit."

"If it's legit." Roger sounded impatient. "She's scatterbrained—making leaps that just don't add up. Now that I know she's hormonal, it makes more sense to me this week than it did last week, I'll tell you that."

"She's hardly scatterbrained," Shay softly defended her partner. "Some of her leaps—as you call them—pose interesting questions. I think it's worth looking into."

"You bring me hard proof, without wasting the Bureau's

resources and manpower and I'll consider it. Until then, Agent, focus only on the tasks at hand."

The conversation had taken a formal turn. She reciprocated as such. "I'm working on that, sir."

He paused, softened some. "Just be careful, that's all I'm saying."

It was the second such warning she'd received that night.

"E-mail me the Governor's case."

"There is no official case," he corrected her.

Funny how when it was his stuff, there was no need for hard evidence to look into it. She rephrased the request. "E-mail me the *details* and I'll book our travel first thing in the morning." Then added with a modicum of sarcasm, "Better consider what you're telling the business office about the expenses I'm filing for your unofficial case."

Shay hung up before he could prove himself to be any more untrustworthy than he just had. She wondered if her partner was safe at home.

In the dark, she checked the kitchen, all the window latches and doors in the house. She crept upstairs, did the same thing there. When she was satisfied that it was empty, she headed downstairs, washed her face and bedded down on the couch.

She lay wide awake, staring at the ceiling and listening. For what, she did not know. She wondered if she could trust Holloway. Hell, she wondered if she could trust her partner. Living in a town called Pleasant was proving to be no more pleasant or restful than living in Manhattan. All in all, it made for a poor night's sleep.

CHAPTER TWENTY-THREE

Her carry-on duffel was packed and waiting in the Jeep. Armed with a single folder, Shay entered the office building. The security line was nil in the early morning hours. She breezed through it and glanced at her watch before heading to the commissary for coffee. It was while she was getting cream that she overheard a conversation in progress. She recognized Agent Buchner's voice.

"You kidding? Williams' old partner is a dyke—who'd have her?"

"I call bullshit," another jock-sounding male put in. "If she's a dyke, so am I."

More laughter. "Go on, laugh. But I guarantee it. Shot me down cold."

"Maybe she didn't want a baby-daddy. Or maybe it was just you, Buchner."

"Are you kidding me?" he pretended to brag. "Look at me. Who in their right mind would turn this down?"

Boys being boys. Shay shook her head, started to go, but was stopped when she heard someone say, "Makes you wonder what Cooper did to get on Holloway's shit list to get paired with Agent Whack-Job."

Shay stepped around the cart and one at a time, the agents noticed her. Three of four immediately grew deathly serious. Agent Buchner, still with his back to her, was deep in his belly laugh when Shay laid a hand on his shoulder. He jumped and the color had drained from his face by the time he turned to see her.

"Agent Cooper, I'm sorry about that," he stammered apologetically. "That was inappropriate. I didn't mean anything."

"It was inappropriate." Shay bent slightly, spoke right into his ear. "Watch yourself, Agent."

She left them in her chilly wake.

In their office, Shay downed half the cup of coffee in a matter of seconds. When her partner walked in, she stood and issued her a stilted-sounding greeting.

"Good morning, Agent Harris."

Kate looked puzzled at her formal tone. Shay put a finger to her lips, followed her to her desk. She waited for Kate to set her bag down, then opened her folder and, one at a time, laid out three note cards bearing bold block handwriting.

Get your things.

I'll explain on the way.

No worries.

Kate's eyes were wide with questions that she didn't dare ask inside an office her partner had deemed insecure enough that she'd just read instructions on cue cards. Shay collected the papers, grabbed her coffee and jacket and followed her out.

In the Jeep, Shay briefly told her about Holloway's late night telephone call. She left out the parts where Holloway discussed her reassignment, or the warning for Shay to keep her nose clean. Obviously, she didn't share information about Ortelli's call.

She feigned some difficulty finding Kate's apartment building, lest it be discovered that she was familiar with the layout from her previous visit. Shay waited in the parking garage while Kate got an overnight bag. She returned in minutes with a bag and two metal bottles of water.

"Want one?"

"Thanks, but I'm not finished caffeinating." Shay motioned toward her coffee. "Short night."

"I hear that." Kate looked wistfully at the coffee. Instead, she twisted the lid off her recyclable bottle and took a long swig.

Within fifteen minutes they were at the airport check-in counter. Shay handled the necessary paperwork to allow them to carry their weapons. Midway through the process, she caught a glimpse of Kate.

"You okay?" she asked her. Kate nodded, but she looked drawn and pale. "Take a seat while I finish this up. We'll board shortly."

Once onboard, Shay summoned an attendant and ordered juice and toast.

"Christ, Cooper. You're starting to annoy me," Kate chastised her. "If I want anything, I can get it myself."

"Me too," Shay said, ignoring the look from her partner. "I wanted you to have something in your stomach, so I ordered it. Awesome how that works, huh?"

Kate drank some of the juice, but in an act of defiance didn't touch the toast. Shortly, she reclined her seat and fell asleep. When Shay was sure she was out, she reclined her own seat, but her congested mind would not allow her the slightest rest. She thought about the case for which it might be worth jeopardizing her job.

Every agent had DNA on file. It was part of an extensive personnel process that included a background check ten miles long, fingerprint series and red tape about every significant relative and even close friends. The paper chase was built to screen for the best candidates for the FBI. On unfortunate occasions, the prints and DNA served to identify their dead. No such identification was ever made for Williams because no body was ever discovered.

She glanced over at Kate who was soundly sleeping. Small beads of sweat dotted her forehead, and Shay resisted laying a hand on her forehead to check for fever. She figured in Kate's current mood, the move would earn her a punch in the nose. Her lust for the woman had temporarily been replaced by overprotective feelings. She didn't like to see her sick, or in danger.

She turned in her seat, closed her eyes, but still saw the maze of plot points Kate had tried to re-create on a map days earlier. She'd used degrees of latitude and longitude that Williams had obsessively included in his reports concerning locations of final evidence. When she'd finished her work, Kate had leaned against the desk and looked like she'd wanted to cry.

"There's no pattern here," she muttered. "Just a bunch of wayward stings."

"I like a good string art," Shay pacified her, then tipped her head, studied it. "I've paid to see worse stuff on display at the Met."

Her joke hadn't helped. "I feel like I'm wasting my time."

"You're not wasting time, you're following your intuition."

At the diner, Kate had confided in her that Williams had a strange, secretive side to him; a side that would make him the type to do something like encode a message in simple degrees of longitude and latitude in those reports. Even if the methodology wasn't spot on, Shay thought her thinking was. They were learning how to profile the alleged star profiler. It wasn't without its stumbling blocks.

Now the larger problem was quickly becoming that Holloway knew Shay was operating under the influence of Kate. He could pull the plug on the whole partnership without notice and then where would they be?

She shifted in her seat again, and stared out the window at the colorful patchwork of landforms below.

He'd purchased his ticket using an alias, and in a ballsy move even for him, he'd followed the pair down the gangway and boarded the plane right behind them. Now, a mere four seat rows back, eyes shielded by the bill of a ball cap and a pair of glasses, he had an excellent view.

His luck must be incredible as of late. But moreover, he

suspected the team was preoccupied. This diversion he'd simply lucked into, and it was working splendidly. People always got sloppy when emotion was involved. On this day, given the stances and expressions, he contemplated the possibility of a waning trust between the women. It was fun to watch it unravel.

The Watcher settled back into his oversized seat and studied Agent Cooper and her pretty, sleeping partner. He'd see what he could do to stoke the fires of paranoia.

Yes, preoccupation was a splendid thing.

The plane shook suddenly, jarring Kate awake. They'd been circling to land for some time, waiting for a runway opening and for a clearing in the sudden rainstorm.

"Just weather. No big deal." Shay's whisper sliced through the noise of the loudly humming engine.

Kate sat up, adjusted her seat and smoothed the jacket she'd been using for a blanket. Her eyes flared with surprise then minor anger when she realized it was Shay's. She promptly folded it and handed it back.

Kate was tired, very sore, and at the moment despite her slight belly, she was feeling extremely pregnant. Still, she forced herself to relax and did what she knew she should do. "I'm sorry I snapped at you earlier."

"We're both a little edgy lately." Shay glanced at her shirt. "At least you have an excuse."

Once on the ground, they took a rental car straight to the hotel. Shay was glad she hadn't informed Kate of her original plan to go directly to Janice Tremmel's house, otherwise her change of plans would have had her partner angry. But she was worried about Kate. Scottsdale was purely dry heat, and yet she sat in the passenger's seat of their rental car with a sweater wrapped tightly around her. It didn't do much to conceal her shivering.

Despite her desire to protest, Kate lacked the will. She leaned back in the seat, grateful that she was on her way to what would hopefully be a decent bed.

CHAPTER TWENTY-FOUR

The blankets were strewn in a haphazard fashion cocooning Kate as she lay in a fetal position. Her condition had taken a turn for the worse while they were still at the airport. Still, until the moment they checked into the hotel, she vigorously maintained a stoic front, insisting to her partner that she was fine.

One close after another, searing pains ripped through her abdomen, shot down both legs, and it occurred to her that she felt like pure hell. In her determination to not appear to be weak, she wouldn't confess the intensity of her pain for anything. Shay said she could trust her, but for Kate, trust didn't come easily.

Several hours later, the pains had died down, and she was angry she'd wasted valuable investigative time. A knock on her hotel room door told her Shay might be thinking the same thing. Kate sighed, threw back the bedcovers and gingerly stepped onto the floor.

She abhorred walking barefoot on hotel carpet. Throw in the bed sheets that had been used by hundreds of other guests and only passably clean bathrooms, and it was enough to make anyone who'd ever worked in a lab permanently give up travel. The places were veritable filth and DNA fluid reservoirs.

She smoothed her hair on the way to the door, unlocked it and swung it wide open. The hallway was empty. She leaned out and checked both ways. Puzzled, she closed the door and went instead to the one that adjoined her room with the next one and knocked.

Shay opened the door, started to speak, and then tried her best not to notice that Kate was standing there in panties and a T-shirt.

Kate took Shay's facial expression as confirmation that she looked as bad as she felt. She rolled her eyes. "Did you want something?" she asked, annoyance in her voice. Shay only looked at her blankly. "Didn't you just knock on my door?"

Shay's eyes went to Kate's door. She pushed past her partner, made a little jump over the discarded bed sheets and yanked open the door. She replayed Kate's earlier action—looked both ways—and then closed the door again. She locked it, dead-bolted it, and then returned to Kate's side.

"Christ, don't answer your door." Shay's voice was pitched with anxiety. "Never, *ever* answer a hotel door."

"Okay, Mom."

"I'm being serious. You know what kind of weirdos there are out there?"

"Yeah. I work with you," Kate answered dryly. But Shay didn't budge or even blink. She toned it down. "Fine. Whatever. This is ridiculous. Look—here we are in freaking..." She waved her arm, her tired brain struggling to recall where in the world they'd just landed.

"Arizona," Shay supplied.

"Freaking *Arizona*." Kate folded her arms across her chest. "And we're wasting time arguing in this hotel instead of doing our job."

Shay softened. "Are you okay, now? You looked like hell earlier, no offense."

"You don't look so great yourself, no offense," Kate shot back. She sighed and plopped down on the edge of the destroyed bed, calmed down some. "I had a touch of stomach flu."

Kate rubbed her neck, drawing Shay's eyes to its soft appearance and the graceful curve that disappeared below the V-neckline of her thin cotton T-shirt. She swallowed hard, forced herself to look away. She asked, "Are you getting enough to drink?"

"Even water is sort of making me nauseous."

"*Is* making your nauseous, or *was*? Because if it *is*, we have no business going anywhere."

"*Was*. And I'm fine now." Kate sounded impatient all over again. "Can we just go to the Tremmel place already?"

"Whatever you say, sunshine." Shay returned to her own room calling over her shoulder, "You might want to put some pants on though. I'm just saying."

Kate looked down. Her cheeks went instantly hot.

When the agents arrived at the Tremmel residence they were stopped at the door by Scottsdale PD. Apparently Governor Tremmel had also called in favors with the locals too. A tough-acting officer immediately informed the pair that the situation was under control, standard response from local authorities when the FBI was called in. They were well-versed in these feelings of animosity between the agencies. Governor Tremmel himself was there, and when he saw the agents, he quickly cleared them for entry. Still, Scottsdale PD regarded them like the plague as they walked into the lavish home.

The governor summarized the situation: no forced entry, no sign of struggle. His focus was on Janice's former lover as well as her current boyfriend. The women cast meaningful glances in each other's direction, indicating that Janice could have left on her own accord. Still, they listened patiently.

"Mind if we have a look around?" Shay asked.

"By all means." That the governor was truly concerned was evidenced by his deeply lined brow and hands that he continually wrung. "You want me to clear the local PD out?"

"No, we can manage." Shay forced a reassuring smile, nodded at her partner.

Together they headed for the kitchen to begin their inspection. When they were out of the governor's earshot, Shay asked, "What do you think? Spontaneous vacation?"

Kate pulled open a few drawers; each was lined with shelf paper that matched the wallpaper. She inspected the glass cabinets, each meticulously arranged with plates and glasses. Nothing curious at all. Nothing indicative in the refrigerator, either. Kate quietly remarked, "This woman is in serious danger of being boring."

They wandered into the bedroom, the most promising room for clues. Shay looked in drawers, behind dressers and underneath the bed. Kate checked the closet. She pulled out a purse.

"Good find," Shay congratulated her.

Kate opened the door all the way up to reveal a dozen more designer purses dangling from the hooks. Still, she took the first one to the bed, dumped out its contents. She shook her head. "No ID. It's probably not her current choice."

Shay stepped out of the closet. "These others are empty save for some gum and old lip gloss." She joined her at the bed. "Maybe she had her ID on her. Not unheard of. I carry mine in my pocket."

Kate shot her a look. "I can't see you with a purse." She took a second look at the pile, extracted a long box that at first glance resembled a tampon holder. She opened it and her expression suddenly became alert. "But I don't think she'd leave home without this." Kate held up her find. "An EpiPen. She's got an allergy that requires emergency treatment."

"You're right." Shay approached her. "So, maybe the gov's onto something."

Someone cleared his throat behind them. She turned to see the same tough guy cop who'd greeted her. He attempted civility. "We've got the boyfriend and ex down at the station. They came in on their own free will to help fill in the blanks."

Shay wondered if the governor had encouraged the cop's shift in attitude. She regarded him quietly, kindly. "I'm sure you're doing everything possible."

He nodded, spoke reluctantly. "We don't have much else, to be honest. Luminal turned up a little blood in the bathtub, could be from shaving. If not, it's probably been degraded by cleanser—you know all the tricks by now. Still, we're taking the trap with us to the lab."

Shay turned toward Kate. "What do you think, partner? Anything else we can do here?"

Kate shook her head. Shay turned toward the cop, handed him the EpiPen for an evidence bag and also her business card. "We're in the Melcher Hotel tonight if you want us."

Shay admired how Kate handled people. Her careful choice of words put the ball in the PD's court, just where the local cops liked it. In the end it always netted the Feds better information.

"And if you get something interesting off that blood, could you keep us in the loop?" Kate dipped her chin, eyes wide, and sweetly added, "As a courtesy, of course?"

"Of course," he said and took the card. The women left.

"You're good at that," Shay complimented her.

But Kate's mood had taken a turn toward frustration. "Why are we here? Is this your way of helping me forget about my hunt for Tony?"

"No." Shay unlocked the car and they got in. "I thought you might want to see what it's like outside that building. Real partners investigating. Together."

Kate leaned back, settled in. She looked disappointed. "Well, there's not much action here."

"I didn't think it would hurt us to get out of that office for a day anyway, given everything you told me at the diner."

"So you do believe me?" Kate brightened some, but tried not to appear obvious about it.

Shay nodded. "But, I don't think it's logical to link each and every case we come across to Agent Williams' disappearance."

"I'm not obsessed with it, if that's what you're saying."

"You are obsessed with it, but I understand why." Shay headed for the highway that would take them back to the hotel. "It just feels like we're creating pieces to the puzzle instead of looking at what's actually there for a solve. And we can't make this a single-minded mission. There's other work to be done."

"Thanks for the vote of confidence." Kate angrily stared straight ahead. "I'm sure you abided by that single-minded credo when your son went missing."

"That's none of…" She started to fire an insult, but tamped down her temper. She took a deep breath, started again, calmly this time. "You lose your job, you lose your access, then you've got nothing at all." She slowed for a stop sign, turned to look at her partner. "Nothing at all. Is that what you want?"

"No," Kate answered at last, no less angry.

"Then you get quiet and you be careful. Get back their respect, get your access. Period."

"Did that work for you?"

Shay calmly stated, "I'm over it."

"You can't tell me you gave up…" Kate's voice lost its edge. "I won't believe it."

"I'm. Over. It." Shay repeated, sternly this time. The car didn't budge for several more seconds despite the fact that the street was empty. "If you have even an ounce of respect for me, do not bring my son into this again."

Kate sat back, tried to relax. She figured Shay's son was already "in this," but it wasn't her doing. She wanted to share her suspicion with her partner, but thought better of it. Not tonight.

They rode back to the hotel in silence.

CHAPTER TWENTY-FIVE

There was a knock on the door that separated their rooms. In the midst of brushing her teeth, Shay unlocked her side and let her partner in.

"Just a sec…" Shay left, spit out the toothpaste, and rinsed. She returned blotting her lips on the upturned hem of her well-worn Quantico sweatshirt. Kate's eyes momentarily flicked to her partner's toned midriff. "Something wrong?"

Kate refocused on her mission and took a single step into her partner's room. She tossed a large envelope onto her bed and promptly returned to her own side of the threshold boundary. Shay sensed surrender or defeat in her; she couldn't be sure which one.

"That came just now via courier from the Scottsdale PD."

"Okay." But Shay sensed there was more.

"And I'm sorry."

Though Shay wasn't quite certain which infraction was being referred to, she nodded. "Accepted."

"You're probably right about me needing to play it cool. I guess you would know best, given your history." Kate's unkempt hair wound into loose, long, concealing waves. "I should probably apologize for a few things, actually."

"Just credit me one or two, would you?" Shay grinned, tried to lighten the subject. Despite the curtain of hair, she could see that Kate didn't look well. "You good?"

"Just fine," Kate assured her with a hint of sadness in her tone. Suddenly she blurted, "I don't trust you, Agent Cooper. I wish I could, but I don't."

Shay felt her chest tighten. She nodded, forced herself to say, "I understand."

"Do you? Because I know you go way back with Roger, and I think he's keeping something from me. Something about Tony. I think he paired you with me to report to him my every move." She had rambled until she was nearly out of juice. For an encore, she quietly added, "And I think the whole thing stinks, and I can't prove a goddamn thing."

Kate looked exhausted by the time she was finished. Shay clenched her eyes shut.

"What in the hell was I thinking?" she muttered at last. She opened her eyes, stared blankly at Kate. "You shouldn't be here, Agent Harris. You shouldn't be flying this late in your condition, and you sure as hell shouldn't be investigating anything when you are so *clearly* screwed up from your own shit."

Kate was too taken aback for anger.

"I may be an asshole—but I'm not the asshole you think I am." Shay shook her head. "And I'm not about to put you in more danger if you're in it already—or endanger your baby if you're not in danger and you're just a flat-out nutcase."

Shay took a step toward her at the same time Kate stepped back. Shay softly chuckled. "Hell, I took this assignment to get you out of the office, to get you out your tiny comfort zone because it's no longer comfortable." She paused. "What the hell was I thinking?"

Kate, angry now, raised her voice. "You're not responsible for me. I take care of *myself.*"

"Okay," was Shay's feeble-sounding response. "Whatever."

"But as far as I'm concerned, we are a pair in the eyes of the FBI only. We're not confidantes or buddies." She took another backward step. "Just partners. Period."

Kate closed the door on Shay and went to draw herself a bath. She hadn't known it was possible to feel less secure than she already did, but that was before she stopped and opened her e-mail. A blind-box e-mail with an attachment indicated that Roger Holloway had not yanked the Lanterman case from them after all. Copies of the report included Shay Cooper's signature on the bottom of each and every page. Her own partner had put the case back on ice. And why the hell wouldn't she have mentioned that to her? Kate had gone to the woman's house to personally deliver the news that it had been yanked from them. Or so she'd thought.

She sank into the warm, sudsy tub, wished away every worry and pain, and closed her eyes.

Shay had been staring at the muted television set for over an hour. She listened futilely for movement from the next room. Kate was probably long asleep. Shay flipped aimlessly through the channels, looking for something to think to. Presently she was thinking about her partner, lying next door, hating her.

She sat up at last, rubbed her neck, got a drink of water—all the preliminary things one does when trying to fall asleep. Her eyes fell on the envelope Kate had tossed into her room. She picked it up and dumped the contents on the floor, got down and rolled onto her belly to look at the mess she'd created.

The Scottsdale PD had certainly filed an extensive preliminary report. That, along with the transcripts from conversations with the two men, and it all added up to a lot of nothing.

She must have fallen asleep. The bathwater was tepid at best when she awoke to the noise. Guarding her footing, she stood up in the tub and wrapped an oversized towel around her. She opened the bathroom door just as the door of her hotel room closed. Shock momentarily paralyzed her. She snapped out of it and hammered her fist against Shay's door.

Shay had momentarily dozed off, but was up in a flash. She leapt over the scattered pile of discarded files and opened the door. "Yeah?"

Kate stood there in a thick terry towel, damp hair messily pinned on top of her head. Droplets of bathwater still dotted her neck. She looked shaken. Shay stepped aside, motioned for her to enter.

"I know you're going to say you weren't just in my room."

Wide awake, Shay straightened her posture. "Someone was in your room?"

"The door was closing as I came out of the bathroom."

"Sit down," Shay commanded.

Kate lightly perched herself on the foot of her partner's bed. Trembling, she clutched her towel more tightly around her.

Shay snatched her gun off the nightstand and flicked back the safety. "Stay here."

Shay disappeared into the adjoining room. In moments Kate heard a door opening and closing, and footsteps up and down the front walk outside. Her partner returned, looking puzzled.

"You're staying here tonight."

Kate felt her cheeks burn, and she suddenly found her nerve. "I can take care of myself."

"Lady, if you were doing such a sensational job of that, you wouldn't be sitting here in your towel, scared as hell."

"I'm not scared," Kate countered.

"Well, if you're not, then that's my first indication you might be off your rocker." Shay motioned toward the other room. "A Peeping Tom? And your stuff's probably been ransacked? What'd you have in there that anyone would come after, huh? You might want to make me privy to that information if it compromises the safety of either one of us."

"Stop it!" Kate sprang up from the bed.

But Shay was furious and couldn't stop. "Maybe you're the one with the secrets, huh? Maybe you're putting this trust crap on me because you're covering yourself!"

Kate went toe to toe with her partner, jamming her index finger in the woman's chest. "What reason would I have for trying to trick you! Tell me that! At least I'm not the one signing off on cases without good explanation!"

They stood face to face, both breathing heavily.

"All right," Shay said at last. The Lanterman case. It made a little sense now, but she wasn't prepared to answer for it, and certainly didn't want to bring Ortelli's name into this already screwed-up scenario. She took a step back, lightly pushed Kate's hand away. Even when she was spitting angry words, Kate's nearness did something almost downright painful to her. Shay grimaced, scrubbed her hand roughly through her hair. She calmly repeated, "All right."

Kate didn't back down and Shay tried again, slightly raising her voice. "Sit down, already. This isn't helping anything. You've got me thinking like you now, because I'm about to say we're probably doing exactly what *they* want us to do—tear each other apart!" She stopped short, muttered with disbelief, "Whoever the fuck *they* are."

Kate's posture slumped slightly. She sat down on the edge of the bed and watched Shay pace the floor in front of her.

"Let's try something different," Shay finally said. "Did Agent Williams ever mention anyone holding a grudge against him? He was an arrogant prick, no offense."

"Would you stop saying *no offense* each and every time you say anything about him?" Kate rolled her eyes. "I never had any feelings for him—and I like him less now than I ever did!"

Shay stopped short, thumbed her chin, furrowed her brow. She dropped into a squat directly in front of Kate, used her most understanding voice despite her confusion. "Make me understand—you are carrying the man's baby."

Kate stared at her for a long time, and Shay could see a mental war playing out behind the woman's eyes. Would she yell at her? Would she tell her the truth? At last, Kate's gaze returned to her classic stony look. "That, Agent Cooper, is none of your business."

"Pardon, but it is my business," Shay corrected her. "When you're my partner, you're my business. If someone's after you, that's my business. Follow me? After your baby? My business again. Do I make myself clear, partner?"

"Not for long." Kate stood up and headed for the door. "Soon enough I'll—"

"I know—that whole transfer to Texas business." Shay plopped down in the space her partner had just vacated. She was worn out. "But while you're still here, you think you could tell me if Williams had any enemies? You know, just on the off chance that you're wrong about him being the nation's worst mass murderer." Her voice reeked of sarcasm. "Maybe somebody actually just killed the son of a bitch and now they want to eliminate you as a witness?"

"Now, how would I know that?"

Shay shrugged. "What's your intuition saying? Is he alive?"

"Intuition makes it that simple, huh?" She turned the game on her partner. "What's your intuition say about your son? Is he still alive?"

Shay's gaze went as stony as Kate's. "No."

Kate hadn't anticipated that answer, but then again she hadn't anticipated asking such a horrible question. She was speaking out of impulse, her words were chaotic, and the result made her feel worse than she imagined it could.

Kate abruptly excused herself and went to her own room.

At Shay's insistence, the door between them remained open. Each lay in her own bed watching the same muted black-and-white movie on her own television.

Together. Apart.

CHAPTER TWENTY-SIX

"Clean as a whistle." The announcement came from Pierre Dunedin, a computer technologist and all around tech geek employed by the FBI. Shay had commissioned him to sweep their office for a bug on the Bureau's time. It wasn't like she could make Holloway any more suspicious of her than he already was.

She snatched up the phone handset, gave it a look. "This too?"

"The phone is the big no-brainer." Pierre's eyes lit up. He loved nothing more than to demonstrate his abilities. He unscrewed the telephone mouthpiece on the ancient-looking landline and held it up for her to inspect. "If there was a drop-in transmitter, it'd be in this compartment. That thing gets its power from the phone itself, then transmits a crystal clear signal to the receiver."

"Impressive."

"Now, if this was a cordless, we'd have other things to look at, like wireless interception, mobile receivers, channels, wavelengths and so forth."

"My ears are bleeding with your tech-speak," Shay complained. But she knew he loved that too. "What about the rest of the joint? Lamps? Lights? The works?"

"I swept your walls and overhead lights for electrets, light switches and sockets for FM transmitters." He walked toward the wall, tapped on an old intercom system. "We don't use these anymore, but for the right occasion, these things make splendid transmitters. I clipped all the wires inside yours, just in case." He gave a good-natured shrug. "Naturally."

"Naturally," she echoed him, smiling.

"I once planted a mic that was three-sixteenths of an inch across—that's all. Perfect transmitter." Pierre's eyes glazed over as he waxed poetic over his triumph. His former illegal life as a phone phreak and wiretap artist had earned him his position at the Bureau. His current job probably wasn't as much fun as his former life, but it kept him out of prison. He snapped out of his moment, got serious again. "Here's what not to do, now. Don't pick up any stray ink pens. Don't swap office supplies. Don't order in takeout food."

She shriveled her nose. "Wiretap in my egg foo yung?"

"I've seen weirder," he whispered.

"Note to self, avoid Chinese food."

"Also, take your meetings in the conference room—it only takes a split second and a bit of chewed gum to mic anything."

"And avoid gum chewers." She amended her earlier note. She grinned brightly. "You're amazing, you know that?"

"I do know that." He gathered his stuff. "I'll sweep your office twice a week until you tell me otherwise."

Shay frowned. "You think that's necessary?"

He shrugged. "Depends. What are you working on?" Pierre was practically salivating. "Anything good?"

"Right now, no." Shay saw his disappointment. "But if it gets good, you'll be the first one to know, I promise."

"Thanks, boss." He happily exited their office, passing Kate on her way in.

"Two things." Shay clapped her hands together. "First of all, we've got a clean office. I just had Dunedin sweep the place. We're good for this day, at least."

Kate set her stuff on the desktop, hung up her jacket. "How do you know he isn't one of them?"

"All this talk of *them* again." Shay hiked an eyebrow. "He's Dunedin. I've known him forever. I'd sooner be one of them than he would be." She hooked air quotes, but when she realized the possibility she'd insinuated, she rolled her eyes, shook her head. "Strike that. I forgot I'm talking to the Queen of Paranoia."

Kate rested her hands on her hips. "What's the second thing? You said there were two."

"Oh, yeah. We got trace." Shay smiled, set the folder proudly before her. "Trace evidence from the Tremmel place." She eyed her, suddenly wary. "Now, that doesn't mean this is associated in any way with Williams' case. It just means that the Scottsdale PD pulled enough clean blood out of the drain trap to type it."

"What type?"

"AB," Shay said. "But don't make too much of it."

But Kate's eyes were already wide, her mind swirling with possibilities. "Less than three percent of the population has AB blood type."

"I know. Calm down." Shay took her seat, then noticed that Kate looked suddenly worried. "What is it?"

Kate shook her head. "The more deeply we get involved in this, the more worried I am that we're going to be right about it all."

"Slow down and put one foot in front of the other," Shay calmed her. "Science, that's your bag, right Harris? We form a hypothesis, check it, and accept or refute, am I right? That's all we're doing. If your theory's wrong, maybe we'll discover something valuable along the way. Nothing lost."

Kate stared into space a moment. Finally she nodded. "We're running this through CODIS, right?"

"Pending the lab report, and they're backed up for a few days." Shay's expression turned serious. "Now that we're sure no one's listening, have you got anyone you can stay with for a while?"

"What for?"

"In light of what happened in Scottsdale, and now that we've got our hands on some secondary blood—" She stopped short to insert what was becoming her standard disclaimer. "Not that I'm saying this is relative to Williams' case. But in the event that it is, I hate the idea of you being alone."

"And where should I be?" Kate dipped her chin, her eyelids fluttering with her exaggerated sarcasm. She put on a faux whisky voice. "With you, perhaps?"

Shay sat up a little straighter. She wondered if she was putting off inadvertent vibes about how attracted she was to the woman.

"Don't mess with me," Shay practically croaked. "I'm asking if you have family nearby. A...boyfriend?"

Kate folded her arms, stood like a smallish tower of stone before her partner. "Since you seem hell-bent on finding out about my personal life—I never had a boyfriend. I had a very long-term girlfriend. A girlfriend who wanted a baby, just not *this* particular baby, and therefore she's now a very *ex* very long-term girlfriend. Any more mysteries I can clear up for you, Agent Cooper?"

Shay felt her stomach drop at the spontaneous admission.

"You're a confusing woman, Harris," she muttered. Her eyes wandered to Kate's belly, then back. "You're standing there with your turncoat partner's baby in your belly, making some kind of a lesbian confession—and I'm the untrustworthy one?" Shay chuckled softly. "I can't top this. Hell, I need a scorecard just to keep up with you."

"Fuck you."

"You first." Shay was suddenly very serious. "No matter what you think of me, listen to me anyway. An old...*contact* of mine warned me that you may be in danger. I don't want to leave anything to chance."

Shay hated calling Ortelli her contact almost as much as she hated informing Kate about any of this.

"A contact," Kate echoed in disbelief.

"That's right." Shay sighed. "And as long as we're making big-ass confessions, agreeing to reexamine these cases with you wasn't entirely out of the kindness of my heart."

"Of course. It was the contact." Kate nodded suddenly. "The contact whose warning was more reliable than the information I gave you."

"I should have known that's how you'd take it." Shay rubbed her forehead. "My apologies."

"Thanks for the trust, *partner.*" Kate grabbed her briefcase and jacket. She headed for the door.

"FYI," Shay said in a bored-sounding tone before Kate stormed out. "I'm a phone call away if you need me."

"Fuck you," she only repeated. The door slammed so hard the windows rattled.

"Thanks. Good talk. See you later," Shay muttered to no one. She yanked open her top desk drawer and pulled out a bag of sunflower seeds.

Kate emerged from the elevator in her apartment building and nearly tripped over the fattest tabby cat she'd ever seen. She caught herself, scooped up the cat, and carried him down the hallway. Her next-door neighbor threw open her front door before Kate could press the buzzer. She snatched the cat out of Kate's arms.

"Shame on you!" she chastised Kate. "Trying to steal Mr. Kittens. Poor baby," she cooed. "Poor, poor baby. I'll protect you."

She issued Kate a death glare. Kate only rolled her eyes, returned to her own apartment door. "You really need to keep an eye on your cat, Ms. Dupree. She's going to get outside one of these days."

"You really should get your own pet instead of running around trying to steal other people's babies!" The old woman was clearly out of her mind. Kate shook her head, pushed open her door.

"Never mind, crazy unwed mother! You're unfit to parent a cat, even!" She raised her voice. "Men and women coming here at all hours of the night! You're nothing short of a full-fledged trollop!"

Kate considered her words for a moment before stepping back into the hallway. She cleared her throat, causing the batty neighbor to turn around to face her.

"I don't take guests, Ms. Dupree." And it was true, though she didn't care at all what the old woman thought of her. Kate hadn't had a single visitor in the months since she'd moved in.

"Malarkey!" Ms. Dupree scoffed. Her white curly hair looked a little wilder than usual. Kate wondered if the old woman had already been into the box wine. She wondered how her neighbor had mastered the art of swearing and insulting in such a sweet sounding tone. "Men, women—the whole gamut! You're a tramp."

Kate mined the information out of the insult, and she was curious. She took a small step toward her nutty neighbor, gently asked, "Can you tell me what they looked like?"

"Oh brother." Ms. Dupree rolled her eyes. "The man was one of you secret agents, spying all around here like he was waiting for a rendezvous."

"Just a minute." Kate left her long enough to snag her briefcase out of her apartment. She rifled through it, extracted a Bureau picture of Agent Williams. She returned to the hallway, held it out. "Is this him?"

She peered at the photo. "I don't know. Could be. I can't keep up with all your callers." Ms. Dupree opened her door and dropped Mr. Kittens inside, intending to follow her cat.

Kate stopped her from going inside so quickly. "Wait—and the woman?"

"How would I know?" Ms. Dupree raised her arms high, let them fall to her sides. "I can't keep track. Tall, dark hair, dressed in a man's suit, pale as a ghost…"

Shay Cooper.

Kate let the neurotic, rambling woman go. She went into her own apartment, into the bedroom and tore everything out of her closet until she came to the overstuffed folder. It was Agent Shay Cooper, A-Z, about a hundred printed pages of background. Weeks earlier she'd stuffed the information in her closet where she intended to keep it until she could destroy it. That was back when she felt she could possibly trust her partner.

With renewed interest, she laid every piece of paper out in a grid on the floor. She'd comb each one until she felt confident she knew who the real Agent Cooper was. She sank into the only chair. It was hard to believe her instincts had failed her again.

CHAPTER TWENTY-SEVEN

Chicago had given its residents an early glimpse into summer, but Kate wasn't in the mood to open her windows. Having real air in the house used to give her such a sensation of easy-going freedom. Now, it felt like a security breach.

Still in her work clothes, she had made a nice study of Shay Cooper for the better part of the day. The information created a chaotic timeline and she wasn't sure what she was supposed to learn from it.

"You're an investigator," she told herself, taking a sip of water. "So…investigate."

She re-read details about the huge New York drug bust, Cooper's signature achievement with the Bureau. Len Ortelli's clan was a major force to be reckoned with in the drug world and Shay had virtually single-handedly exterminated the entire operation. The courts had awarded Ortelli amnesty in exchange for names. In the end, everyone went to prison and Ortelli went deep underground.

Then Christopher Cooper vanished. Shortly afterward, Shay transferred to Miami and Kate wondered why. On a hunch, she ran Ortelli's mugshot through the facial recognition software and in moments had a positive match. A farmer's market in Miami regularly photographed all patrons as they came and went for immigration and law enforcement purposes. Ortelli would no longer raise a red flag with the authorities, thanks to his crafty trade for civilian life. But it told Kate something. Shay had a vengeful streak in her. She'd gone to Miami to settle the score.

She considered what she did know, that strange things seemed to happen to her whenever Shay was around. Then there was a matter of this mystery contact. Who was she protecting and why? Was it possible that Shay had also tied Tony to the disappearance of her son? If so, was she willing to trade Kate's safety for information about the missing boy?

Kate's stomach lurched and her head spun. She took another sip of water, swiped her damp lips on the back of her hand. These suspicions, whatever their worth, utterly undermined the glimmer of faith she had in Shay Cooper.

Feeling sickly and paranoid, and without a clue what the late night office visit would yield, Kate grabbed her briefcase and headed for the door.

The Watcher knew things were quickly coming to a head. Fear was preeminent and mistrust was the soup of the day. He knew their habits by now, knew where each woman was; he'd effectively alienated each from the other, and as a result both were amply paranoid for no good reason.

He considered how much fun it had been watching events build, but soon enough it would end. He'd never had better candidates.

The government boasted that it invested one hundred thousand dollars training each agent for CIRG; they were built to infiltrate and flush out varieties of domestic and international evil. They endured grueling background checks, batteries of tests, more training, more physical and psychological challenges—no losers allowed here, no way.

The Watcher considered that if his former game was checkers, he'd raised his own bar to chess. Still, there were smarter, more prominent pawns out there. As for this match, he was about to checkmate.

Sitting on a worn-out bed in a dive hotel, he finished cleaning his gun and put it back together. It was vital that he make no mistakes, for this game had an added catch he'd not anticipated and the tiniest discrepancies could bear the most catastrophic results. Strangely, it didn't bother him like he thought it might. And that made him feel even more invincible.

At home, Shay grabbed a beer and wandered down to the basement. As she did for about ten minutes every night, she watched the computer software still hard at work, still spinning number and letter combinations, trying to crack Williams' password for the virtual file parking space.

She unscrewed the bottle top with the edge of her T-shirt and took a swig. She recalled once reading a profile that Williams had composed about a bomber who had a penchant for leaving tidy little explosives in elementary school garbage cans. In this rare case, Williams had actually saved the day. He'd scouted out the device and it had taken him only a minute or two to defuse the crude structure—despite the fact that Williams had no experience with such things. It made better sense now; Williams had probably created the device himself.

In Williams' profile for the alleged bomber, he'd claimed the male had an intense fear of commitment, was a victim of abuse, and the product of a fatherless home where religion ruled and children were silent. The perp had a fascination with law authorities, was a fire truck chaser, a non-smoking, unmarried, businesslike-appearing, oxford-wearing everyday schmuck. He even went so far as to say the man had been a former bed-wetter, didn't swing his arms when he walked, and that he resented his mother. The perfect recipe, according to Williams' rambling report, for a head-case closet hater of childhood authoritarians— hence a school would be his natural choice.

For Christ's sake—where did the man get this stuff? Was it a true composite of himself? Or was he just frigging with everyone? Shay figured Williams was a walking, talking contradiction to the FBI code of ethics. It made it difficult to understand a man she was trying to get to know strictly on paper.

She sighed, ran her fingers through her hair, and turned to a different computer to check her public e-mail account. The subject heading on the topmost message caused her to lean forward for a better look.

Check your other screen.

Shay opened the blind box e-mail, but the body of it was blank. She leaned back in her chair, and as she contemplated it, her eyes wandered back to Agent Williams' computer screen.

ACCESS GRANTED.

Shay sat up so quickly she sloshed a spot of beer on her shirt. She set the bottle aside, and gave the screen her undivided attention. Her eyes went wide when she saw the single line of text worth the elaborate password protection:

Tonight she dies.

The words stared her in the face, buzzed through her head. In an instant it vanished, replaced by a million tiny letters dancing in a nonstop chorus line of mockery.

HAHAHAHAHAHA...

Shay stood up so quickly she knocked over her chair. Someone knew she had the hard drive.

She went to the nearest basement window, checked the seal, but found no evidence of a break-in; saw no peering eyes outside to witness her harried behavior. She went to the next window and the next checking the seals, the screens—everything. At the fourth window, a thin security wire jutted out from the rubber stripping, clipped and covered with tinfoil. She ran her finger over it, flicked it off the end, exposing the end of the wire. Immediately her alarm system detected the circuit interruption and started beeping loudly to report the perceived security breach.

"Son of a bitch," she muttered. She thought about the office and the bug sweep, but had never considered that she'd need one for her own house. She wondered if he was listening to her at that very moment. Fury coursed through her every vein as she screamed, "Son of a bitch! Williams!"

Shay fished her cell phone out of her jeans pocket and hit autodial on her way upstairs. She grabbed her jacket and headed for the Jeep. It went straight to Kate's voice mail. She tried four more times on her way toward the highway. At last her wary sounding partner picked up.

"What do you want, Agent Cooper?"

"Harris—thank God." She veered her Jeep onto the entrance ramp bound for Chicago. "Where are you?"

"On my way to the office. Why?" Her tone reeked of paranoia that Shay didn't have time to dance around.

"Don't go there. Go somewhere else and I'll meet you. Someplace public, okay?"

"What are you talking about?"

Shay could hear traffic in the background of the call. In her escalating panic, she yelled, "Don't go to the office! Do you hear me?"

"I'm almost there."

"Well stop! Go to a coffee shop or something until I can get to you!" She cut a Hyundai off and swerved onto the on-ramp. "I need to see you."

Kate sighed. "If this is about the files I commissioned from New York and Miami, I've already seen them. I know all about it."

Puzzled, Shay said, "About what? This isn't about files! Christ—don't give me the runaround. Not right now—don't do it!" And when her partner didn't answer, she yelled, "Hello? Can you hear me?"

"I think I'm finished listening to you, Agent Cooper," Kate announced. "I'm very, very finished."

The sound of a dozen or so cars laying on their horns blasted as Shay bypassed even those in the passing lane via the shoulder of the highway. She dropped the gas pedal, and tires squealing, literally left them in her dust.

The line went dead. Shay tossed the phone in the seat beside her. She swiped her hand across her damp forehead, stomped the brakes then the gas alternately, swerved around another line of cars, and hit the shoulder again to fast-track the normally lengthy drive.

Kate turned down a side street on the hunt for a parking space. A coffee shop was nearby, she wondered if she should simply make the call and meet Shay. Her partner had sounded utterly desperate on the phone. But it was getting harder to trust her instincts. Her phone rang and she glanced at the screen. It was a private line. She punched the talk button.

"Agent Harris, speaking," she politely answered, in case it wasn't her neurotic partner. And it wasn't.

"By all means, do not trust Shay Cooper."

The whispered voice was difficult to hear over the non-stop horns of downtown Chicago traffic. But the message was unmistakable.

"Who is this?" Kate asked, but there was no answer. "Hello?"

The line was dead. She dropped the phone in the seat beside her, stared at the traffic light for a while before realizing the honking horns were aimed at her. She swallowed hard and pressed the accelerator, bypassing all notions of coffee shops.

Who was her hit-and-run caller? The supposed *contact* of Shay's?

She made an illegal U-turn and headed for the office.

CHAPTER TWENTY-EIGHT

Being around Agent Harris always made Lou a nervous wreck. She repeatedly scanned the woman's parking permit and felt more flustered than ever when the computer wouldn't accept it.

"That computer still giving you problems?" But Kate was hardly in the mood for conversation.

"Sure is." Lou tried to manually punch the numbers in again. Finally, the light turned green, and Lou breathed a sigh of relief. "I know you're not going to believe this, but this machine only seems to do this to you and your partner."

"You don't say?" Kate absently remarked. She accepted her pass back from the attendant.

"Weird, right?" Lou grinned at her. "Oh well. Have a good night, Agent Harris."

Kate nodded and started up the parking ramp to level four and her assigned spot.

Having thoroughly pissed off fifty percent of all Chi-town traffic, Shay's Jeep nearly ramped the parking garage entrance. Were it not for the spikes at the entrance that would have pierced a dozen holes in her tires, she would have busted right through the wooden arm and barreled down the garage ramp. As it was, she rolled down the window and breathlessly fired a single question.

"Harris here yet?" And when Lou gave her a strange look, she spoke more clearly. "Has Agent Kate Harris been here?"

Lou made an upward motion. "About two minutes ago. Level four."

Without another word, Shay jumped out of her car and left it idling behind the parking gate. Astonished, Lou watched her run toward the stairwell.

An agent entered the parking garage on foot. Lou started to call to him, but he beat her to the punch.

"Good evening, Lou."

The deep voice triggered recognition, but Lou couldn't place it. She desperately tried to see his face, but it was shadowed by the hood of a Quantico sweatshirt. "How's it going?" she called, trying to buy a sentence or two more from the odd fellow. She stepped outside the booth and watched him pass. He kept a safe distance.

"Going good," he said without establishing eye contact. By now he was headed toward the up-sloping ramp. "Have a good night."

She left the booth entirely, and jogged a few half-hearted steps after him, still trying to place him. As he passed beneath a security light, she was able to read the last name stitched on the back of his official sweatshirt. Her mouth gaped.

In her hurry, Kate got out of her car and promptly dumped her briefcase and its contents onto the garage floor. With some effort, she knelt down to assess the damage; stuff was scattered everywhere, rolling nearly under her car. She sighed, but stopped short when she heard what she thought was the sounds of shuffling shoes. Nothing. Casting small glances over her shoulder, she hurried to collect and reassemble her belongings.

Lou ran back into the small booth and picked up her portable radio.

"Security, come in." No one answered. She smacked the side of the thing against the countertop and impatiently tried again. "Security? Come back?"

Still nothing. She thought about the stranger.

"Holy fuck." She frowned deeply. It didn't make sense. "It can't be, right?"

She started out of the booth, doubled back and grabbed her measly Taser gun, the only weapon she was qualified to carry. The Bureau would have her ass and her job if they found out who she'd let into the garage. She took off toward the same stairwell Agent Cooper had disappeared into. She'd heard rumors about paranoid Kate Harris. Perhaps they weren't rumors at all...?

She picked up her pace, hit the stairwell and took the steps two at a time to catch up with them.

Kate crammed her things into the briefcase and snapped it shut. The sound of the metal door smacking against the cement wall drew her attention to the stairwell several yards in front of her. She slowly stood, felt for her gun.

Shay emerged, showed her hands flat in front of her when she saw that her partner had her gun at the ready.

"Kate!" she called to her, relief evident in her tone. "It's okay—it's me!"

The confirmation that it was Shay had Kate bring her gun front and center. She didn't raise it, yet.

"Oh, shit..." Shay mumbled. "Kate, it's not me you're after—you have to know that."

Kate's voice trembled. "Why should I believe you?"

"Someone is fucking with both of us. You've got to trust me. You *can* trust me." She swallowed hard, took a step closer to Kate. They moved in a slow circle.

Kate's voice was quiet. "I know Holloway put you up to keeping tabs on me. You're trying to ruin me."

"No, I swear that's not true." Though Shay secretly wondered if it that was Holloway's true intention.

Kate shrugged. "Is it? Do I look stupid?"

"No, no you don't," Shay pleaded. She shook her head. "Please, I'm asking you to listen to me. You're in danger—"

"No! You listen to *me!*"

"Kate—" But Shay's gravelly voice was cut short when Lou burst out of the stairwell door behind her. For the second time in minutes, the metal door crashed against the stairwell.

"Agent Cooper!" Lou's Taser gun was pointed over Shay's shoulder, aimed at the opposite stairwell. She ran ahead of them. "Get out of here! Both of you!"

A sharp twang echoed throughout the top level of the garage. Lou's body jerked with the impact and she slumped to her knees. Shay's gun was out of her holster and trained on the dark shadowy stairwell. She blindly fired twice. Both bullets made hollow sounding clinks as they struck cement, then pinged to the ground.

"Harris—get down!" she screamed, running for the stairwell. She was dodging fire she couldn't predict, firing at a target she couldn't see. She lunged for the emergency box and slammed the button which bellowed a nuclear-sounding alarm that resounded off the cement structure. She dropped to the ground near the stairwell.

Shielded by the guardrail, Shay slowly rose up when all sounds of gunfire ceased. In the distance she could see her partner crouched beside her car, and poor Lou, flat in a bloody pool on the floor. Shay emerged from her place and checked the stairwell. With the alarm still blasting, it was impossible to hear any footsteps. She ran down several flights, stopped breathless on the landing, but heard and saw nothing. She fished her phone out of her pocket and phoned medics as she hiked back up to the top level.

She went to Lou and crouched over her. The useless Taser gun lay unfired, several feet away. Shay hurriedly bunched her own jacket up and used it to staunch the wound in Lou's chest.

"No worries. Help is on the way, kiddo."

She unbuttoned the top few buttons of the young woman's coveralls. Lou wore a Superhero T-shirt that was shredded and bloodied right in the center. Shay felt even worse about the woman's chances of surviving. She swallowed hard, pulled the coveralls back together so Lou herself couldn't see the horrible injury, and pressed her jacket against the wound. Shock was settling in fast and she heard Lou gurgle.

"Lou, stay with me. Stay with me, hon." Shay looked around them at the still empty garage and screamed over the alarm. "We need a fucking medic!"

Despite her best effort to suppress the gushing wound, the woman was bleeding out. Lou's eyes grew fuzzy. Her lips moved, and Shay knelt very close to her. She whispered something vague before closing her eyes. Tears sprang to Shay's eyes.

Kate stood over them. She was shocked, but otherwise unhurt. Using every drop of strength she had left, Shay pulled the dying woman onto her lap and gently rocked her. She repeated the same words against the background of the alarm and approaching sirens.

"You're a big hero, Lou. Very, very brave…"

Within seconds, rescue vehicles invaded the garage. The young woman was out of her arms, strapped to a gurney. Shay stood there, blood-covered. For the second time in weeks she'd be surrendering her clothes to the lab. Before she could answer any of the million questions being fired her way, she looked over at her white-faced partner, who promptly crumpled to the ground.

CHAPTER TWENTY-NINE

AD Holloway couldn't be reached at home or via cell phone. Agents scoured the parking lot-turned-crime scene, searching for a shooter. Others were posted at St. Anne's Hospital where Agent Harris had been taken by ambulance. In borrowed hospital scrubs, Shay paced the hallway in front of the holding bay where her partner was sleeping.

It was just as well that Holloway was MIA. No way could Shay tell him what she'd found on her computer. Not without admitting she'd stolen a hard drive from the evidence locker. Plus, Holloway could be a part of it. If the partnership was axed, who'd protect Kate? Shay paced some more. She was firmly and deeply locked into the game.

The garage scene relentlessly rolled around her brain. Kate had pulled a gun on her partner. Kate didn't trust her; the jury was out on how much she herself trusted Kate. But one thing was sure—whether or not hormones were to blame, Kate's instincts clearly sucked. Shay was furious that Kate dared hold her—her *partner*—at gunpoint. Kate's apparent stupidity was more than a little alarming.

The low hum of monitors and medicinal smells filled the darkened hallway of the triage wing of the hospital. Shay had already been there for two hours. The doctor had been in the room for half that time. Shay practically ambushed her when she finally exited the patient's room. Dr. Michaels glared at her as if she were the single-handed cause for the night's events.

"What's the scoop on my partner there?"

"I've ordered bed rest. No ifs, ands or buts." Dr. Michaels started to walk away, but Shay kindly stopped her.

"What are the risks?"

"She's vulnerable to pre-term labor. For reasons unknown, Kate periodically demonstrates signs of labor. The baby needs more time to develop. I need her off her feet indefinitely." She folded her arms, stood solidly before her, as if waiting for the next challenge to rebut. "For the moment, she's stable."

Shay nodded. She peered over the doctor's shoulder at her sleeping partner.

"She'll be checking out now." Shay made the announcement in a firm tone of voice. "So make any necessary preparations."

The doctor glared at her. "You can't make that decision for her."

"You said she's stable." Shay arched an eyebrow. "Did I miss something?"

"No," Dr. Michaels curtly replied. "But she'll have to sign herself out, and right now, she's sleeping. I'll have to warn her of the possible consequences of that action should she choose to do it."

The time for courtesy had long passed. Shay stepped very close to her, whispered, "Lady, you can talk until you're blue in the face, but in ten minutes, I'm taking her out of here."

The doctor issued her another death glare, but by now Shay was accustomed to ignoring those.

She stepped inside the room and went to Kate's bedside. She

softly squeezed her partner's arm, rousing her from sleep.

"We need to talk," Shay quietly said. Groggy, Kate started to sit up, but Shay stopped her. "I need to take you someplace where you are safe."

"It's safe here," Kate whispered.

"Anybody can walk into a hospital. It's too big a risk."

Kate's eyes were heavy with concern. "What about the parking lot girl...?"

Shay only shook her head. Kate's eyes filled with tears and she swallowed hard.

"Trust me, please."

Armed with explicit instructions from the doctor, Shay drove her sleeping partner carefully through the city. She constantly checked her rearview mirror to make sure the SUV was still behind her. Another nondescript car tailed it, two agents she'd personally selected herself to escort them on this mission of safety. Lou was dead, but Kate was alive. Guarding her was Shay's responsibility now. She was taking the woman to the only place where she felt in control and safe.

Half an hour later, both vehicles stopped in front of her house in Pleasant. Shay got out first, entered her home, and checked every room, window and door. She came back and nodded all clear to Agent Buchner, who gently carried Kate into the house.

In the downstairs bedroom, Shay drew back the down comforter and sheets on the bed and stepped aside for the agent to enter. Buchner lay Kate down and promptly vacated the room to take his new post at curbside.

Earlier, she'd summoned Dunedin from bed. Accompanied by another agent, he'd swept the place for bugs prior to their arrival. He'd even repaired the sliced security wires before calling her and eagerly proclaiming the place bug-free and secure.

Kate was dazed and barely helpful as Shay removed the thin cardigan that covered her hospital gown. She slid her sandals off, and then covered her partner with blankets. Shay went to the window, double-checked it, then watched as Buchner got into the SUV. The other car was down the block. Yet she was disturbed by a presence she couldn't account for. Perhaps her instincts were working in overdrive. Despite everything inside her home being in its rightful place, it felt different; it felt like the enemy had been there.

Shay drew the curtains closed and quietly dragged a chair to the bedside. Too tired to change out of the borrowed scrubs, she dropped into the chair and settled in for a restless night's nap.

The Watcher studied Shay's house from down the block. He winced at the trouble his arm was giving him and rolled his sleeve above his elbow to inspect his wound. It had bloodied right through the bandage, again. Now, it was achy.

He'd been cleanly grazed by a bullet and lucky for him, he'd managed to find and pocket it, despite his aching arm, before running back down the ramp of the parking garage. He'd gone to one of his makeshift residences—a crappy ramshackle hotel in the worst part of town—where he'd doctored his left bicep wound with mesh tape. More than it just being painful, it pissed him off that he'd let anyone get that close to him. He'd never been shot before.

Poor timing, too. There was work to be done, and carrying it off without so much as an occasional painful wince would be a challenge. He squeezed a few Tylenol out of a blister pack and chased them down with water. He craved something a bit stronger, but dared not take anything that would cause him to be jittery, or worse, fall asleep. He'd made enough mistakes for one day.

He was laying the groundwork for his new life. He hated to take a scar with him, but at the same time it was a gentle reminder of what happens when one doesn't take care of problems the first time around. Now he was left cleaning up old messes simply to move on.

He stripped off the old gauze, rolled it up and shoved it into a plastic bag, then tucked it into his jacket pocket for disposal at his own discretion. He was careful with details like that. He squeezed a line of antibiotic ointment on the wound, then peeled off a length of fresh gauze. He wrapped it around tightly, flexed his arm muscle a few times and muttered curses.

The more he killed, the freer he felt. Nothing could stand in his way. Things were difficult, but not impossible. He'd have to step up his campaign for ultimate freedom.

He reclined the driver's seat as much as he could, leaned back, still with a perfect view of the two-story house in Pleasant. He fixed his eyes on a particular window and breathed in and out, mentally lifting himself up and out of the pain. He chanted his new mantra.

Timing is everything. Breathe in, breathe out.

CHAPTER THIRTY

Shay Cooper was out of the house long before her partner awoke. Confident that Kate was in good hands, Shay knew there were other things to attend to before the rest of the world could fully caffeinate.

She'd answered what felt like a million preliminary questions and surrendered her service weapon the night before, post chaos, per protocol. There were sure to be more inquiries from Internal Affairs very soon. But Lou's wounds had been created by a different, stronger caliber, and she'd be cleared of the shooting, at least, by Monday morning. Still, she had to go to her office and fill out her own separate report. She'd had much opportunity to think about it during her sleepless night, and in the end, she'd decided to paint it simple: Lou tried to intervene in a mystery shooter's random attack. For that, she truly was a hero.

Shay had refrained from injecting personal suspicions. She'd numbly signed the paperwork, placed it in an envelope, and slid it under Holloway's office door for his Monday morning review.

Before heading back to Pleasant, Shay drove to Kate's apartment. She only had to flash her badge for the desk clerk to summon someone with a master set of keys. The old guy walked and talked as they took the service elevator to her floor.

"This girl's got some lifestyle, huh?" He shot her a sly grin. "What's she...? Undercover CIA or something?"

"Something like that." Shay humored him.

"Yeah. It's the second time in so many months that one of you types has come in for a key. I figure she must be either the world's biggest troublemaker, or way deep undercover." He shrugged. "I figure I haven't seen her name in the paper, so it must be the undercover thing, if you know what I mean."

The doors parted and he made a grand sweeping gesture for Shay to exit, but she didn't just yet. She stared at the old man in coveralls.

"What do you mean second one of my type?" she asked him. "Someone else had you open this apartment?"

He nodded, eyes glancing up, then right. Visual remembrance. She was about to hear his version of the truth.

"Medium height, dark hair, well-built fellow." He squinted. "He wore gloves, which surprised me a little. I mean it was early spring, but not cold, if you know what I mean."

"And he showed his badge?"

"Yes, ma'am." He nodded. "Not to me, but to the desk clerk."

"Is that logged in somewhere?" She took out a notebook, prepared to write down a name.

"No. We only log in deliveries and such. It's not our business who's coming and going." The old man glanced right, then left, which told her he'd been carefully instructed about how to answer to such an inquiry. His voice dropped to a whisper. "We have quite a few important folks who have...how can I say? Special *friends*—meaning not-their-wives, if you know what I mean."

She helped him along. "Mistresses."

He nodded. "Our policy is absolute confidentiality. If we track one, we have to track them all. Not good for business, if you know what I mean."

Shay put her notebook away, nodded. "Thanks, I appreciate this."

"No problem. Anything for our government, if you—"

"I know what you mean," Shay interrupted him. She flashed him a tolerant grin and closed the door on him.

Agent Kate Harris's apartment was largely empty. She wandered around, noted perfect vacuum lines in the rug, not a drop of dust. She took inventory. Fluffy toss pillows situated on a single chair in the center of the floor. Two boxes, looked like books. No table or chairs or usual dishes, pots and pans in the kitchen. Only plastic utensils and paper plates.

Shay took prenatal vitamins out of the cabinet along with two freshly filled recyclable bottles of water from the otherwise empty refrigerator.

She sauntered into the bedroom. She opened her partner's closet and found the usual work clothes in plastic dry cleaning bags. A plastic bin contained a few T-shirts and other things that looked appropriate for nightclothes. She gathered them up, stared at the panties that lay neatly folded beneath the T-shirts. Swallowing hard, trying not over-think it, she scooped the lacy underthings out of the box and set them on the bed. She found a simple overnight bag and placed her finds gently inside.

A blue glowing nightlight powered by a rectangular solar bar remained on despite the fact that it was daytime. Shay unplugged it, looked it over. She peeled back the rectangle which wasn't a solar bar at all, but a sticker concealing a tiny camera lens. Shay's eyes wandered over to the mattress, the single piece of furniture in the room. She imagined her partner sleeping there, unaware that she was under observation. Her pulse quickened with her anger. She dropped the lens and crushed it under her heel, then picked up and pocketed the remains.

Shay grabbed the overnight bag and headed for the door. She saw a bulging red folder next to the bed and doubled back for it. As she flipped through it, her cheeks grew warm. She hastily stuffed it in the bag and made her exit.

Back in Pleasant, she parked her car and nodded at Buchner, who was keeping a curbside vigil. He gave her a wave as she passed him on her way to the house. Shay wasted no time, marched into the bedroom, and tossed the thick folder onto the bed of her sleeping guest. It landed with a significant thud and startled Kate awake. She groggily sat up, looked first at Shay, then at her surroundings. It was clear she didn't remember much from the previous night.

"You're at my place." Shay's greeting was void of compassion. She plopped down on the edge of the chair next to the bed waiting for her partner to fully wake up.

"Why?" Kate finally asked. She looked down at her clothing, a hospital gown, and pulled the blanket around her as if to shield herself from Shay.

"There is an agent sitting down the street in an unmarked car, another one in front of the house. Then there's me." Shay glared at her as she stated the facts. "That makes you safe."

"Why can't I go to my own—"

"Your place is under surveillance," Shay cut her off. She extracted the remnants of the tiny camera from her jacket pocket and tossed it onto the bed next to the folder. "No, I'm not paranoid."

Kate looked at the folder, saw her own overnight bag near the door. She folded her arms across her chest, angrily asked, "You went to my place?"

Shay laughed softly. "Sister, I am in no mood to tolerate your holier-than-thou princess ass anymore than you are in the mood to put up with me. Deal with it."

Kate stared her down. "And if I refuse?"

Shay's lips formed a thin smile and she pointed toward the door. "Then walk right out of here."

"Fine," Kate practically spat. She threw the covers back and sprang out of the bed, entangling her feet in the sheets and nearly losing her balance. She looked for her shoes.

"You are in danger." Shay calmly stated the fact. She watched as Kate finally located her sandals poking out from underneath the bed. Her partner performed a hop-balance maneuver as she slipped them on and then looked around until she spied her cardigan draped over the back of the chair. She gave it a tug, difficult since Shay was sitting on the sleeve.

"Do you mind?" She looked exasperated.

"I do," Shay told her, firmly. "Sit down, sunshine."

"Don't sunshine me! First, you signed me out of the hospital," Kate said in an accusatory tone. She gave the sweater a final successful yank and the sleeve went flying.

"You signed you out," Shay corrected her.

Kate drew the sweater around her, saw that one sleeve was longer than the other. "You told me I was going someplace safe."

"You did. You are."

"Your place is safe?" Kate was breathless from her efforts. She looked around, waved her arm. "Was I drugged? What the hell was I thinking?"

"You were thinking about what's best for you and your baby."

Kate started to open the bedroom door, but in a single move, Shay was in front of her, pressing the door shut with the heel of her hand. She glared down at her partner.

Suddenly, pain streaked down Kate's left side, causing her to almost double over. She didn't waver, refusing to acknowledge her discomfort, especially to her partner. She hoped she didn't show it as she sat on the edge of the bed. She hated feeling weak. Moreover, it was clear she wasn't going anywhere, and she hated that too.

"Come on." Shay helped her back out of the sweater. Kate glared at her, but allowed it. She got back into bed and Shay drew the covers over her legs. She knew something was wrong, but knew better than to ask. Instead, she toughened her stance and launched into her instructional monologue. "You're on complete bed rest, do not get out of bed. Those are Dr. Michaels' orders."

She fluffed the pillow behind Kate. "A nurse will come visit, we'll arrange days and times. Same with a nutritionist. Here is a bell if you need anything."

Shay picked up a little brass bell, jingled it for demonstration purposes, but yanked it high out of Kate's reach. "Use it for emergencies. I'm not your maid, hear me?"

Shay set the bell on the bedside table. Kate sighed loudly. Shay started for the door.

"Cheer up. I brought your reading material for you. That should keep you busy for a while." Shay smiled sarcastically, gesturing toward the bed. "You'll find it all there—the reason I fell off the grid for three months in Miami, my records, my son's case. I even added some things—threw in my performance reviews from all offices, you know, for good measure."

"Agent Cooper—"

"That's what you wanted, right?" Shay opened the door. "That should just about answer all those questions you asked me while you were waving your gun in front of me last night."

Kate glared at her throughout the embarrassing confrontation. As Shay left the room, she grabbed a pillow and threw it as hard as she could against the closing door. The sound of it slamming shut canceled out the expletive Kate yelled behind her.

Shay leaned against the wall, rolled what had happened around in her brain. Part of her was happy to have reduced the woman in the bedroom to childish curses. But the more sensible part of her was always aware that having Kate as a guest was not about pissing her off, but keeping her safe. Safe from an enemy who was out there, somewhere. She had much work to do.

CHAPTER THIRTY-ONE

Since her departure from the Academy, Shay's opportunities for cardio exercise or time in the sun were few. For that reason she'd head off to the track and join the students on their midday run each Sunday. This particular weekend, she craved the workout—nothing but the sound of her shoes against the track and her own breathing in her head. It was a safe place to purge her anxiety; and as she was a teacher amongst her former pupils, they knew better than to ask questions beyond the common courtesies. Now they especially steered away from conversation regarding the shooting or the mysterious circumstances that had resulted in a colleague's death. Still, she felt the stares and realized to her dismay that word had traveled fast.

When she arrived back home, Agent Buchner was just where she'd left him, parked in front of the TV in her living room. He turned it off and hoisted his brawny form off the couch to greet her.

She cast a glance down the hallway. "How's it going?"

"She's been quiet." Then he whispered, "But thanks for your earlier warning."

She'd instructed Buchner to steer clear of Kate unless there was an emergency. She hadn't elaborated beyond, "She's in a mood."

Buchner's smile faded. "I've been meaning to ask you, how's your side?"

The agent had apologized a hundred-plus times for the drug house shooting.

"Like it never happened," she lied. And when he still looked rueful, she moved to reassure him. "I wish you'd forget about it, kid. It was just a graze. I might have been killed if you hadn't been there." She started for the hallway and stopped short when she smelled a hint of cinnamon in the air. "Cook been here?"

"Come and gone."

"Good enough." She grinned at Buchner, effectively dismissing him. "See you tomorrow?"

Buchner nodded and made his exit.

Shay wiped the remaining sweat off her forehead, bypassed Kate's room and headed for the shower. Fifteen minutes later, she poked her damp head into the bedroom. A food tray was still sitting on the ottoman next to the bed. Shay made a face, went over to it.

"What's this?" She began lifting up food covers. There was untouched veal cutlet, new potatoes, broccoli and soft rolls. She smirked. "So you're Gandhi now that I kidnap you and force you to stay in the comfort of my home? What a damned terrible person I am."

"I don't have an appetite." Kate answered, wanly. "And I don't eat meat."

"So you told me," Shay sarcastically commented. "Amongst your many strange confessions."

Her partner didn't acknowledge the joke. Shay plopped herself into the bedside chair and studied her. Kate's hair was strewn casually around her shoulders, little wisps softly curling around her eyes, and actually it would have been quite elegant had she not been searing her with the glare from hell. Shay moved onto other business.

"I signed off on the Arizona case." Then she pretended to catch herself. "It's okay that I turned that one over to the local authorities, isn't it? I didn't think you'd want to fly anytime soon."

Kate remained glaring.

"I'll take that as your consent." Shay folded her arms. "And for your information, the Lanterman case was a ruse designed to get me alone. Len Ortelli—" She eyed the bulging red folder on the bedside table. "I'm sure you've read all about him by now? He waited for you to be a no-show, then he told me you were in danger. Hence, the mystery contact is revealed." She appeared pleased with herself. "I'm all about transparency these days. Seems if I don't tell you, you'll just go pecking all over the Internet anyway, leaving a trail of virtual breadcrumbs right back to us, possibly further endangering our asses."

Kate rolled her eyes. "I get it, okay?"

Shay grinned. "Good. We finally understand each other."

"You could have told me about all this earlier, and I wouldn't have been pecking around."

"You could have told me about this earlier," she pointed at Kate's belly, "and maybe we wouldn't be getting shot at, huh? We're even."

They stared at each other, then sighed in chorus.

"Let's just call it a draw." Shay was suddenly too tired to argue.

Kate looked confused. "Why would this Ortelli character tell you I was in danger?"

"Don't know." Shay had been contemplating the same thing. "Maybe he's trying to pay me back—you know, your kid's safety because he took my kid?" It sounded surreal. She scrubbed her hands through her damp hair, whispered, "I don't even know what I believe anymore."

Kate nodded, looking unexpectedly sympathetic. "I just want you to know I'm sorry about Christopher."

They locked eyes. Shay rarely heard the boy's name

mentioned aloud. The very sound of it still pained her, even after all these years. She felt her courage growing, but just as it always did when she built herself up, it took a defensive detour through anger. She abruptly stood up.

"Anyway, enjoy your reading. And the good news is, when I'm gone, you can sneak around and go through my drawers, see what else you can find, huh?" Shay chuckled. "Convenient, right? Holed up in the home of your primary study?"

She took the tray and left a bewildered Kate behind her, even slammed the door for good measure. It was her way of telling her how badly she received comfort. Anger kept her safe.

She left the tray in the kitchen before wandering aimlessly around the house. She ended up in the living room before the muted television.

It was nearly dark when Shay awoke to a sound in the hallway. She grabbed her gun off the coffee table and released the safety. Rising up, she carefully crept toward the doorway in time to see a woman with a medical bag emerging from the bedroom and closing the door behind her. Shay breathed a sigh of relief, secured her gun and slid it into her back waistband before the leggy brunette could see it. The woman approached her, smiled brightly.

"You must be Agent Cooper. I'm the nurse, Lisa Kenner. Just checking in on our patient."

Nurse Kenner was dressed very un-nurse-like in a short skirt and sweater that showed off curves Shay had only seen on nurses in movies. People would hurt themselves on purpose for a nurse like her. Shay swallowed hard, pretended not to notice. Her libido was way out of control these days.

"Well, how is she?"

"She's fine. I'm going to plan my visits for Tuesdays and Thursdays from here on in. Dr. Micheals will be scheduling a day as well. Any objection?" Her teeth practically sparkled when she smiled.

"None," Shay told her. She steered her thoughts away from

the nurse's cleavage-revealing V-neck, wondering if Kate had noticed it too. That notion sidetracked her and she got back to business. "What about those contractions the doc mentioned?"

"Those symptoms are gone for the time being. Sometimes they're a fluke, but I'll keep an eye on her." Her big green eyes softened to match her voice, "She's a little sad, though."

Shay nodded, looked away. "Yeah, well. She's like that."

After the nurse had gone, Shay stared at the bedroom door. She went to her makeshift office and gathered her paperwork, then made herself march back to Kate's room. She knocked before pushing open the door.

"It's me," she said.

"Really?" Kate blandly remarked.

Shay took the chair. "I figure there's no sense in my working these cases alone. You're here, right? And we are partners."

"Only for a while longer, Agent." It was Kate's new anthem.

"I know. Dallas." She humored her. Shay's eyes locked on hers and her voice grew quiet. "Is that why you haven't put anything together at your place for the baby?"

Kate looked thoughtful. "I suppose so."

"I see." Shay nodded. "Do you think a move now is practical? I mean, you're due in a handful of months."

She turned utterly melancholy. "I don't know anymore."

After a spell of silence, Shay whispered, "Even without the bed rest order, it would be hard to start over someplace far away with a tiny baby. That's what I'm thinking."

Kate shifted slightly in bed, looked uncomfortable. She changed the subject "I'm going to be tired of sitting here soon enough."

Shay smiled. "That's the breaks, sunshine." She set a folder on top of Kate's blanket-covered legs. "Meanwhile, you want to work this with me?"

Kate looked unsure. "Tony was the star profiler, not me."

Shay nodded. "Well, it's your domain now. It gives me the creeps."

"Why?"

"I don't dig getting inside the heads of monsters. Killers and sex offenders, child predators…" She shook her head. "It's a deep, dark place and I'm not interested."

"You have to learn to purge it from your brain at the end of the day." Kate tipped her head, appeared to think it over. "I suspect you'd actually be quite good at it."

Shay wasn't sure whether or not to be offended. "What makes you say so?"

"Because you hate them so much." Kate's eyes were intense. "And hate is a powerful motivator."

So is love, Shay recalled. She suppressed a shiver. "I've brought home our chart of vics with common denominators."

Kate took a look at the tri-fold chart they'd constructed in the office. Previously, they'd devoted a column to Tony Williams as a potential victim in the name of open-mindedness. Now his name had been thoroughly marked through with a Sharpie. Kate shook her head. "Tony came back off the list? I'm confused."

Shay leaned forward, quietly summarized events. "You had a hunch, you shared it with me at the diner. I was slow on the uptake, I admit. I'm a skeptic." She sighed, looked suddenly sad. "Lou confirmed it."

Kate's eyes grew wide. "What?"

"She told me it was Agent Williams. His name was on his sweatshirt. She was trying to save your life."

Kate's eyes took on a dreamy, blank quality.

"Don't blame yourself," Shay whispered. Then she did what she did best, which was to move toward action. "I'm considering that all serial killers seem to have in common one thing—they like to save something. A memento, or souvenir. I cross-referenced all the evidence in lockup to the reports, and it all checks out. Nothing appears to be missing from the crime scenes."

Kate only nodded.

"So, if it is Williams, maybe you're right about a possible encrypted message in the reports. How safe is that? A private screw-you that only Williams knows about." Shay pushed the folder across the bed, left it next to their chart. "You want to give it a look? Only you know him."

Another feeble nod.

"I'm prepared to set into motion crews of agents to follow up on whatever we find here. When it happens, we're going to move quickly. We need substantial evidence to present to Holloway or he'll shut us right down, possibly split us up. Maybe you don't care, but I do."

Their eyes met again in the dim bedroom light. Kate was processing her partner's strange confession. She looked away. "Can we trust Holloway?"

"I don't know. But what choice do we have?" Shay dipped her chin, met her partner's gaze. "I need your help on this. We can get him."

"I'm helping you on this fishing expedition enough already, aren't I?" Her words sounded abrupt and cold. Kate nestled back into the pillows, and faced away from her partner. Her soft voice cut through Shay like a knife. "I assume I'm your lure."

Shay had already considered this. At last she nodded, despite the fact that Kate couldn't see her.

"I guess that does make you the lure," she admitted. "But if he comes after you, yeah, I want the first crack at him."

Kate's voice was muffled. "I'd like to be alone now."

It was becoming her new nightly ritual. After sprawling on the couch for an hour or so, Shay would wander into the bedroom where her partner was asleep. There was a car posted curbside, an agent at the ready, but she needed to be at Kate's bedside. Something about her steady breathing soothed Shay's nerves and allowed her to get a bit of rest herself. She took her usual post, and noted that, more than on previous nights, Kate's sleep was fitful.

Shay considered her own poor timing, involving Kate in crime solving. Perhaps she thought the woman was enough like her that she'd need to feel useful, especially under such confinement. Kate was a big girl. A bright, strong FBI agent.

But Shay knew that in fact they were very different. Add to that, Kate was pregnant, a delicate situation itself aside from a million other gentle differences that existed between them. Maybe it had been too much for her.

Shay thought about the barren Chicago apartment and wondered what kind of mother Kate would be. She recalled too well that Rita, her ex-partner, had not been terrific at it. Rita was resentful of her pregnancy right from the start, something the doctor assured Shay was normal. But her ex was a career woman, a fashion photographer, and pregnancy didn't bode with her jet-set lifestyle. She complained that it was tough shooting beautiful people all day long when she, herself, felt like a beached whale. Shay thought she looked beautiful. She was certain that once Rita held their newborn, her maternal instincts would kick in and soothe her quirky ways. When it still hadn't happened after Christopher's first birthday, Shay was forced to admit that Rita just wasn't the motherly type.

Shay figured she had subconsciously blamed Rita for their son's disappearance. She wondered if God was punishing them both for Rita's disinterest in parenting. Though she knew it was probably only her imagination, Shay felt that Rita didn't grieve Christopher's disappearance as she should have. It made her wonder if a small part of Rita was happy to be relieved of parenting duty. It felt like the whole world had gone mad. Months later, Shay relieved her of their relationship as well. She'd heard Rita was now trying life on the other side of the lens as a fashion model, something Shay suspected she'd long wanted. She was glad Rita could put it all behind her. Glad and resentful as hell.

Kate stirred, mumbled something incoherent in her restless slumber. Shay reached across the bed and gently clasped her hand. Kate settled down for the moment. Sighing, Shay stroked her small, smooth hand. It was the best she could do.

CHAPTER THIRTY-TWO

Special Agent Shay Cooper had lived in New York until she'd applied for a transfer to the Miami division. There she'd enjoyed another successful run, hunting drug dealers and shutting them down. She had a tremendous success rate. Then the information got a little hazy.

Though she felt sneaky for actually reading the files, Kate was glad for the alone time to give them a look. Was it sneaking now if Shay knew that was what she was doing? Still, it did little to soothe her guilty conscience.

It was all there for her perusal—applications, reviews, records, and then something unexpected. Kate squinted at the poorly photocopied paperwork. It was a doctor's chart sprinkled with enough medical terms to make for thoroughly exhausting reading. But there in the meat of the report, in black and white, were words even a lay person could recognize. Words like aneurysm and coma. Hence the three months of missing material. Frowning, Kate set the report down. Shay was hard-headed and tough as nails. In her wildest dreams Kate couldn't see her falling victim to anything—medical or not. It softened something inside her—or maybe it was just the fact that she didn't feel all that great to start with today.

When she heard the front door close, she ashamedly stuffed the folder under the bed.

Shay knocked and entered, but when she saw Kate, her smile promptly disappeared. She looked puny, even paler than usual. Instinctively, she felt her partner's forehead, muttered, "You're warm."

"I'm fine," Kate softly protested. She wriggled around beneath the covers.

"You're a bad patient." Shay cut the toughness from her voice. "Are you having those pains again?"

"No."

But it was clear Kate was lying.

"I'll call Dr. Michaels."

"I said I'm fine. I promise." She sat up against the pillows, pointed at the bedside table. She thought about Shay's health and didn't want to worry her. "Could you just hand me that water?"

Shay did what was asked of her and sat on the edge of the bed as Kate gingerly sipped from the metal bottle.

"Take it easy," she warned. Kate nodded. She took a few more sips and handed the bottle back to her partner. Shay fluffed her pillow, tried not to act like a terrible softie. "Why don't you rest."

Kate nodded and nestled into the pillows. As soon as Shay was in the hallway and safely out of earshot, she called the doctor.

Agent James Buchner was determined to get back in Shay Cooper's good graces. He'd been hand-selected by her to help guard Agent Harris, and that was a good sign, but he was haunted by memories of Holloway's favorite agent reprimanding him in the cafeteria after he'd caught him gossiping about Agent Harris. He wanted to win back Agent Cooper's trust and really show her what he was made of. Therefore he'd eagerly accepted her challenge.

He stared at the information laid out on the kitchen table of his tiny studio apartment.

As an "extracurricular" assignment—meaning unpaid—Buchner was to review Williams' cases for a fresh perspective that might help them crack the missing persons files. She told him to lean toward certain numbers in accordance with a suspicion she had. By agreeing to take on the cases, Buchner had immediately earned his way into the secretive Cooper-Harris office.

There were dozens of cases, all yielding nothing. No bodies, no arrests. Buchner liked puzzles—he'd been known to spend hours turning computer games inside out—but so far, he was only able to confirm a few of Agent Cooper's patterns: three days, three final evidence locations spaced evenly apart over the course of a one-hundred-mile radius. The locations had never been regarded as actual crime scenes, but only secondary scenes, as it was clear the evidence was planted. She claimed it was a long shot, but Buchner understood that Shay Cooper needed bodies.

He rolled everything around in his brain, then scooted his chair away from the table and looked at the mess before him. The cases were starting to run together in his head and that was certainly not a good thing. He thought about his orders.

He had to stay local. There was no budget for travel as of yet. So he started with a Springfield case of a missing military sergeant. A thorough canvass of Bluff Park had turned up the man's ring and a single tennis shoe. Buchner glanced at his watch. It was after six. He grabbed a hiker's GPS tracking device and jacket and headed for the door.

It took every drop of self-control for Shay to stay away from the bedroom door during Dr. Michaels' visit. She tried to busy herself at her desk, but ended up pacing the floor, waiting for the doctor to make her exit. When she did, Shay all but jumped on her.

"How is she?" Her gruff voice hardly conveyed the passing interest she hoped it would.

"Why don't you ask her?" Clearly the doctor had not forgiven her for checking Kate out of the hospital.

Shay watched the doctor leave then knocked on the bedroom door.

Kate looked better and brighter than she'd seen her in weeks. Shay sighed with quiet relief. The last thing she needed was to have Kate's sickness on her conscience. After all, she had talked her into prematurely leaving the hospital.

"I guess it was just cramps," Kate told her before she could ask.

"Is that normal?"

"Yeah, it can be." Suddenly Kate smiled a big smile. "It's a girl. Dr. Michaels just told me."

Shay beamed at the unexpected news. "You're kidding me? That's great."

"Yeah." Kate's cheeks slightly pinked. The silence between them was awkward.

"Can I get you anything?" Shay finally asked. "You or...your girl?"

Kate actually laughed. "No, we're good."

"Juice, maybe?" she persisted. "Or something to eat?"

"No, I've got water. Thanks."

Kate nervously prattled on about baby things, but Shay's focus had shifted. She stared at the bottle on the nightstand, picked it up, flipped back the cap, gave it a little whiff. It didn't smell of anything in particular.

"Where did you get this?" she interrupted the giddy narrative.

"Pardon?" Kate was caught off guard.

"This water?"

"The water from the bag you brought me from my place. It's a special filtered."

"What kind of filter?" Her interest was growing by the moment. Kate had been drinking water all three times the cramps had occurred. Coincidence?

"Standard charcoal. Enriched with calcium and other stuff." She shrugged, wondered where Shay was going with it. "It's good for the baby. Why?"

"How long have you had this filter?" Shay shot her a look.

"Three years." Kate chuckled and shook her head. "You think I'm being poisoned now? Wow, the wheels never stop turning, do they?"

"Never do," Shay muttered. She grabbed the bottle and stood up. "Could I have your apartment key?"

Kate knew better than to protest. She was starting to recognize the look on her partner's face that said she'd find a way inside the apartment, with or without her help. Kate nodded toward her bag and Shay retrieved it for her. In moments Shay had the key and was out the door.

Agent Buchner sat in his car in the middle of Bluff Park studying his surroundings. He plugged in the GPS coordinates listed on Williams' old report, the reported location of final evidence. Buchner compared it to a grid map. The brush was too thick for driving. Armed with GPS, he left the car and took a walk.

He found the spot within minutes, but stopped short. A large tree, with a trunk twisted from disease, was front and center. He could feel the bumps from the old, sprawling root system underfoot. Buchner made a face, looked again at the case file picture of a smooth, grassy terrain with a single shoe lying atop it. The case was five years old. He stared at the tree which was at least a hundred years old. He already knew it didn't add up.

He found a long stick and ambled around the grounds, poking it into overgrown brush. He considered Williams' anal reputation. The guy never made mistakes. Buchner read the first lines of the report again. The evidence had been discovered in Bluff Park, at 5:04 a.m., by Agent Tony Williams—who'd have to be a hell of an early bird to be poking around for a body at that hour. According to the time stamp on that same date, trace evidence was turned in at the lab at noon. Yet the pictures he

held were taken in daytime with clear eastward-cast shadows—
late afternoon shadows if Buchner ever saw them. He shook his
head. It was sloppy work on Williams' part. How could the agent
think anyone would buy this?

Buchner walked back to the vehicle, leaned against it and gave
it a think. He thought of other things too. Like his girlfriend
who disapproved of him taking extra hours, especially without
pay. He was supposed to meet her in an hour.

But suddenly he had other things on his mind. He smelled
a game, and Buchner loved a challenge. He removed the tie
leftover from work and tossed it into the car. He rolled up his
sleeves, and laid the grid map out smooth on the hood of the car.
He considered a famous quote by Williams, one he'd memorized
from his texts when he was still a student in Quantico: *Timing is
everything.*

Buchner already knew it was. And now because of it, he was
going to be a hero.

His brain was suddenly alive with possibilities of 5:04.
Knowing that five degrees north or south and four east or west
would have him hundreds of miles off track, he'd turned his
attention to feet, yards and miles. My, how serials loved to leave
clues, he thought, whether they were ever discovered or not.

He thought about the papers Agent Tony Williams had
authored—he had read them all. His study had been more
about the man than his writing. Buchner had even revisited the
old basement office in preparation for this case and this very
moment. Long ago cleared out, the only evidence that the
basement room had been anything more than a janitor's closet
was a single postcard that remained tacked to the corkboard. It
was a scenic train bridge surrounded by crisp leaves emblazoned
with the caption, "Northwest."

He remembered the day Williams had tacked it up. Buchner
hadn't pegged the agent as an avid vacationer and the card with no
handwriting and no postmark made him curious. He'd smelled a
game. It really was a simple card that had changed…everything.

He pulled the postcard out of his jacket pocket and ran his
fingers across it, as if he could glean some second-hand Williams
confidence from it. In addition to a postcard, the senior agent

had bequeathed many ideals to Buchner. He felt simultaneous excitement and a creeping frustration for what he was about to do.

Buchner tucked the card back into his pocket and instinctively headed out, to go north five miles, then west for four.

CHAPTER THIRTY-THREE

The same woman was always on evening duty at the Bureau lab. She was a heavyset, extensively tattooed woman who rolled her eyes when she saw Shay enter her suite. She promptly raised her hand in a halting motion and cut her off before she could speak.

"No way, no how. We are backed up and cannot even look at it this evening."

Shay glanced at the woman's nametag. "Frannie, this is priority evidence."

Frannie sighed heavily and exhibited preliminary signs of surrender. Shay smiled sweetly, set the paper sack on the countertop and removed the bottle. She handed it over.

"Could you push this through chem-tox, see what you find?"

"What are we lookin' for here, Agent?" Using a gloved hand, Frannie picked it up for her inspection. "Bottle, lid or contents?"

"Yeah," was her blanket reply.

"Some help you are." Frannie rolled her eyes.

"I don't want to give you any preconceived scientific notions."

"Please." Frannie grinned so deeply her arm fat jiggled. "Sugar, you haven't got a scientific notion in your whole body."

Shay was quick to respond. "You, on the other hand, are brilliant."

"What a lube job." Frannie shook her head. "Fine, you talked me into it."

She dropped the bottle back into the bag and started toward the rear of the lab.

"Thanks Frannie. I owe you."

"You bet you do," she called behind her. "Worship me with Whoopie Pies from Sweet Mandy B's. On Webster Avenue, MapQuest it. Don't show your face here without 'em."

Kate Harris stood at the window. It was a lovely night, she could tell, and this was as close as she would get to it. Indefinitely. She sighed, turned and surveyed her room. Its whitewashed walls and high ceilings and soft, flowing curtains hinted at a nice sense of style. Nothing she would have ever guessed out of her dark, rugged partner.

She thought about Shay with her messy hair that flipped up boyishly on its ends. Her home was a display of unexpected elegance from a woman whose idea of jewelry was a leather cord necklace with some Zen-type symbol dangling from it. Kate had caught a glimpse of it one day against pale skin, riding barely beneath her standard crisp white collar. For some reason, she'd expected Shay's home décor to be utterly minimalist, dull and earthy.

If she had to be parked in a bed somewhere indefinitely, it wasn't too bad that the surroundings were so homey and spacious

The room was beautiful, and Kate was sure she was the first and only one to sleep in the bed. The firm mattress still had its "Do not remove" tags and the pillows were new and plump.

She turned back toward the window, but dared not open it in adherence to the specific orders laid out by her partner. Down the street she could see an unmarked Bureau vehicle and she knew she was safe. She wondered when Shay would be home and couldn't believe how anxious she was to spot her Jeep. Her thoughts turned to Shay's deep-set, dark eyes and her earnest demeanor. The thought of Shay suffering a profound loss, then life-threatening illness, moved something within her. She appeared no worse for wear on the surface, but Kate was getting a glimpse into a different, deeper side of Shay. She'd taken on the world and had nearly been ruined for her efforts. As an encore, she'd taken on the responsibility of first keeping Kate employed, then alive. Kate sighed and dropped back onto the bed.

Despite her nearly lifelong personal credo of trust no one, Kate couldn't help but trust her partner.

Shay went back to Kate's apartment. Using a key this time, she entered and went straight to the kitchen. A fountain-type water dispenser had been installed on the sink ledge, and she followed the line beneath the countertop to the source of the filtration system. Shay dislodged cartridge and dropped it into a plastic bag. She stuffed it in her jacket pocket.

Her mission complete, with some guilt she perused the vacant apartment again, this time for her own curiosity. She poked into mostly empty closets and leafed through a few books lying about. She stopped short when she came across a small department store bag. She opened it and pulled out a tiny one-piece pajama set with matching socks. She stared at it for a long time. It was the only sign that a baby would ever inhabit the place.

Shay felt the soft fabric between her fingers and then buried ⁿ it. It smelled clean and sweet and for a moment she orted back to the days of folding laundry for her own sweet baby boy. She felt her insides shift, her chest felt tight. She replaced the clothes in the bag and carefully set it back inside the closet as she'd found it.

She turned to go and caught a glimpse of a leftover piece of the nightlight she'd destroyed days earlier. Anger flared, provoking steely determination within her. She would find Williams and stop him. She would give her partner back her life and her security, for her and her baby, whether she stayed in Illinois or moved to Dallas.

Shay locked the apartment door and headed for the elevator. It wasn't without reservation that she made the admission to herself: she hoped Kate would stay in Illinois.

Agent Buchner stood atop a tiny clearing in a section of tall pines of Bluff Park. Using moonlight as his guide, he entered the new coordinates and watched the blips on the screen as they scrambled to reformulate a position not far from where he stood. Now it was time to show everyone how smart he was.

He went to the car trunk and rummaged through miscellaneous camping equipment until he found a foldable shovel. He was grateful that recent rain had softened the ground considerably. Agent Buchner returned to the clearing and plunged the steel blade into the dirt.

The lab results had taken longer than she'd counted on and it was well after midnight when Shay arrived back home. She quietly slipped into her partner's room and found her still awake.

Shay sat on the edge of the bed. "How are you feeling?" she quietly asked.

"Where have you been?" Kate sat up straighter against the pillows.

"Do I actually detect a note of concern in your voice?" Shay arched an eyebrow at her. She handed her partner a single printed page. "I was at the lab. Look what I found."

Shay turned on the bedside lamp so that Kate could read the report. She frowned. "Misoprostol? What is it?"

"Well, used *normally*, it counteracts gastrointestinal upset for folks on aspirin regimens—stuff like that."

"And why am I looking at it?"

"Because it also can cause cramping in pregnant women, spontaneous abortion, premature birth, depression—the list goes on." Shay held up the bag with the remains of the filter in it. "I found it in your water system."

Kate recognized the cartridge, muttered, "Oh my God."

"Yeah, my God too." Shay felt tired. She set the bag along with her jacket on the floor. "Who knows how long you've been drinking this stuff. Incidentally, I faxed the same report to Dr. Michaels' office."

"All I drink is water."

Shay nodded. "And one of Misoprostol's side effects is thirst, so that didn't help."

"Surreal."

"Also, I had the lab take an 'unofficial' look at the perp's sample on file from the Arizona case—no need to red flag Holloway. It's sort of a reverse DNA to aid in identification. You know, genetic markers." Shay paused before adding, "Keep in mind this would never hold up in court."

"Okay." Kate's interest was piqued. "What did you find?"

"Caucasian male, dark hair, dominant gene for brown eyes."

"That could be anybody, though." Kate's voice contained very little hope. She knew they were closer to finding the truth than she ever wanted to be.

Shay turned out the lamp and sat on the edge of the chair. "That's right, it could be anybody. But understand where I'm at here. If even one piece of blood evidence is discovered from Williams' old cases, the files will be reopened."

She leaned in close, continued speaking in a soft, sympathetic voice. "And if it's reopened under the assumption that Williams is the unsub, they're going to want proof. He knows this and so do you—you told me yourself that night at the diner. Your baby is the only remaining bona fide blood evidence that can tie him to those crimes."

"There's no stopping him." Even in the dark, Kate's eyes looked wide and tearful. She whispered, "He will make sure this baby is never born."

"That won't happen." Shay settled back in her chair, fixed her eyes on an imaginary point in the ceiling to avoid looking at her sad partner. "I promise that will not happen."

By four a.m., Agent Buchner had three more agents on the scene at Bluff Park. Spotlights boldly illuminated the designated section of ground. A black body bag was center stage as it was slowly being filled with fragments of rib cage, a femur, pelvis and a skull.

Buchner could hardly wait to inform her. He ran to his car and fished his cell phone out of his discarded jacket pocket. Wiping a dirty arm across his sweaty forehead, Buchner waited for Agent Cooper to answer.

Shay's cell phone jarred her from a soft sleep. She hurriedly fumbled with it, punched it on, hoping to avoid waking her partner. She whispered, "Cooper, here."

Shay listened to the caller for several seconds before she raised her eyes to Kate, who'd awakened and was now sitting upright in the bed, waiting. At last Shay punched the off button, set the phone beside her chair. She leaned forward, rubbed the back of her neck, dreading sharing the news.

"Tell me," Kate insisted.

"Agent Buchner just got his first body. He went off Williams' documented time. It's not time at all, it's miles north and west of the listed evidence location. Buchner cracked it."

Kate swallowed hard. They were quiet.

Kate's touch surprised her. In the darkness, she'd reached for her hand. Shay's heart slammed against her ribs as her partner moved it to rest on her belly. When Kate looked at her, she was fighting her own panic about the unexpected intimate action.

It had been years since Shay had been so close to another woman. In her lifetime she'd said important words and nurtured true feelings; she'd loved deeply and fearlessly. As a result, she'd been broken on so many levels, she'd sworn off it all for good. Concerning baby bellies, she'd only touched one other in her life, and that was a lifetime ago. Her own horrific past flashed before her eyes and she closed her eyes hard, willed it away. She breathed deeply, but felt herself tremble.

Kate held her partner's hand there. Shay could feel the smooth warmth of her skin through her thin nightgown. Simultaneous feelings of fear and desire for her touch combined to torture her. It was a very human reminder of everything they were fighting to protect.

When Shay finally opened her eyes, Kate pretended not to notice they were glistening; she pretended not to know what pain she was clearly inflicting upon her partner. In a manner that she was unable—or unwilling—to define, she needed Shay.

"Could you stay?" Kate asked, breaking the silence. She was unable to disguise the tremble in her voice. A nervous, quick smile dismissed a tear down her cheek. She hurriedly wiped it away, softly chuckled. "If you want to know a secret, I don't like to be alone at night."

Shay studied the woman in the darkness. Against her better judgment, she finally nodded.

Shay quietly dragged the chair as close as possible to the bedside, never removing her hand from where Kate had placed it. She purposefully calmed her breathing, and when she spoke, her voice was soothing.

"If you want to know a secret," Shay confessed, "I'm here every night."

CHAPTER THIRTY-FOUR

The following day, Agent Buchner was quietly dispatched to Missouri on a recovery mission. He'd met with Shay Cooper early that morning and had sworn to her he'd play it close to the vest. Eager to impress her even more, he agreed to continue the search using his same method.

It was possible that the location of the first body could be a coincidence, and forensics hadn't yet determined if the vic was their missing person or not. But two finds using the same technique would give them enough evidence to present to Holloway to reopen the cases under a larger, even scarier umbrella. With her partner's safety at stake, Shay didn't have time to wait for forensic results. They were hunting a serial killer who was very likely one of their own.

It took everything Shay had to leave her partner and go

to the office that morning. It took even greater self-control just to stay there. She spent eight hours engaged in seemingly innocent study of completely unrelated cases, anything to stay off Holloway's radar of suspicion. It was difficult to act as if possibly the biggest case of her life wasn't quietly breaking open in Missouri. She would focus on avoiding raising more eyebrows than she already had by sending Agent Buchner to Missouri on a mystery mission.

She watched the clock strike five, yet waited until a quarter after to avoid looking too eager to leave. Then she waited in throngs of traffic to get to Pleasant by nearly seven. Finally at home, she gave a little wave to the substitute agent manning Buchner's usual curbside post.

Shay dumped her briefcase on the hallway table and went to shower away the office stench. When the bathroom was steamy and sauna-like, she turned the water off and grabbed a towel. The sounds of a scuffle from the next room had her scrambling for a T-shirt and pajama pants before she'd even completely dried off.

She grabbed her gun off the hallway table on her way into Kate's room. Shay pushed through the door and trained her weapon on a man she'd never seen before. Kate was staging a verbal protest, cowering on the opposite side of the bed.

"Hold it right there!" Shay's look was no-nonsense. "Hands where I can see them."

"What the hell?" The man drew back and for the first time, Shay was able to see that he had a syringe in his hand. The color drained from his face as he weakly stammered, "I'm...the nurse."

Shay edged toward the pair, gun still raised high in front. She held out her free hand, made a give-me motion. "ID," she demanded.

The nurse carefully reached into his front pocket and tossed her his wallet. She briefly inspected it without altering her steady aim. She tossed it back, glanced at the syringe in his frozen hand. "What's that?"

"B-12 injection."

"What's that for?"

"We give them to all strict vegetarians who are pregnant. It's normal, swear to God." He swallowed hard and his eyes practically bulged from their sockets as they flitted toward her hand. "Hello? Big scary gun?"

Shay lowered it, secured the safety.

"Thank you," he said in a huff as he gathered his things to go.

"Where's the regular nurse?" Shay asked him, her tone suddenly casual.

"Day off? Who knows," the nurse muttered as he hurriedly capped the syringe. He brushed everything off the bed into his bag in a flippant manner. "Maybe she doesn't like your brand of hospitality—who can say?"

"Save the attitude." Shay nodded toward her wary partner. "She made me immune to sarcasm and scary looks long ago."

The nurse headed for the door, reprimanding her as he left, "Dr. Michaels is concerned about Ms. Harris's stress level. I'll be sure to note this little incident in my report to her."

"Send her my love," Shay said as the bedroom door slammed shut.

"Did you run out of bath towels?" Kate asked her. Shay looked down at her own T-shirt, which stuck to her in large, damp spots. She smiled.

"Yeah, well, I was interrupted by my neurotic houseguest having it out with her nurse." She shot her partner a look. "You knew that was a vitamin shot, didn't you? I was going to shoot him over it, you know."

Kate shrugged. "It was a little fun to watch."

Shay ignored the remark, plopped down on the edge of the bed. Concern suddenly showed in her eyes. "You stressed out here?"

"Not when your gun is holstered." But she saw Shay was serious and cut the sarcasm. "I'm kidding. I'm fine."

"Okay." Shay nodded and combed her fingers through wet hair. She started to get up off the bed, but Kate's touch stopped her. A particularly damp spot on her shirt made it transparent and easy to see the scar from the recent bullet graze. Kate gently traced her finger along it. Before she could say anything, Shay moved to eclipse her guilt. "Stop worrying about that, would you? I'm fine."

"No thanks to me," Kate softly said. "It could have been even worse."

"Could have, might have—stop already." Shay gently removed Kate's hand, held it midair, mindful of her electrifying touch. She gazed at her partner with earnest eyes. "You don't need anything else to be stressed out about. Everything's fine, get some rest."

Kate sighed. "Easier said than done."

"Yeah, well I'm going to have to answer to Dr. Michaels if you don't chill out." Shay looked nervous about that prospect. "Frankly, I'd rather march back into the drug house."

Kate cracked the smallest smile. "Honestly, I'm as relaxed as I can be."

"Somehow that doesn't offer me much comfort." Shay plumped the pillows, looked thoughtful. "All right, let me see what I can remember about this stuff. Lean up a sec."

Kate did as she was told and Shay scooted onto the bed behind her, a leg on either side of Kate. She placed a pillow between them, forming a nice, safe barrier, and nudged her partner to lean back against it. She felt tension throughout Kate's stiff body, got a whiff of her flowery scent, rolled her eyes and reminded herself to focus.

"This is Lamaze—you take the little mommy childbirth course yet?" When Kate shook her head no, Shay sighed. "Of course not. Merciful God—do I have to teach you everything?"

She felt Kate's small laugh.

"Okay, now relax." With no small measure of apprehension, Shay began to massage her partner's belly in a circular, sweeping motion. "You're going to breathe in through your nose, two counts, then out through your mouth two."

"I've never understood why—"

"Don't argue with me for once. There's no arguing in Lamaze." She continued to stroke her. "Breathe in two, out two. Good job. When you're in the delivery room you'll find a little focus point on the ceiling and concentrate on it while you're doing this breathing."

After several seconds, Kate interrupted the process again. "You can't seriously tell me this makes childbirth a painless process."

"Only for everyone else." Shay continued in her low, soothing tone. "The more you're concentrating on your breathing, the less you're concentrating on killing the other people in the delivery room. Or at least that's what I've been told."

Kate burst out laughing. It was a wonderful sound. Shay chuckled too, then shushed her. "Less laughing, more breathing."

Within minutes, she felt Kate relax against her. She was nearly overcome by her partner's flowery scent and more than ever, she was grateful for the small pillow barrier between them. Lamaze breathing was providing an entirely different distraction for her. She closed her eyes, concentrated on counting breaths.

"You do this well," Kate said after a long silence.

"We used these same relaxation techniques when my son was born."

Kate tipped her head to the side to see her partner's face. "How long ago was that?"

Shay's eyes flitted upward, pretended she had to think about it. "Ten years ago."

"I don't know much about you, Shay Cooper."

"What do you want to know?" She continued making small circles.

"For starters, your house," Kate drowsily mumbled. "It's nice and…strange."

Shay laughed. "Now, is it nice or strange?"

Kate paused a beat. "Nice. It's just not what I expected." And then, "How many rooms?"

"Two more upstairs besides mine here."

She felt Kate shake her head. "You don't sleep in this room, Cooper."

"How can I?" Shay softly laughed. "You're sleeping in it."

Kate grew serious. "Come on, where do you really sleep?"

"Couch," Shay confessed at last.

"If you don't like this room, why not just pick another one?"

"I do like this room," Shay quietly told her. She resisted adding that with Kate's presence, she liked it better now than she'd ever liked it before. "I didn't rush to finish the others. I figured one person, one bedroom, right?"

Kate glanced sideways at her partner. "You like it that way?"

"I don't know," she answered after a lengthy pause. Kate had grown too serious. Shay softly nudged her. "You okay?"

Her answer was groggy-sounding. "I'm so okay, I'm about to fall asleep on you."

Shay leaned back, felt the welcome weight of her partner's soft form against her. She readjusted slightly, continued the circular strokes, whispered, "Go ahead. It's okay."

CHAPTER THIRTY-FIVE

The Watcher was on the move, revisiting old places with new faces, waiting curiously to see how things would turn out. That had brought him to Missouri.

Agent James Buchner had been a high school or college student when some of the crimes were committed. He was now investigating those same crimes with fresh enthusiasm. He'd made a plan, he followed it to the letter, and it was reaping great results, as he knew it would.

It was somewhat difficult to see the long-held secrets unearthed. At the same time it excited him, brought back fond memories. The FBI had been momentarily outfoxed, and now it was time for a better fox. He could do it, too, but first he had to finish other affairs. He thought about Kate, tucked away in Pleasant, under the constant watch of her pit bull partner and a few underlings, which added a few degrees of difficulty to the task.

As he'd already been wounded once, care and safety were top priorities. The fact that Shay Cooper loved a challenge almost as much as he did gave him no guarantee of either one. He considered this as he watched from his safe vantage point as two local field agents foraged for clues along a ravine that bordered miles of an old, ruined hog farm. The property had recently been acquired for development by the adjacent property, Cactus Canyon Campground. They probably didn't need the publicity of having a body found on their new land. The Watcher waited to see how it would play out. Within an hour, an agent gave a whistle and waved the others over. They tramped across the ravaged land toward him.

The Watcher grinned when he heard one of the young men yell, "I found something over here!"

Her scream split the silence of the dark house.

Kate struggled to escape the arms she'd fallen asleep in; the same arms she'd felt protected by until her nightmare.

Shay fought her struggle in the darkness, wouldn't let her go, talked her down. "Hey, hey. It's me."

Kate's eyes were wide and she expelled a sigh of relief, breathless and damp with perspiration. She fell limply against her partner's chest. Shay stroked her back and shushed her until her breathing leveled out. She wondered if the scream had carried and if the agent posted curbside would be breaking down the door any second. She waited and listened to night sounds.

"It was just a dream," Shay whispered. She pulled her close. "You're safe. I'm right here."

"A nightmare," Kate finally mumbled.

"You have a lot of those."

"I've had them for a long time." Kate sniffed, swallowed hard. "My ex used to send me to the couch."

The mention of her ex piqued Shay's curiosity. "How long were you together?"

"Six years."

"That's a little while."

She felt Kate shrug against her. "It was a relationship doomed from the start."

"Tell me why."

"Different worlds, different ideas." Kate sounded airy and loose. "We spent so much time trying to have a baby, I think we forgot why we were together in the first place."

"I wanted to ask about that," Shay finally admitted. "About you and Williams too."

Kate quietly launched into a brief narrative. "My ex, Elise, and I were in counseling over this baby thing. She couldn't have a baby at all, and for some reason, my body rejected technology and its notions of donor insemination. Figures." She chuckled softly, shifted slightly. "So, on a particularly drunken night out with my good buddy Tony Williams, I closed my eyes and went for it."

"Went for it?"

Kate nodded, clenched her eyes shut, spelled it out. "I used him for baby-daddy sex."

Shay sounded puzzled. "Knowing what we suspect about him, I'm surprised he allowed that."

"Since I'm confessing, it gets worse." Kate sounded thoroughly ashamed. "He had strange habits that should have clued me in that he wasn't altogether *right*."

"Like what?"

"He shaved…everything. That's right." She shuddered. "And he insisted on using a condom which he disposed of immediately in the toilet."

"How'd you get pregnant?" Shay leaned up slightly, looked into her eyes.

"I'd punched a hole in it with my earring."

"Shameless and inventive." Shay teased her softly. Leaned against the pillows.

Kate snapped her fingers. "Worked like a charm."

"I take it Elise was not pleased." Shay continued to stroke her back.

"Would you be?" Kate shook her head, her voice quieted. "It

was a stupid move on my part. Frankly, I'm surprised Tony even went for it. And in the end, look at the mess I created. I hit every low, like some depraved dog."

Shay considered it, softly said, "So your methods weren't spot on. Your intentions were good. In your defense, it's not like you *knew* he was a total psycho."

Kate's watery eyes locked with Shay's. "I'm advancing his sick gene pool."

"Don't even do that to yourself." Shay stopped her. "Do not do it."

"This baby is half his."

"And half *yours*," she firmly reminded her. "And you'll raise her to be a wonderful person."

"Evil genetic code," Kate numbly whispered.

"That's a myth, sunshine." In a natural, unpremeditated move, Shay pressed a kiss into Kate's hair. She stroked her back. "Williams is a bad seed, that's all there is to it."

"What if he's not...?"

"Don't—don't do this, please." Shay stopped her from succumbing to her own worry. "No single genetic based factor has ever been clearly tied to evil. If that was the case, we wouldn't have jobs because they'd be predicting genetic code, not profiling behavior."

After much quiet, Kate softly said, "I know I've not been the easiest person to be around. You've been very good to me."

Shay pulled her closer yet, stroked her back. "It's time that somebody is."

CHAPTER THIRTY-SIX

The bodies were rolling in and Holloway had given his reluctant blessing to reopen the cases. Buchner was at the helm, traveling midwest cities, a soldier on a single-minded recovery mission. He'd fly in, recruit assistance from the local field office for the day, track down the remains and send them home to Chicago. The paperwork it generated kept Shay at the office for hours longer than normal each day. She wondered if perhaps that wasn't such a bad thing.

Surrounded by case files, faxes and pictures, she sat in their office facing her partner's empty desk. She remembered the days when she'd dread coming in, dread nasty looks and cynical comebacks. These days Shay dreaded being in the office because Kate wasn't there. It gave her plenty to think about.

Lustful feelings were one thing, but she wondered if she

could truly be falling for her. The thought of Kate's wide eyes and smooth, soft skin lit fires in long cooled places within her. It was nothing she'd planned on, and given the circumstances, she figured there couldn't be a worse possible scenario in which to fall in love. Plus, Kate was a splendid mixture of hormones at present. Her eyes sparkled with wishful thinking, and her expression was nothing short of adoring whenever she looked at Shay. It turned Shay into pure jelly on the inside. But did Kate need Shay, or did she just need her protection? Would things change once the baby was here?

Once again, Shay's thinking would come full circle; Kate's safety was job one for her. If she allowed her ridiculous heart to guide her, her primary focus could slip, and that just could not happen. The idea of losing control scared the hell out of Shay. The idea of losing Kate scared her even more.

She leaned across her desk and snagged the nameplate off Kate's desk, and twirled it slowly between her fingers. She willed logic to prevail. Number one, she couldn't afford a relationship with her colleague; not someone who counted on her to save her ass. Her choice was to resign as Kate's partner or turn the job over to someone else. She didn't trust anyone else to know how to think like Williams did. By now, Shay suspected she had him figured out pretty good. There was no two ways about it; she was the best candidate to keep Kate safe.

Kate was soft and gorgeous in the right places. It was a distracting package, and in Shay's experience, distraction generally resulted in errors. She sighed loudly, set the nameplate back on the desk. She'd take herself off the damn case if she became too distracted to protect her partner.

And Kate had said she was going away.

Shay reached into her desk drawer, drew out the slick scan ultrasound picture. She ran her finger across it as she considered a silent promise she'd made to the third member of their thrown-together team. Kate had said it was a girl.

Failure wasn't an option. She dropped the scan back into the drawer and lay her head down on her desk for a little rest.

Hours later there was a sound at the doorway. Shay jerked awake and blinked the sleep out of her eyes. She assumed it was Buchner, who was due back from a long day perusing the countryside for yet another body. "Why don't you go home and get some sleep?"

When she looked up, her smile promptly disappeared. Without a key, Ortelli had entered the office and was standing directly in front of her desk.

"Ah, I wish I was home, Agent Cooper." He leaned onto the scepter top of his new cane. He looked even worse than he had before. He grinned broadly, stretching the thin skin of his face. He looked like a skeleton. "I was thinking about Manhattan again this morning. As you know, it's been five years since I was there."

Shay flew out of her seat and to the doorway. She checked both directions in the hallway for witnesses, then slammed and locked the door behind her. She muttered curses all the way back to her desk.

He appeared amused. "Are you keeping me in or prying eyes out?"

Shay plopped into her chair, whispered harshly, "How did you get in here?"

"I was taking a tour." He glanced innocently enough toward the door. "I got separated from my group."

"Tour doesn't come to this part of the building." She winced. "You look terrible."

"You, on the contrary, look good." His thinning hairline expanded with his broad smile. "Athletic build, nice skin, dark, brooding intensity. I would go so far as to say that you're quite pretty."

She glared at him.

"Presiding over a top-notch crew too. Your Agent Buchner is a real go-getter." His dark eyes sparkled. "I must say, I do like the person you've become."

"A compliment from you. The best kind," she sarcastically remarked. She watched as his eyes roved across the casework that spanned two desks and she quickly swept it aside with a broad stroke of her arm. "You're not supposed to be here. This is confidential casework."

With no small effort, Ortelli shuffled over to the back wall, and examined the pictures and map tacked to the corkboard.

"Looks like you're well on your way to solving the case of the decade." He shot her a pleased look. "You may have even outdone your New York work."

"What do you want?"

"Conversation?" Ortelli got no response. "How are things between you and your partner these days? Looks...cozy from where I'm standing."

Shay watched him dab the sweat off his forehead. He looked like walking death, and she hoped he wouldn't drop dead right there in her office. That would be interesting to explain.

"Why don't you sit down before you fall down," she half-ordered him.

He dropped onto a chair situated in front of her desk.

She leaned back in her seat, folded her arms behind her head. "I don't get it. Are you here to make amends or just get one last shot at screwing with me?"

He ignored her inquiry. "It's nice that Agent Harris has done well with the residuals from her father's book. He originally left her with nothing at all. I wonder if she hated him for that?" His tone turned to one of concern. "What about you? Did you hate your father?"

"I never knew him." She rolled her eyes. "Am I really supposed to put up with this nonsense just because you're on your last leg?"

"Then why do you do it, Agent Cooper?"

In truth she didn't know why she did her job, or for that matter, why she was hearing him out. "I'm a profiler, now. Maybe I'm trying to figure out what makes you tick so I can stop the next one of you that comes along."

"I thought maybe you enjoyed my stories." He grinned again. "Did I ever tell you about my family?"

She only stared at him.

"I married my wife for her father's booming import-export business."

"Ah, the import-export biz." She smirked. "Yes, I'm familiar with it."

Ortelli continued his tired-sounding summary. "We had an adequate life together. I worked while she raised our son. She had her charity work while I made frequent business trips. We had more of an arrangement than marriage."

"Figures."

"On one such trip I met a wonderful woman. Dee was her name. For a while I saw her every chance I could. I believed I was in love with her."

Shay grimaced. "I could do without the vision of you engaged in geriatric jiggy. Thanks."

"I wasn't born old, Agent Cooper." Ortelli paused. "Anyway, ours was a short-lived romance because I had responsibilities. My own family."

"How noble of you."

"Dee had a child by me."

"So much for nobility."

"I sent her money over the years and always made sure they were okay." Again he quieted. "She turned out to be a much better mother than my own wife was."

"So, your wife ever find out about your bastard child?"

"As it turns out, my wife had been engaged in extracurricular services with her charity minister. Sadly for her, it was the last bad decision she ever made."

Shay rolled her eyes. "Well, that's got to be cheaper than a divorce, right?"

"I didn't kill my wife." A thin glaze formed over Ortelli's hardened eyes. His face was thin and drawn; he looked small and ruined. "My son did."

She shrugged; she wasn't surprised. "Apple, tree...all those clichés."

He leaned forward, studied her. "He'd discovered our infidelities and set out to clean house, so to speak. I suppose he thought he was erasing our sins. He'd discovered my other family as well. I was able to stop him before he quite finished the job." Ortelli looked uncharacteristically troubled. "I was forced to institutionalize him. He stayed there for two years and was released on his eighteenth birthday."

Shay feigned only moderate interest. "So what? Did it take?"

Ortelli's eyes were emotionless, flat disks. "No."

Shay sighed deeply, leaned forward onto her desk. "What's the real reason you're here?"

"Would you believe I'm still minding the nest after all these years?"

She raised her eyebrows. "Not really."

"You think I'm made of stone, Agent Cooper? That I don't have a care to protect my people?"

She gave a low chuckle. "Given how you turncoated on your people in New York? Or how you finalized operations in Miami? No, I don't."

"There is a very big difference between business and family." He lowered his chin, looked her squarely in the eyes. "I thought I'd taken care of things with my son, but the problem evolved into something I hadn't anticipated."

"All this talking in riddles." She shook her head. "When you kick off, I'm sure the ghost of Confucius would like his tongue back."

"You want some advice?"

"From you?" She laughed. "Oh, you know it."

He rose out of his seat, leaned over her desk and whispered, "Do everything in your power to protect what's yours, Agent Cooper."

"That's funny, coming from you. Considering how you bailed on both your families." But her argument had lost its bite and the air in the office suddenly felt different. She watched him tiredly lumber toward the door.

He paused before making his exit.

"Agent Buchner seems to understand Anthony Williams quite well. I'm not sure I like that."

She shook her head, her voice was a monotone. "Why are you telling me this?"

He hesitated only briefly before departing. "I'm protecting what's mine."

CHAPTER THIRTY-SEVEN

Shay pushed through Kate's bedroom door carrying a large paper sack. She sat down on the edge of the bed and proceeded to arrange three tiny white take-out boxes between them.

"What's the occasion?" Kate asked, smiling.

Shay noticed her partner was wearing one of the nighties she'd picked up from her apartment. It was gauzy and white, innocent, yet enticing. Shay tried to focus more on the food she was laying out and less on the smell of soap and baby powder that permeated the room as it often did these days.

"I canned the cook. I hope you don't mind." Shay glanced at her before plunging a fork into an open container of rice. She handed it to Kate. "You weren't really eating her food anyway."

"I really wasn't," Kate said, looking puzzled. "This looks great. Thank you."

"We've got Buddhist Delight—all veggies and tofu, no MSG. Then there's brown rice and spring rolls." She handed her an ice-cold carton of milk to top it off. "From the soy cow, of course."

Kate grinned as she took it. "You really thought of everything."

"I did." She rose from the edge of the bed and started for the door. "And now I've got to get some work done."

Kate's smile quickly faded. Her shoulders fell.

"What is it?" Shay took a tentative step toward her. "You good?"

"I'm fine. I'm just bored, that's all." She reached down and massaged her slender calves, and Shay tried not to be too distracted; she needed to make a run for it. Kate calmly droned on. "And I've been in bed for so long my body is sore—my legs are killing me."

"I'll ask Dr. Michaels about that." Shay went for the door.

But Kate didn't dismiss her so easily. "Wait a minute—what's wrong?" she asked her, oblivious to her own allure and the impact it was constantly making. She shrugged. "Did I do something wrong? You don't come in here much anymore."

"I'm just…busy." Shay sighed, ran her hands through her hair. "I think Buchner's role in your old office was seriously undercredited. He went from being scribe to chief body hunter within six months." She smiled, added, "Now I'm his scribe."

"You could bring it in here," she offered. Then Kate's voice softened, as did her eyes. "I know you'd rather be out in the field with him. I'm sorry all this babysitting of me has turned you into an office worker—it's not your style."

"No, no…" Shay started toward her, but stopped, refocused on her mission of getting the heck out of there. "Look, there's all sorts of time to get out there. I want to be here. Besides, Buchner's enjoying his time in the sun. Let's let him."

"Okay." Kate nestled back in the pillows and faced the wall, ignoring the food.

Shay glanced at the door. "I'll just get some things done and check back on you in a bit."

Kate nodded, still facing away. Shay tried not to notice how sad she looked; she tried not to feel as awful for being responsible for it. From behind, Kate's pregnancy was concealed beneath the airy gown. Her figure moved softly with each breath. She was beautiful.

Shay dipped her chin as she considered what she would say. There was no pretending she wasn't avoiding Kate. She'd been doing it for days now.

"Kate, believe me when I say you didn't do anything wrong."

There was only silence. Shay's brain cranked out an internal *Jeopardy* theme. On the last note, she rolled her eyes and snagged a chenille throw from the walk-in closet. She tossed it at her before she could change her twisted mind.

"Put this around you. My air is wonky—it's colder in the living room."

Kate turned to look at her, eyes wide.

"Put it around you," Shay ordered. She went to her, put an arm around her partner's waist and guarded her footing as they walked toward the living room. When Kate started to protest the assist, Shay cut her off. "Don't be a pain in the ass, sunshine. You're supposed to be off your feet. Dr. Michaels will have our asses if anything goes wrong."

Kate's eyes were practically sparkling by the time they made it to the living room. She sat on the couch, and Shay looked around before handing her the TV remote.

"Wow, should I be nervous about you bringing me to your real bedroom?" Kate teased her, but stopped when she saw the terrified look on her partner's face. "I'm kidding—just a little joke."

"Consider this your big outing." She disappeared and returned in seconds with an armload of Chinese food containers. She laid them out, picnic style, on the coffee table. They ate as Kate flipped through the channels.

"Ah, *Planet of the Apes*—the original."

"A classic," Shay mumbled between bites of fried rice. "I can't stand the new one."

"Me too." Kate took a few bites of tofu then set the container aside. She rested her hand on her belly.

Always at the ready, Shay asked, "Something wrong?"

Kate shook her head. "There's just not as much room in there as there used to be. I can't eat much."

Shay cast little glances at her belly which was more visible than normal through her thin nightie. "I'm glad we figured that water thing out. Your color's back—you look really good, Kate."

"You figured the water thing out." Kate smiled at her. She arched an eyebrow. "And I look really big."

"That's normal." Shay blotted her lips, set her container beside the others. "Babies literally double in size in the last three months."

Kate settled back, smiled in the blue light cast off by the television set. "Is there anything you don't know about babies and...stuff?"

"Maybe I overstudied." Shay laughed when she thought about it. "My ex wasn't exactly enthralled with pregnancy or parenting. I guess I tried to overcompensate for that."

Several seconds later, she still felt Kate's stare on her. She smiled. "What?"

"I bet you are a great mom."

There was something heartbreaking about her tone, and the fact that Kate indicated *are* instead of *was* wasn't lost on Shay.

Shay slid her arm across the back of the couch, paused for two deep breaths, then tentatively rested her arm around Kate's shoulders. She held her breath and counted to ten. Kate seemed aware of her partner's insecurity about the move. She smiled encouragingly and snuggled in closer.

After more than an hour of nodding off, Shay tiredly asked her, "You sleepy yet, sunshine?"

"I lay around all day, you'll remember." Kate lowered the TV volume and situated a toss pillow across what was left of her lap. She patted it, sweetly insisted, "Please, I'm practicing my maternal instincts."

After only a moment of hesitation, Shay stretched her lanky form across the couch and rested her head on Kate's lap. Minutes later, she lurched in near-sleep and caught herself. She reached one hand up and gently patted Kate's belly, whispered, "Sorry, ss."

She closed her eyes again and drifted into deep sleep. Slightly taken aback, Kate moved to stroke Shay's hair. It was a robotic move that became more natural with each passing second. She turned off the television and sat in the dark, thinking.

Princess?

The word sounded soft and sweet coming from Shay's lips. Kate didn't remember much about her own parents, only that they'd been academic types; certainly not the kind to employ such silly endearments. The very idea that she was going to have a child of her own was strange. She'd been barely parented herself as a child. Now, it seemed like she was getting a second chance to discover what childhood could be. It was as if someone had handed her the Lindbergh baby with instructions to do it right this time, save the baby, save herself...

Elise had been terribly critical of her. Funny, as much as her ex had wanted a baby, and try as they had to make that happen, Kate had never been able to envision them as a family. Fantasies of family spontaneously expanded whenever she looked at Shay, as if Kate was making up for lost time. It was ridiculous. It was... wonderful.

As she gazed over her sleeping partner, Kate was forced to realize she was getting another chance at other emotions that had also been long dormant. Perhaps they'd never been properly attended to in the first place. Confusion ruled her head, but not her heart. Without a doubt, she knew she had fallen in love with Shay.

CHAPTER THIRTY-EIGHT

The view through binoculars was poor, and a poorly placed streetlight would have blinded him had he employed the night vision binoculars he'd brought along. The Watcher kept his car at a safe distance, aware of two unmarked FBI vehicles parked curbside several yards in front of him. One agent was reading a newspaper. The other had been still enough to qualify as asleep. All eyes, tired or not, were trained on the Cooper house.

He dropped the binoculars back on the seat next to him and snorted. How quickly Kate had managed to get on with her life. He wasn't sure what anyone, men or women, saw in the woman. His feelings of indifference, self-control and confidence were making a record fast segue to hatred. He thought of the time he'd spent in the office next to Kate. For as long as he'd known her been a smug bitch. Too smug for a mere office worker and sometimes lab rat. She'd been too stupid to realize the important work he was doing. Thoughts of showing her empowered him, gave him incentive to finish the job.

He left his vehicle parked down the block.

The commotion awoke Kate from a sleep she didn't even know she'd fallen into. She sat up straighter, shook Shay's shoulder.

"Something's wrong," she whispered.

Shay came around quickly. She sprang off the couch and went for her gun. Someone was frantically hammering on the front door. Shay ran to it, threw it open, and stared at the agents standing there.

"What the hell's going on, guys?" she blurted. They stood in the doorway conferring in ragged whispers. Despite their secrecy, Kate understood that someone had attempted to enter the house through a window and had run off when confronted. Shay noticed her listening. She pulled herself out of their powwow long enough to address her. "Get back in the bedroom."

Shay crammed her feet into sneakers, preparing to leave. She saw Kate still standing there, wide-eyed. "Room, please? Now?"

Kate nodded and headed down the hallway. She heard the door shut behind her. From the bedroom window she watched blue-tinted flashlight beams bounce through the night and the chase for the mysterious almost-intruder was on.

Three agents spread out and canvassed the immediate neighborhood on foot, huffing through yards and hurdling low fences. The low-key neighborhood was bedded down for the night, unaware that anything was amiss.

Shay was operating at an extreme disadvantage; she hadn't seen anyone peering into the house windows like the others had and she had only a partial clothing description. This was the story of her life as of late. It was haphazard as hell, like the night when she was blindly firing shots into an empty-looking parking garage. She figured she would recognize Tony Williams if she saw him face to face. She only hoped she would see him first and not the other way around. And she wanted him alive; she needed him to account for the bodies they'd been unearthing for more than a week.

Lights went in three directions for several blocks. More than ten minutes later, the agents reassembled on her front lawn. Shay leaned over to catch her breath, fought a stitch in her side from having sprung fresh from sleep and sprinting all over the neighborhood. She looked at the others, similarly surprised and breathless.

"Was there a vehicle?"

"Don't know." Agent Durham looked utterly puzzled. "Too many cars parked on the street. Didn't notice anything new."

"Did we get anything, guys?" She shook her head when they looked blankly at her. "Tell me—was it Williams?"

There was only silence until Durham spoke at last.

"Ski mask. And don't bother to print—he wore gloves."

"Dammit!" Shay said, angry and loud. She swiped perspiration off her forehead, then laid out nonnegotiable instructions. "All eyes on this house tonight. I don't want you to blink, get me? If you're tired, get a replacement. Make sure everyone knows this is priority one. This guy has killed many and now he's after one of our own."

Everyone voiced agreement before returning to their designated posts. Shay went into the house, reset the alarm and checked to be sure she had a clear phone signal. She leaned against the door until her breathing leveled off. Then she made her way through the dark house toward the bedroom. She gently pushed open the door to see Kate standing at the window. Shay froze.

Kate's profile was illuminated by the bright moonlight streaming in through the window. The short gauze nightie wasn't designed for a pregnant belly, no matter how small. It rode especially high on her thigh. Shay was grateful to be unnoticed. It gave her a moment to gawk unapologetically at Kate's form through the ghostly material. She swallowed hard.

Instinctually, Kate spun around.

"You're supposed to be in bed," Shay blurted in her raspy

voice. She roughly crossed the floor to stand before Kate. Their eyes locked.

"What's going on?" Kate's eyes flitted toward the window and back to Shay. "What happened?"

Shay had every intention of persuading her partner back to bed, chastising her for posing like a target in the large window. Instead, she heard herself stammer, "Nothing. It turned out to be nothing."

Kate started to lose her patience. "Nothing had you running all over creation?"

Shay stepped closer, raised the hem of her T-shirt and swiped it across her damp forehead.

Kate didn't miss seeing her trim physique. Nor did she miss the fact that her partner was breathless for reasons she figured had little to do with a late night she'd been abruptly thrust into.

"You're supposed to be off your feet," Shay started, but her tone fell flat, her intentions of bullying her all but vanished. Before she could offer further protest, Kate's lips were on hers.

Shay kissed her back tentatively, then deeply in response to Kate's soft, encouraging whimpers. She made a possessive, thorough exploration, and when they finally drew back, they were mutually breathless, glassy-eyed, fearful.

Shay came to her senses first, scrubbed her forehead, took a step backward.

"I can't do this," she muttered looking truly regretful. "I have to keep you safe."

"I am safe," Kate whispered. "Shay, trust me."

She reached for Shay with plans for round two. She easily went to her and their passion quickly escalated to graceless groping until Shay twisted herself out of the entanglement, and forcibly pulled herself away a second time. This time she cupped her hands over Kate's shoulders, firmly holding her at arm's length.

"I can't do that to you," she said, troubled beyond all measure. She whispered, "I don't know what's gotten into me. I'm truly sorry."

Conflict showed in Kate's eyes. "You're not doing anything to me I don't want you to. I'm a big girl."

"I do know that." Shay took her hand, led her back to bed. She assisted her in, tucked the blankets around Kate's legs, then sat on the edge beside her. "You're needy right now, I get that— I'm needy too, even without the extra hormones."

Kate defended herself, felt a developing undertone of anger. "It's not just hormones."

"Okay." Shay hesitated, looked embarrassed. "I just don't want to take advantage of any feelings coming out of left field because you're pregnant and emotional."

"You aren't taking advantage of me."

"I hope that's true," Shay whispered. She gathered her strength. "But what you need most is my protection. I don't want this guy to get you."

Shay sensed Kate withdrawing from her and she moved to stop that downward spiral. "I swear to God it's not personal. But I'm bad as hell at relationships. I haven't had one since my ex and I busted up—I just resigned myself from it."

"That's a bad excuse." Kate sounded hurt.

Shay reached for her hand, squeezed it. "It's not an excuse. I don't want to hurt you or your baby in any way—emotionally or otherwise." Her tone took a grim turn. "And I'll die before I let anyone else have a shot at it."

Kate looked numb and Shay was out of words. She figured she'd worn out her welcome and started to leave her alone for the night.

"I'm scared." Kate's quiet admission sliced through the dark room and stopped her.

Hidden by darkness, Shay winced. She approached the bed. With much apprehension, she lay down next to Kate, on top of the blanket, creating a safe barrier between them. She awkwardly folded Kate into her arms.

"Me too," she whispered.

She spooned her body around Kate. Her own body ached with need. Kate's wonderful smell and soft skin that could be felt through the gauzy nightie didn't help matters. She attempted to focus on Kate's motherhood instead of her womanhood, but one was evidence of the other and only served to amplify her desire. Shay clenched her eyes shut and willed every ounce of goodness in her body to cooperate and simply get through the night. She laid a protective arm across her partner.

At six a.m., Shay wasn't ready to get up. Kate was nestled in tight, having slept soundly for the first time since coming to the house. She felt Shay's movement and her eyelids fluttered open. Recognition, not startle shone in her eyes, and a small smile played on her lips.

"What are you doing?" she whispered.

"Watching you." Shay gently brushed the hair from Kate's eyes. "I just want to remember you...soft and peaceful like this."

Kate raised her hand and drew her fingertips along her partner's arm, sending a chill through her. Shay caught her hand, kissed her fingers, and tenderly pushed her away. She hated what she was about to do.

"I told you, I need to keep you safe," Shay gently explained. "And I've decided without a doubt that I can't do that when I have other things on my mind."

"Other things?" Kate looked confused.

Shay softly chuckled. "You...are the other things."

"Yes. You pretty much told me that last night." She forced a polite thin smile. "I'm hormonal, not stupid."

Shay sat up straight, aware that she'd offended her partner. "I have never, ever said or even thought you were stupid. Never."

"You obviously don't think I make good decisions. You don't have faith in me." Kate shrugged, whispered, "I can't believe in someone who doesn't believe in me."

"That's not—"

Kate moved forward with business. "I'll make arrangements to return to my place as soon as possible."

Shay felt her heartbeat quicken. She began to stammer. "You—you're not safe at home, and you know that."

"I think I can make a few phone calls and get the proper resources," she said, dipping her chin. "I can surely manage that in my hormonal state."

And like that, Shay had offended her yet again.

"I beg you to reconsider."

"I appreciate everything you've done for me, but I've got it from here, Agent Cooper." She rolled over to face the wall. "You better get to work."

She nodded behind Kate's back and quietly slipped out of the room.

CHAPTER THIRTY-NINE

Agent Buchner would be the FBI's new golden boy. He was on his seventh case in as many days, turning in skeletal remains hand over fist. He could do no wrong.

Buchner had suspected the code was nothing short of an idiot's game about halfway through his days under Williams' tutelage. Of course, he never asked about the odd time stamps. If what he'd suspected about the senior agent was true, and he was a maniacal killer, he feared he himself would be dead, his final resting location coded within a time stamp that might never be cracked by a lesser agent.

Acting on instinct, he'd carefully, discreetly collected a set of Williams' prints during their time together. Call it insurance. He knew an animal like Williams would not have his own in the system. That was just another solid fact Buchner had been right about.

For now, Buchner would continue to follow the code, collect the bodies, and bait his superiors with the "what-ifs" of Agent Williams. He knew for a fact that there'd be more prints recovered. Then he'd produce the drinking glass he'd collected from the office long ago. He was going to single-handedly solve this mystery. By the time it was over, his achievements would far overshadow those of his colleagues. He smiled as he thought about it and actually laughed out loud as he recalled his last employment review. He'd actually been written up for what Holloway referred to as Buchner's cowboy behavior. Not a team player, he'd said. Holloway certainly seemed to know where to poke the stick and give it a twist. Damn the son of a bitch anyway. He'd put them all to shame. Particularly Shay Cooper.

"Agent Cooper-who? What drug bust?" he mocked in a smug tone. He'd been waiting for this his whole life and he knew exactly what to do with it. There would be interviews, promotions, more books than Williams or Holloway could ever dream of producing. Possibly he'd get a profile on the Justice Channel with that sexy interviewer Laney Howard. He allowed himself only a few moments to gloat before getting back to his files, neatly laid out on his hotel bed. He'd flown in early that morning, found a body right on schedule, and was preparing to go back to Chicago. He placed the files in his duffle carry-on bag for the flight back.

Williams was out there, somewhere, and he wanted to find him. Buchner wanted to draw him out, call his bluff, see him squirm and suffer and break. Thinking about it brought him even more enjoyment than the prospect of simply being heralded as the FBI's golden boy.

He thought about the two pieces of evidence in existence that could tie Williams to those crimes: a baby's DNA and a handful of fingerprints. Concrete proof. He hated to share glory; after all, he'd waited for it for so long. He wanted to spring his trap on his own terms when the time was right. He'd bring them all down. He was sure Williams was nervous by now, wherever he was. Buchner would prove himself the champion. Perhaps he should get a lawyer, even a publicity agent...

He'd hang on to the information a while longer. He was reminded of the postcard he carried and the words of his former mentor.

"Timing is everything."

Shay reviewed two more cases Agent Buchner had turned in. It was quite the lackluster ending for the Lanterman case; the Senator's daughter's remains were discovered, oddly enough, buried in a park not far from her childhood home. It crossed her mind that she had believed her mother had known something about the case, therefore advancing her own overt fascination. Now Shay doubted it. She was disappointed that she didn't feel the closure she'd thought she would upon the close of that particular case. Or maybe that's because the closure she'd truly craved concerned her mother's own disappearance.

Shay scribbled her name across the form and sighed. From her office they would go to AD Holloway, who seemed only barely thrilled at having to reopen the cases anyway. She wondered why.

Her desk phone rang jarring her from her thoughts.

"Cooper."

"Special Agent Sam Feldman, New York office."

She sat up in her chair, slid the case file off to one side.

"How can I help you?"

"Some coordinates were forwarded to me yesterday afternoon by an agent in your charge."

She nodded as if Feldman could see her. "Yes. Agent Buchner. I'm familiar with those cases."

"Tell him congratulations—we found his bodies."

Shay drew in her breath as she drew a pair of folders out of a different pile. She smoothed her finger over a thumbnail picture of a small boy.

She quietly said, "Go on."

"Male, mid-thirties in upstate New York."

She swallowed hard. "The other?"

"Male child, Long Island."

Her shoulders heaved forward with unbearable dread. She hadn't wanted to believe Kate when she'd proposed a link to her own son's disappearance. Still, she'd pulled the official case, kept it aside, but had avoided looking at it until now. Her voice cracked as she asked, "Whereabouts in Long Island?"

"Under the asphalt of the Dueling Building, you know the place?"

She did. It had been a mere construction site when she used to take Christopher there to see the bulldozers. He would wear a plastic yellow hardhat. She bowed her head, rubbed her moist eyes. "Yes, I know the place."

Unaware of her agony, the agent droned on with a relative degree of insensitivity. "The bodies are obviously severely degraded. They're with our ID guy now. You contact the families?"

"I'm faxing you a case file number to cross reference along with the name of a dentist there in the city who can provide records. Can you get that to your guy immediately?" Shay used a Sharpie marker to write the case number on a fax sheet. She knew it by heart. Her voice remained steady, despite simultaneous explosions in her head and chest. "Can I get confirmation by this afternoon?"

"That's pushing it."

"The families are desperate to know."

After a brief hesitation, Feldman said, "I'll do what I can."

She hung up and went to the fax machine where she punched in the New York office's number. With a heavy heart and dreadful premonition, she pressed Send.

Kate Harris used her cell phone to dial the office and was momentarily caught off guard when Agent Buchner answered. She recalled Shay telling her that the junior agent had set up camp in their quarters once again. She hoped he'd be gone before she made it back; his gung-ho attitude was becoming increasingly harder to tolerate. She forced herself to sound cheerful.

"Agent Buchner, it's Harris. I'm looking for Agent Cooper."

"Hey there, Agent Harris." He sounded genuinely glad to hear from her. "She took out of here about an hour ago. If she comes in I'll tell her you called, how's that?"

"Sounds good," she said, preparing to hang up. She stopped, frowning as she mentally tabulated his comings and goings. "Agent Buchner, weren't you just in Des Moines this morning?"

"Yes, ma'am. And I'm on the redeye tonight for Wisconsin."

"Don't you sleep, Agent Buchner?"

He laughed. "Sleep is for wimps, Agent."

She chuckled softly. "Jesus, you remind me so much of my old partner."

His enthusiastic tone said he perceived her statement to be nothing short of a glorious accolade. "I'll take that as a compliment."

CHAPTER FORTY

Shay didn't arrive home until after midnight. She cruised past the agents in unmarked cars without acknowledging them. She assumed their presence was a sign Kate Harris had been unable to work her magic to get herself out of Shay's prison-home. She sighed, punched in the security code, and headed for the kitchen. She took everything out of a low cabinet until she found half a bottle of scotch. With trembling hands, she poured a little into a glass tumbler and carried the bottle with her to the living room. Sitting on the couch, she cradled the glass, consumed by the tragedy that had become her life.

"Shay?" Her partner's voice startled her and she raised her eyes to see Kate in the doorway.

"You shouldn't be out of bed," she gruffly remarked. "I tell you and I tell you..."

Shay refused to look at her. Seeing her in whatever alluring getup she was wearing tonight would only add to her profound misery.

But Kate crossed the room, knelt onto the floor on front of her, leaving Shay no choice but to look into her eyes.

"I talked to the New York office. They called me when they couldn't get you." She softly told her, "I'm so, so sorry."

Shay took another drink. She looked like the world had won. Kate took the glass away from her, clasped her partner's hands. Shay received her intended comfort for only a moment before she abruptly rose off the couch and pushed her hands away.

"Let's get you back to bed."

Kate also stood up, held her ground. "No. I'm here for you."

"No." Shay forced a sad laugh. "I'm here for *you*. And if you can't do what I tell you, you're going to have to leave."

"What happened to me is not your fault," Kate said firmly, also rising. "What happened to Christopher was not your fault. Don't you see?"

"I see that you're trying to make me feel better." Shay shrugged, finished the drink in one swig. Her eyes watered as she swiped her hand across her lips. "And it's really not working."

"You need to talk about it."

"I don't need to talk about it."

"Your son—"

"My son is *dead!*" It was a long overdue explosion. She shrugged off Kate's intended touch. "He's dead. I knew that. Now I know for sure."

They stood in the darkness, staring at each other.

"Would you please, *please* go back to bed now?" Shay begged her. She dropped back onto the couch, covered her face with her hands.

Kate sat down next to her. She put her arm around her partner's shoulders, squeezed her tight. "Please, let me take care of you." She laid her cheek against Shay's shoulder. "Please let me."

In a sudden move, Shay pulled her onto her lap and held her tight. She buried her face against her shoulder and cried. They sat there for a long time.

Kate stroked her partner's back, whispered in her ear, "I'm right here. I promise."

He was the king of the body hunters.

High above the city, Special Agent James Buchner stared out the window of the aircraft. His plane had departed O'Hare and was now at cruising altitude; the seatbelt light had finally switched off.

He'd defied orders to wait for clearance and had gone ahead with the case on his own. For it, he'd send body number twelve back to the lab by the next day. DC would soon get involved, then there was no keeping it from the press. Sweet recognition. Others were thinking of this as well, judging by the e-mail he'd received from AD Holloway prior to boarding. Buchner was to report to his office first thing upon his arrival home. It wasn't exactly a ticker tape parade, but his day in the sun would come. Thinking about it made him smile.

He'd made discoveries that went way beyond raking the leaves off a few crusty bones. His biggest and best discovery had been made before Williams had vanished, and that was simply finding out what kind of a monster he truly was. He wasn't the mathematical genius everyone had heralded; in truth, Williams knew as much about math as Buchner did about knitting. He was nothing but a sick, twisted liar employing a ridiculously juvenile code.

Despite his penchant for creating his own work, Buchner knew he owed his success—and inevitable fame—to the missing agent. To Shay Cooper as well, he supposed. There was another super pain-in-the-ass rock star. Buchner remembered the day Cooper had confidentially shared her suspicion about Williams with him. She'd given him a simple objective: follow the breadcrumbs, unearth the bodies, uncover the truth. He'd thanked her, praised her brilliance, then smirked after she'd left. Like Williams, Cooper was an amateur.

iffuse light in the cabin of the plane was cast off by nt reading lamps. Buchner didn't have a particular aversion to flying but it was getting old as of late. He'd be glad to get back home when this was over. Maybe he'd take a little vacation and revel in his newfound glory.

He pulled the window cover shut and fluffed the tiniest pillow in the world. He didn't like his apartment either, maybe it was time to upgrade. Maybe it was time to buy. He tried to close his eyes but his mind wouldn't wind down. He was exhilarated.

Shay woke up and felt guilty when she discovered she'd made her pregnant partner sleep on a couch, tucked into her side. At the same time, it was wonderful to see her there. To feel her against her. The wave of relief rolled out and dread rolled in to take its place.

She would receive the official report on her son's remains today. Then she'd be forced to talk to her ex after all these years and share with her the long-awaited news about their missing child. The closure the discovery provided her wasn't the tremendous relief she hoped it would be. And how could it be?—her son was dead.

She stood up and tried to shift Kate into a more comfortable position on the couch. She tucked the blanket in around her.

"Don't go to work today."

Kate's whispered request startled her. Shay took a seat back on the edge of the couch. "I have to."

"You need time," she pleaded with her. "Please. Stay with me today."

Shay's eyes found a focus point across the room. Her voice was low and haunted when she finally spoke. "I always knew he was dead, you know? But I couldn't help hoping I was somehow wrong."

Kate clasped her partner's hands, remained quiet.

"I guess that's why it was easier for Rita to get on with her life. She acknowledged what she felt." Shay felt and sounded tortured when she added, "She felt like he was gone."

"You had hope," Kate whispered. "It helps keep you going, if only for a little while. Sometimes you just need that."

Shay looked at her partner. "When I said I didn't want to compromise your safety by getting involved—"

"Not now," Kate stopped her.

"Let me explain," Shay insisted. She wet her lips. "I can't stand to lose…people. I lied to you about my family. I lost my mother when I was eight years old. She was murdered in our house while I was at school one day. Or at least I guess she was. They never found her body, just…so much blood…"

"How awful, Shay." Kate took her hand, whispered, "I'm so sorry."

Shay nodded, forced herself to continue. "Then Christopher, then Rita. Hell—a sick part of me hates it that fucking Ortelli is dying, I'm getting so used to losing people." She looked momentarily sidetracked. "I'd blamed him for so long for Christopher."

"I know." Kate looked deeply troubled. She laid a hand on her belly. "How do you honestly feel about this baby now knowing she belongs to your son's killer?"

"She doesn't belong to him. She belongs to you." Shay didn't even feel remotely tense; she didn't feel sad or angry; she only shook her head. "I feel about this baby the same way I feel about you. It would kill me if anything happened to either one of you."

They remained locked in each other's gaze.

"I shut my feelings off so long ago, for everyone, for this very reason." Shay swallowed hard. "I can't stand to lose anyone else."

Kate touched her partner's cheek, looked at her adoringly. "You've taken very good care of me. Dr. Michaels came to see me yesterday. She gave me the all clear." Kate grew quiet. "I was going to leave, but then I heard the news."

"I don't want you to leave here, Kate." Shay was suddenly serious again. "I can't take that chance. Please understand."

"What happened to your son wasn't your fault."

"I should have protected him."

"Not from minds far more devious than even you or I could imagine."

"I could have at least…found him." Shay felt utterly defeated.

She sighed, stood up and offered Kate her hand. "Let me help you into the bedroom, okay? A few more days of laying low, please? Just humor me?"

Kate studied her a moment. Then she nodded.

It was the first time Shay had talked to Rita in nearly five years, and from her experience at the Bureau, she well knew it wasn't the kind of conversation anyone ever hopes to have. She tonelessly informed Rita that Christopher's body had been found a mere ten blocks from their old apartment. Rita seemed sad, but oddly removed. She'd obviously spent their years apart processing any grief she had. Shay realized she'd only deferred her own.

Despite their shared pain, Shay felt nothing tugging at old heartstrings. Nothing about Rita felt familiar—she had wondered how she'd feel upon speaking to the first and longest love of her life; the mother of the only child she'd ever have.

Rita was caught off guard only by mention of the burial arrangements. It angered Shay that Rita didn't have any interest in working together on it. When Shay told her she'd handle it, Rita had the audacity to mention a small life insurance policy. It crossed Shay's mind that her ex had lost her mind. Shay told her, "Keep it," and hung up. Probably her ex could use the money for new rugs or art for her fancy apartment recently featured in a New York magazine.

The exchange was revoltingly shallow. She wished she'd had someone else inform her.

Kate was back on the case even from her bed. She contacted the lab in Arizona to see if there was any news about the blood discovered in the drain of Janice Tremmel's bathtub.

Her contact's tone was impatient, gruff. "No hits in CODIS."

"I wonder if you could e-mail me that case number and lab

link?" Kate conjured up her sweetest voice. "It would surely be a big help to us here in the Midwest office."

"I could do that." He softened at her kind request. "Go on, give me your info."

She typed in her password to connect with the Bureau's network. In fifteen minutes she was downloading the full case file and lab results. She ran the results through the national database again for her own confirmation but no perps came up. She sighed, stared at the screen. She punched in a new search to include new parameters. Within seconds, she had two alerts.

Kate moved closer to the screen and her eyes grew wide.

CHAPTER FORTY-ONE

The welcome home sounded more like an interrogation.

"Where were you? Didn't you get my calls?" Kate anxiously asked Shay when she walked through the door that evening. "You didn't answer."

Shay eyed her warily. She shrugged out of her jacket and dropped it on the hallway bench. "You didn't leave any messages and I was already on my way home." She looked over Kate's shoulder. "Could we please take this conversation into the bedroom? You're getting all stressed out, which is stressing me out."

"Listen to me," Kate firmly ordered, but Shay was already behind her and had begun steering her down the hallway.

"I promise I will listen to you, but not before you are in that bed, okay?" Shay pointed toward the hallway. "I insist. You're humoring me, remember?"

Kate sighed loudly and when they reached the bedroom, she plopped down onto the bed in a show of obligatory compliance. She presented her case.

"First, the blood evidence from Arizona." She handed her the paper she'd been clutching. Shay briefly read it over.

"What am I looking at here?"

"No easy hits in CODIS, so I had them send the info to me. I linked up to the mainframe and ran it through the Bureau database." She made a singsong voice. "Got something."

"You're kidding me?" Shay frowned. "Who?"

"Ran it against vics, unknown perps—the works." She cut her explanation short and instead handed Shay a fax-quality report with Len Ortelli's mugshot on the top of it.

"Are you saying Ortelli's not out of business yet?" Shay shook her head. "I've seen him—he's practically dead. No way he could—"

"This is only a familial match," Kate cut her off. "Do you understand what I'm saying?"

Shay looked confused. "Right now, I can't wrap my brain around anything."

"It means that the perp in the Arizona case is a relative of Ortelli's." Kate nodded. "They have certain markers in common. Family alleles."

"Jesus," Shay whispered. She made rapid recollection of the conversation with the old man in her office, days earlier. "Ortelli said he had a bad kid."

"There's more." She produced another file. "An old file from the Missing Children's database. It was recently pulled for comparison in the New York lab. I knew you wouldn't believe it unless you saw it for yourself."

Shay's eyes narrowed, she shook her head. "Impossible. This is…just not possible."

"Ortelli and the unknown blood from the bathtub share common markers with your son. Your *son*, Shay." Kate emphasized it, dipped her head to capture Shay's fading attention. "According to this report, your son is Ortelli's grandchild. We need to talk to your ex, now."

Still reeling from shock, Shay's voice was quiet, scratchy. "That's not necessary."

"What do you mean?" Kate drew back, surprised. "We have no choice. According to this, Rita is Ortelli's daughter."

"No, she's not." Shay paused, looked at Kate. "Rita carried Christopher using donor sperm and *my* egg."

Kate was stunned into silence.

Struck with inspiration, Shay rose up and began rummaging through the top drawer of her bureau. She found an antique box and brought it back to the bed where she dumped its contents on the comforter.

Kate quietly watched her frenzy as Shay sorted through pins, tiny pictures, old watches, a few rings until she found what she was after. She held it up like a prize; it was a gold locket dangling from a tarnished chain. She gently pried it open with her fingernail.

To D, my truest love.

"Fuck me," Shay muttered. She looked at Kate. "I thought he meant Dee—but Dee wasn't her name at all, it was her initial." She swallowed hard, laid it back on top of the pile. "My mother's name was Diane. Jesus, he practically told me all this."

Kate found her voice at last. "Did he say anything about his other child? About you?"

"I suppose so," she admitted. "Some kind of master detective I turned out to be."

It was well after hours when Buchner showed his face at the office. Lucy, a woman from the secretary pool, knocked on the door of the office where he'd set up temporary camp alongside Cooper. Lucy's sleek form, spike heels and ponytail bump made her appear as tall as the doorway.

"AD Holloway would like to see you as soon as possible."

"Tonight?" Buchner glanced at his watch, scowled. "It's after eight."

"He's waiting for you."

Buchner nodded then smiled. Perhaps his accolades were going to come even sooner than he'd planned.

Shay pushed through the bedroom door carrying a dinner tray loaded down with plates of pasta and bread and a juice glass containing a single rosebud. Kate was wrapped in a thick terry robe, the ends of her hair wet from the shower, and she hurriedly hung up her cell phone when her partner came in.

"I borrowed your robe. Hope you don't mind," Kate informed her.

Shay grinned. "No, not at all. It looks good on you."

"Pasta? This looks fabulous." Kate made a quick assessment of the tray. She then spotted the flower. "That's beautiful."

"I found it in the backyard," Shay told her, lest Kate would think she'd gone through a lot of trouble, or that she'd officially brought her flowers. She shook out two napkins and arranged silverware on either side of the tray. "It's a jungle out there, but there's some real hidden beauties when you get a good look."

Kate smiled at her. "Isn't that the case with pretty much everything?"

"Yeah." Shay's cheeks pinked slightly. "I guess so."

"You know, we could have done this at the table," Kate told her. "Dr. Michaels said I can be vertical, remember?"

"I kind of like seeing you in here." And then when Shay realized what she'd implied, she dipped her head, looked away. "I hope you're not planning to go back to work until after your leave. You've only got a month left anyway."

"Don't worry, I plan to lay low until then."

"Good." Shay raised her water and they clinked glasses. "To baby."

"Hear, hear." Kate sipped her water then twirled the pasta around her fork tines and popped it in her mouth. She closed her eyes, savored the flavor. "Delicious. Where did you get this?"

"Kitchen," Shay nonchalantly informed her. "I spent a month undercover as a chef in an Italian restaurant. Learned everything I know."

"Are you serious?" Kate's eyes grew wide.

"No, not at all." Shay chuckled at her partner's uncharacteristic gullibility. "It's just a little pesto I whipped up."

"Nice job, little liar." Thunder rumbled, rattled the house windows. Kate playfully arched an eyebrow at the timing of it. "I think you're about to be struck down."

Shay grinned at her, blotted her lips. Her eyes went to a pile of fax papers beside Kate. "What's that?"

"I checked your DNA against Ortelli's and the mystery blood from Arizona, just for the sake of efficiency." Kate waved a hand as she explained it. "Also a familial match, as we figured it would be."

Shay looked suddenly serious. "I called a buddy of mine in New York, had her check the system for juvenile offenders named Ortelli. Four popped in a two-year timeframe, but only one showed up for a name change on his eighteenth birthday. Any guesses?"

"Anthony Williams." Kate's eyes were wide with disbelief.

"Formerly Anthony Ortelli, Jr. Guess he liked his first name."

"Jesus, this is too much." Kate set her fork aside, rested her hand on her belly. "Do you realize that it's possible you're almost as related to this baby as I am?"

A noise from the front yard deferred Shay's response. She sprang off the bed and in seconds was out the front door of the house. Her appearance effectively interrupted a shouting match unfolding between Buchner and a rookie agent manning his post. Buchner's face was slick with rain. Seeing him start after her, the rookie raised his walkie to call for backup.

"Wait! We'll handle this." She made a halting motion at the rookie, she squinted her eyes in the rain, looked at Buchner.

"Holloway took me off the case!" he spat, his eyes burning with fury aimed at her. Rain came down in a noisy, steady curtain around them. "He said you recommended it!"

"Calm down." She wondered why Holloway would tell him any such thing. In truth, the AD had asked her opinion and she'd given it. Nothing more, and certainly it wasn't a recommendation. She shook her head. "Let's just calm down and talk about this."

"All that motherfucking work I did for you? All the shit—and this is how you repay me?" As he stood over her, the rain did little to suppress his body odor, a telltale sign that he'd been working nonstop, without sleep, on his recovery quest. Dark half-moons underscored his eyes and he was trembling with anger. "That was *my* work! *I'm* the one! Me!"

"Go home and get some sleep." But he wasn't listening, and in his present state, he was making her nervous. Thunder rolled through the neighborhood and she yelled to be heard over it. "I'll talk to Holloway about it tomorrow. I promise that much."

"You see this?" He waved a wet piece of paper in front of her that looked as if it had been wadded up and subsequently smoothed out for her review. "Suspended! Because of you—you glory-seeking, narcissistic bitch!"

"Calm the hell down," she said firmly, locking eyes with him. Her tone and stance made the order nonnegotiable. Raindrops dripped from her shaggy bangs and she swiped them away. "You're out of control. This is completely inappropriate—all of this!"

Buchner was seething, his shoulders bobbed with his uneven breaths.

She laid out succinct instructions. "Get out of the way for a while, and let me deal with Holloway, okay?" When he didn't answer, she repeated herself, "Okay?"

Buchner took a step closer to her, jammed his meaty finger into her shoulder. The sound of the rainstorm couldn't drown out his ragged whisper, ripe with warning. "You better get out of the way."

He turned and stormed down the sidewalk, got in his car and peeled away from the curb. Shay took the front steps two at a time, strode past the rookie who was wearing a yellow rain poncho and still clutching his walkie.

"Nobody hears about this, understand?" she told him. He looked too nervous for her taste. "Don't let that ruin your day, kid, or this job will be your own personal hell."

Kate was waiting for her return, practically ambushed her when she came through the door. "What was that about?"

"Buchner got suspended." Shay raked her hands through her hair, flipping little drops of water everywhere. Kate handed her a towel. "Needless to say, he's a little pissed off."

Kate looked confused. "But that's not your fault."

Shay's shoulders slumped. She was soaking and miserable. "Look—I sent Buchner out there on a hunch with nothing more than a map and some numbers. If I'd had clue one what he'd find, or how quickly, I would have sent a team. It's too much for one agent. Period. That's not how we do business."

Despite her wet clothes, Shay plopped onto the edge of the bed. Kate sat down next to her partner and began rubbing her back. "It's out of your hands. It's between Buchner and Holloway now."

"He wasn't prepared for this. He's cocky to start with and impulsive as hell. He fancies himself the Lone Ranger. Too many bodies, not enough sleep…" She thought about Tony Williams. "Look what happens to our guys when we don't keep an eye on them."

The remark inspired silence between them in the dark room.

Kate cleared her throat. "What about you?"

"What about me?"

"You were pretty much a one-woman operation looking for your son's killer."

Shay finally, sadly nodded. "That's true. But it wasn't for guts or glory. I just wanted my son back."

"What about your ex?"

Shay's tone was bland. "She's…my ex."

The dark mood took an unusual turn, forged by Kate's whispered words. "Why have you been alone for so long?"

Shay blinked the rain off her lashes, stammered. "I'm…better alone."

"You really believe that?"

Shay licked her lips, nervous. "I have to."

Kate asked the question that had been niggling at her brain for weeks. "Are you still in love with your ex? Is that why you don't want me?"

"Oh, God no." Shay's response was automatic, vehement. She

wondered how Kate could possibly believe she didn't want her. It wasn't a matter of want, it was a matter of heart. She softened her tone again. "Trust me, you and Rita are...night and day."

"Then what is it?" She moved her hand from Shay's soaking back and laid it upon her baby belly. "Does this remind you of her?"

Kate looked warm, inviting. Shay swallowed hard. "Nothing about you reminds me of her. She wasn't cut out to parent." It was a strange confessional coming from someone who'd spent so many years being loyal, then as many years protecting her past. She looked at Kate. "You are going to be a great mom, I can tell. It's really one of the...sexiest qualities you have."

Kate licked her lips. "You think so?"

Shay nodded, became intent. "You've restored my faith in people."

"You've restored my faith in this baby," Kate admitted. She smiled faintly. "You overcame genetics, she will too."

Shay rushed to reassure her. "This is going to be one fantastic kid, okay?"

Tears sprang to Kate's eyes as she made her own confession. "I'm mean."

Shay moved closer, curious. "Pardon?"

"That's why I'm alone," Kate supplied the finish.

"Bullshit." Shay chuckled softly. "That's just what you do to keep yourself safely away from people, that's all."

Kate leaned dangerously close to her. "Like how you've convinced yourself you're a loner?"

Their lips came together in an electrifying kiss.

Shay slid her hands all the way down, supporting the small of her back. When their lips finally parted, they breathlessly stared at each other. Kate's cheeks were wet from Shay's hair. Her gaze roved to the front of her gauzy nightie now damp and nearly transparent where Shay had leaned against her.

Shay rose up from the bed. "I should go get out of these clothes. I got you wet."

Kate also stood up, leaned dangerously close to her ear, whispered, "That fact has nothing to do with your clothes."

Shay stared at her, blinking. Such seductive words coming

from such an innocent-looking woman. She felt her cheeks warm, dipped her chin slightly and glanced away.

Kate surprised her by clutching the hem of her T-shirt. She waited for Shay's silent go-ahead before she gently rolled the soaking shirt upward. Shay stopped her, but only momentarily, before she peeled the shirt off herself.

She stood before Kate, her smooth skin goose-pimpled in the chill air conditioned room. Kate stood before her, taking in her slim physique and pert nipples. Kate herself looked like a small child standing there in her gauzy white nightie. As wide blue eyes locked onto hers, Shay felt like she was about to pluck an innocent flower. She swallowed hard.

"Come here," Shay whispered.

Kate stepped close enough that Shay easily wrapped her arms around her. She nestled Kate's cheek against her chest, felt her warm and welcoming skin through the thin nightie. She stroked Kate's back, swaying slightly with her as they stood in the center of the room. "You are beautiful."

Kate drew back enough to see her, whispered, "You're pretty beautiful yourself."

Shay shook her head, but before she could protest, Kate's lips were against hers again. They kissed more deeply this time, pressing their bodies together. Shay trembled with desire, wondered why the feeling of Kate's belly pressing against her own flat one was such a turn on.

Her thoughts shifted back years ago to life pre-Rita. Shay's rocker good looks and the fact that she carried a gun made for fantasies stripped straight from a steamy paperback romance novel, and she'd had no shortage of lovers. Then came Rita for so many years. Then nothing. Since their breakup, Shay had been resolutely celibate. The reason for her sudden insecurity was obvious.

"Tell me what's on your mind," Kate said softly.

"This is foreign territory for me," Shay admitted in her low, raspy voice. "I'm nervous."

Kate's quiet respect was reflected in her eyes. Her hand went to Shay's and she squeezed it, smiled. In a voice that hinted at teasing, she asked, "Afraid you've lost your moves?"

"I guess I thought it would all come back, like riding a bike or something." Shay's laugh and her smile quickly vanished as she gazed into Kate's eyes. "But it feels different with you."

Kate leaned close, put her lips to her ear. "I've only ever been with one woman. Ever."

Her confession unzipped something inside of Shay, and she felt her stomach quiver and drop out. The words triggered an almost perverse pleasure as she gazed at the innocent-looking, nightie-clad nymph before her. She was offering herself, but she was offering something more. She was offering her trust, and Shay knew it was the only thing of value she had left.

Shay gulped, clenched her eyes shut, and quietly vowed surrender. With sudden assuredness, and taking great care, she took charge. She kissed her. Her tongue hungrily moved around Kate's mouth, exploring and tasting. Kate softly moaned, reciprocated the initiative. Shay felt Kate's soft, warm hands tease the top of her jeans, tugging. She shoved her hands away, unsnapped and peeled the wet jeans until they were in a soaking heap next to her similarly discarded T-shirt.

Shay rested her hand on Kate's belly, while the other firmly held the small of Kate's back pushing them as close together as their bodies could get. The obvious physical resistance only served to stoke fires of desperation within. Kate felt small, soft, and deliciously receptive. Shay guided her to the edge of the bed and knelt before her. She studied Kate's eyes for encouragement every step of the way.

Her hand slid up Kate's soft thigh, beneath the gauzy nightclothes near her panties. She kissed her belly, nestled her cheek against it. Every move was purposefully and lovingly made.

Shay's body ached for Kate, to feel her, to be loved by her. Instead, she transformed her need into giving as she stroked and teased her way along Kate's inner thighs.

"Please," Kate begged. "Touch me, please."

Shay saw the desperate longing in her partner's eyes. "Don't close your eyes," she whispered.

Kate nodded. She locked eyes with her as Shay at last softly stroked her through tiny cotton panties. Kate's eyes shut and she rolled her head slightly back with delight, but Shay reminded her, "Look at me."

Kate opened her eyes and she watched as Kate stroked her, then slid a hand inside her panties. Kate's tiny moan of appreciation gave Shay encouragement.

"You're so soft," Shay whispered with painful delight. She felt her insides churn with need.

"Shay, please…"

Shay cupped one hand around Kate's buttocks, holding her firmly. The fingers of her other hand softly stroked and teased the wetness she'd created. At last she slid into her wet center, watching Kate's eyes. She got only lovely sounds of approval.

"I need you," Kate raggedly whispered. "Please, Shay."

Shay's slow circle-making caused Kate to writhe against her hand, but she refused to speed up the process, refused to plunge deeper or harder. "Don't close your eyes. I want you to see me loving you."

The storm had picked up and raged outside, forming a natural orchestral background to the love they were making. Kate struggled to keep her eyes open, she wanted to hold her partner, reciprocate, but Shay only resisted her.

"Not yet." She whispered encouragement. "This is about you. Come to me, Kate. Let go, it's okay."

In that moment, Shay felt a lightning force throughout Kate's body. Her wet center tightened then softened and quivered around her touch. Afterward, Kate's head bobbed slightly back in a display of pure exhaustion. Her full breasts heaved beneath gauzy material. She sobbed.

Shay softly pulled out, kissed Kate's inner thigh while holding her and stroking her belly. She raised up to see Kate's tearful eyes. Gently, she assisted the trembling Kate onto her side. Shay crawled onto the bed and lay facing her, cocooning her body around Kate's.

"I've got you. I've got you both," Shay assured her again and again. She stroked her back. "I promise I'm right here."

Kate nodded, pressed her tear-streaked face against Shay's bare shoulder. She cried with release and relief.

"You make me feel safe," Kate whispered.

Shay hugged her tightly. "You are safe. I'll make sure of that."

"You make my heart feel safe, Shay." Kate moved slightly to see her partner's eyes in the dark room. She was tearful, scared. "I'm falling in love with you."

Shay drew a comforter over them both, held her until Kate's breaths were long and even. When at last she spoke, Shay's words permeated the stormy background and drew Kate slightly away from the edge of sleep.

"I love you too."

CHAPTER FORTY-TWO

At nearly four a.m. Shay heard movement in the room. She moved to put an arm around Kate, but the bed was empty. In an instant she was up, sheet wrapped around her, heart pounding wildly as she darted for the door.

"I'm here."

Shay blinked until her eyes adjusted to the near-black room. She saw the barest outline of her partner standing at the window. She went to her.

"You okay?" Shay asked. Kate nodded as Shay pulled her into her arms, whispered, "Then why aren't you asleep?"

"I've got things on my mind, I guess."

Shay was suddenly nervous, pulled back slightly. "Is it—God, did we go too fast?"

"No, not at all," Kate rushed to reassure her. Her tone

changed. "I was thinking about Tony. What if we don't catch him?"

"We'll find him. I promise you that much."

Kate frowned. She felt weariness throughout her body. "But if we don't, what happens?" Tears sprang to her eyes. "How are we supposed to be normal? What am I going to do? Keep an agent posted outside this baby's bedroom door indefinitely?"

"No." Shay's answer was firm. She turned thoughtful, her eyes flitted toward the ceiling. "However, you may want to do that when she turns sixteen."

Despite her tears, Kate smiled. "You are ridiculous."

"I'm just saying…"

"You know how to make me feel better, you know that?" Kate relaxed in her arms and her genuine smile shone beautifully in the dim moonlight.

Shay dipped her chin, nibbled Kate's neck. "Like this?" she murmured. Kate nodded. Shay kissed a path over her collarbone and gently cupped one full breast, leaned into her. "And this?"

"Yes," Kate whispered. She smiled at the sensation. "You make me feel attractive."

"You are attractive," Shay muttered between sweet kisses. Her mouth covered Kate's nipple through her nightie and she licked and suckled her. "Insanely attractive."

"Really?" she murmured with a chuckle. "Attractive like a barn?"

"Nonsense." Shay abruptly stopped, raised her eyes to Kate's. "A very, very small shed. At most."

Kate's laughter was like wonderful music. She caught her breath as Shay began kissing her all over again. "Don't stop."

Shay's only focus was comforting and pleasuring Kate. She caressed her belly, moved her hand downward and cupped her warmth. Kate raised her leg slightly for better access and soon they were moving against each other again. She felt Kate's center, teased her there, felt she was close.

Kate backed away suddenly, breathless. She shook her head. "No. Wait."

Shay found her back literally against the wall. The sheet feathered down her sides, landed at her feet. Kate admired Shay's athletic build and her firm breasts. She licked one, then the other, until wide nipples were erect. Then she knelt in front of Shay.

"Don't, no...I don't like to see you on the floor," Shay pleaded with her. Kate looked up at her, smiled. She looked playful, nymph-like, and incredibly seductive.

"Just keep your eyes open," she whispered. "I want you to see me loving you."

Shay grinned at hearing her own words right back at her. She pressed her head against the wall, felt greedy with love and desire, and willed herself to watch. Kate's tongue pointedly teased her until her legs trembled and threatened to give. She clutched the chair back to remain standing when at last Kate entered her warmth. Kate's tongue and fingers made alternate thorough explorations, a sensation that conspired to send Shay over the edge.

She avoided closing her eyes as she'd promised, and instead watched Kate kneeling before her, loving her with her incredibly gifted mouth. She focused on the softness of her tongue and her gentle movements. She admired her, loved her, and moments later nearly buckled over with the most powerful orgasm she could ever recall. Her slim body was pressed against the wall, heaving with relief and delight. She slid down the wall until her forehead pressed against Kate's. Her partner looked as satisfied as she felt, perhaps even a little smug that she'd been tremendously successful in her efforts.

"That was insane," Shay muttered. "I don't know how..."

"Shh," Kate hushed her. She kissed her deeply.

At last Shay broke away, warily stood up and assisted Kate off the floor. She helped her into the bed where she spooned her body around Kate's, snuggled in close.

"Tell me something," Kate broke the silence. "Did you know about the baby the night of the raid?"

Shay hesitated only a second before making her confession. "Yes. I found the ultrasound when I was nosing through your desk."

"You checked me out?" Kate stiffened slightly, feigning offense.

"You checked me out," Shay answered, chuckling. Kate went

soft in her arms again. "So, we're both paranoid and we're both liars."

"And after your thorough investigation, what did you discover, Agent Cooper?" Her tired sounding voice said she was close to sleep again.

"I discovered that you're probably the only person who trusts people less than I do," Shay said. She swallowed hard, stammered through her next words. "And that I...am completely in love with you."

"Tell me again," Kate demanded.

"I do love you."

Shay drew Kate closer, grateful that she could feel the warmth of her skin and every dip and curve. It was better than in her dreams. Every bit as erotic, but with underlying trust and love.

"I do love you," she whispered again to Kate.

CHAPTER FORTY-THREE

AD Holloway was put off by the hammering on the door of his apartment. He squinted at his illuminated watch and saw that it wasn't quite five a.m. Cinching his robe around his waist, he stumbled toward the living room.

"Coming!" he weakly informed the hammerer. He was more thankful than ever for having tucked his wife away in a nice beach house, far away. He couldn't wait to join her. What would she think of these recent late night shenanigans?

He checked the peephole, unlocked the door and promptly turned his back on his guest. Holloway plopped onto the nearby couch and aimed impatient eyes at the man. "I told you not to come here anymore."

"You told me a lot of things." The Watcher smirked, perused

the perfunctory living room, eyed a painting above the dry bar. "More than anything else, you told me to shut up."

"Shut up," Holloway told him again. He shrugged and dropped his hands into his lap. "See? It never works. I don't know why I trusted you this long."

"Drink for you?" The Watcher asked as if they were old friends.

"No." Holloway watched him go to the bar. The Watcher selected scotch and Holloway noted his hands, and mockingly asked, "Should I be nervous that you're wearing gloves?"

"Should you be nervous at all?" The Watcher asked, savoring the sound of his own words, relishing the nervous anticipation his very visit had inspired. He found a glass and poured himself two fingers before settling into the chair facing Holloway. "You got me out of there fast enough. Tell me, are you planning to make me vanish too?"

"Don't be stupid. That's not my line of business." Holloway nervously looked away, muttered, "I'm far too busy covering for you fools to do any real damage myself."

"And you don't like to get your hands dirty." The Watcher smirked, tossed back his drink and went for another. "You're a glory-seeker, Holloway. Nothing more. One day this world will know what you let happen on your watch on your mission of self -fulfillment."

"No. Three months and five days to put up with this bullshit." Holloway's thin lips formed a smile. "After that, you can blow this story up all you want and I'll be basking on an island, giving a shit less about your problems."

The Watcher swirled the amber liquid in his glass, looked thoughtful. "This is your mess. These are your problems. You think they go away when you do?" He laughed. "You're as ruined as I am."

Holloway's smile faded, he leaned forward, rested his elbows on his knees. He wrung his hands together. "I should never have let you talk me into this."

"Me?" The Watcher scoffed. "You knew what was going on and what did you do to stop it besides pen a personal memoir ostering genius in your division?"

Holloway nodded in concession, looked away. "I took my opportunities."

"At the risk of the tax-paying public?" The Watcher feigned shock. "A fine representative for the FBI you are. Lies covering lies covering lies."

He leaned forward in his seat, all business. "I come along, sniff you out, cover your ass, remember? Shay Cooper comes along and sniffs out even a hint of your inadequacies, and *I'm* suddenly the bad guy here?"

"What was I supposed to do?" Holloway shouted. "It was going to break open at some point. We might as well cover our asses where we can."

"Cover *your* ass, you mean." The Watcher settled back in his chair, looked casual. "Throw me under the train, won't you? Simon and Schuster isn't banging down my door for a tell-all."

Holloway trained his glare on his visitor. "I'll fix this."

"You better. You think your little bit of hush money is going to buy me the same cushy retirement you'll enjoy?" He settled back in his seat again and eyed him. "Doubtful."

Holloway whispered, "What do you want from me now?"

"You look desperate, Holloway." The Watcher grinned. "And you're starting to look old. It's catching up to you."

He repeated himself. "What do you want?"

"Full apology and explanation to everyone above you, regardless of the consequences to you." The Watcher succinctly had laid down his terms. "Resurrect me and my career."

Holloway looked pale. He shifted in his seat. "Impossible. You know that."

"What I know is that a monster was freely operating under your nose. You profited off Dr. Jekyll while ignoring Mr. Hyde."

By now, Holloway was sweating. "And which of those two characters do you most identify with, Agent Buchner?"

The young man stared at him for a while. In a sudden move, he withdrew his pistol and aimed it at the Assistant Director. He made careful study of the man's instantaneous silent transition from disbelief to fear to panic and finally death when he shot him twice, point-blank.

He finished his drink and pocketed his glass, then stood to survey the body in a bloody slump on the leather couch. The silencer had robbed the game of pure thrill. He recalled from numerous autopsy reports that Williams' choice of weapon was a knife, up-close, personal and bloody. Perhaps he was onto something; perhaps that drew out the thrill. He'd wanted more than anything to speak with Williams about his methods; he'd do it once he managed to draw the missing agent out of the woodwork. Obviously it had been too much for Williams, a superhero existing among suited up pencil-pushing stiffs. He didn't know how that conversation would go, but either way, Buchner would proceed. He'd make his own way, his own code, his own fortune and fame, and really, he only had Agent Williams to thank for it all.

Buchner studied his boss and recalled his first kill, months ago. The vic had been an eighteen-year-old kid on his way home from football practice. He'd performed the act quickly and recklessly, long before he'd had a chance to appreciate the artistic process of the soul vacating its shell. Fascinating.

Buchner started for the apartment door, but remembered his boss's last inquiry. He dropped back, addressed the dead man on the couch.

"Mr. Hyde, I believe."

CHAPTER FORTY-FOUR

Shay intended to work from home the next day, but that was before the call from Tess. She listened to what Holloway's secretary had to say, sighed, cursed under her breath, and proceeded to disentangle herself from Kate and the bed sheets.

"What's wrong?" Kate drowsily asked her. She sat up in bed and watched Shay gather her still damp clothes from various piles along the bedroom floor. "I thought we were sleeping in?"

"I did too." Shay shook her head, looked tired. "That was the office. Holloway didn't show for the morning meeting. He's not answering any phones, either. Tess has a bad feeling about it."

Kate shoved long blond tangles out of her eyes, looked concerned. "Tess has been with Roger almost as long as he's been with his wife."

"That's what I figured." Shay stood in the center of the floor, her nakedness shielded only by the small damp pile she carried in front of her. "I'm going to jump in the shower then go check it out."

But she doubled back toward the bed where she kissed Kate once, then twice. She pulled away and grinned. "By the way, good morning."

"Good morning to you, too." Kate smiled and plopped her body back against the pillows.

She'd been called in just as he knew she would be. Despite his roster of achievements inside such a short time, Agent Buchner knew that, in truth, Shay Cooper was Holloway's right-hand "man," post-Williams. Buchner had spent three years earning his place at the CIRG, then another two kissing Williams' ass. The apparent crowning of Shay Cooper as the Bureau's golden child was strictly honorary, undeserved. It was bullshit.

Buchner watched Shay as he sat in his old Toyota. She pulled a blazer over her T-shirt and skipped down the stairs outside her home and in moments she was in her car, headed in the direction of the freeway. He made note of the two other agents parked curbside in their unmarked, yet very obvious Bureau vehicles. He checked his gun and silencer, wished he had his service weapon—a kick-ass Glock—but he'd been forced to turn it in upon his suspension. As if the Bureau needed it. The lazy bastards were more interested in parading around in striped ties and suits. That just wasn't Buchner's style. He craved more involvement.

He sighed. It wouldn't matter after today anyway. He'd use his personal gun twice more, then never again. He was becoming an artist. He mentally reviewed his plan.

His first and second shot would go into the left temple then chest of the closest agent posted curbside, Agent Jacobs. Buchner had brought with him a striped Portillo's bag which would surely prove to be a hit in the distraction department. He'd give it a little wave and the window would come down. If these younger guys thought of anything more than sex, it was food. A good

Chicago hot dog would be a shoo-in diversion for Buchner to administer his first kill shot.

Shots three and four would occur less than a minute later, also into the left temple and chest, this time of Agent Hunter. He'd utilize the same beloved striped bag and the rest would similarly fall into place. It was like shooting fish in a barrel. Then Buchner was as good as inside.

He would not kill Kate Harris inside Shay's home, no matter what her struggle. He would not leave behind a hair, fiber, or blood droplet—no single clue from which to go on. Then later he'd kill her on his own terms, slowly, no gun this time, everything necessary so that he could savor the moment when her life slowly trickled, then utterly abandoned her shell. This was a thrill that was sure to last. Simply knowing he'd bequeathed Shay Cooper with yet another lifelong brain-prison full of what-ifs was enough to keep him hard indefinitely.

He'd keep Tony Williams' game alive. He was far too invested it now, but it had become too important to let Williams continue it. He'd draw the son of a bitch out, show him his good work, and to protect it, he'd ultimately have to kill him, too.

With Holloway, Harris and Williams out of the way and Shay a broken-down wreck, the Bureau would beg him to come back. He'd negotiate his own cushy salary and then one day, he'd "recover" the body of the fallen lovely, Agent Harris. He'd publicly damn evil Agent Williams, even write a book or two... It gave him chills to think about it.

True to form, he'd plant whatever evidence necessary, as he'd done before. Like when he'd transferred an old, degraded bit of Williams' blood to that bathtub drain in Arizona. He remembered the mystery wound on Williams' upper arm after one weekend. It had given him an idea. How stupid for Williams to discard his gauze and bandages in the Dumpster outside his apartment. Hadn't he ever heard of Dumpster diving? Truth was, the Bureau believed whatever the evidence told them. Buchner had a lot of evidence.

He'd far surpassed his teacher.

He recalled Williams dictating to him case details, getting off on the sweet smell of smugness in the room during their lengthy sessions. Williams seemed to believe everything he invented. He was bold, charismatic, and the chicks loved him. For being a mathematical moron and a pure fraud—not to mention a psychopathic serial killer—Williams was a genius.

Buchner cleared his throat, tapped his fingertips on the steering wheel. It had begun to sprinkle rain. The timing was perfect. He adjusted the hood of the old Quantico sweatshirt with Williams' name emblazoned on the back of it. Smiling, he got out of the car, heard his own singsong voice.

"Come out, come out wherever you are, Agent Williams."

Buchner was on the move. Constrained excitement bubbled within him, coursed through his veins, touched his extremities. He became more invincible with each step he took toward the first undercover. Jacobs turned in his seat and looked slightly startled before recognizing his hooded colleague. He smiled, sighed with evident relief, and rolled down the window.

"Just me." Buchner grinned and teasingly waved the Portillo's bag. "Hungry?"

Shay would have gone to Holloway's apartment herself had she not received orders to report to the lab ASAP. She sat impatiently in the holding room, and wondered about the agent she'd sent in her place. For the millionth time, she considered Holloway's quirky behavior of late. She had it on good authority that he'd sent his wife to the Caymans on a supposed vacation, and a check of his local bank showed no deposits of his book residuals. He was funneling them elsewhere. One less person to trust. She closed her eyes and leaned her head against the cool cement wall.

"Agent Cooper?" A woman in a blue lab coat entered the drab waiting area. She perched herself on the edge of the bench where Shay was seated. "Sorry to keep you waiting. I have something you'll want to hear."

Shay gave the woman her full attention. "Go ahead."

"A construction site in Milwaukee unearthed remains a few months ago but couldn't make ID. No dentals, no DNA in [S, you know the story." The tech laid out the scenario.

"Okay." Shay nodded for her to continue.

"Yesterday you entered your own DNA into the system for a different case comparison."

Shay nodded. She wondered if they'd at last found her mother.

"I hate to be the one to tell you, but we have a familial match." The lab tech's voice was low, her eyes wide with sympathy. "Since you were comparing swabs, I'll assume you were looking for someone."

Shay thought of her long-missing mother. She swallowed hard. "Go on."

"I believe we may have found him."

Him? She thought of Ortelli. "My father?" But the tech had already told her the body was months old. She'd just seen him. It didn't add up.

The tech shook her head. "Twenty-five percent common markers makes him a half-brother."

"Not possible." It was an about-face of everything washing around her brainpan at the moment. Pieces slowly revealed themselves, took their lazy time finding a place in the ever-evolving puzzle.

"A body was recovered recently up north. Adult male, six-one, approximately two hundred pounds, familial DNA match to you." The tech dipped her head, waited for whatever reaction would come. "I'm sorry to pressure you, but they're anxious in Wisconsin to make ID."

"How?" Shay stood and wobbled toward the door. "The son of a bitch can't be dead…"

"I'm sorry, Agent Cooper?"

Shay aimed hazy eyes at the tech, muttered her obligatory thanks.

"I need that name, agent," the tech persisted.

Shay ran her hand along the wall behind her, clamped onto the cool steel door handle. Her pulse surged and her head hurt.

"It's Williams," she numbly said, pushing through the door. "Anthony Williams."

Her brain was congested with notions of chasing a ghost. How could she keep Kate safe when she didn't know who she was protecting her from? She pressed redial on her cell as she headed for the elevator. Her partner picked up immediately, issued a question in front of her greeting.

"Did you find Holloway?"

"Not yet." Shay stepped inside an empty elevator and waited for the doors to close. Her voice was low, wracked with paranoia. "Somebody should be at his place. We should hear any time."

"Okay." Kate sounded concerned. "Are you good, Shay? You sound funny."

"I'm just worried about you, that's all."

"Don't be. I've got good people here. There's no way Tony's getting near me."

Shay scrubbed her forehead, wondered how she was going to explain this one. She swallowed hard, stammered, "About that. There's been a development."

"I know." Kate's voice intended to sooth her. "Buchner said you'd tell me about it when we get there."

Shay suddenly perked up. "Buchner…?"

"Yes. He's bringing me to you right now."

The final piece of the horrific puzzle clicked into place.

"No! For fucksake *no!* Don't go anywhere with him!" she spat. "Do you hear me?"

"Hey there, Coop buddy." Buchner's smiling voice was suddenly on the line. "Don't worry about a thing. I've got it from here."

"No! Kate—*no!*" she shouted into the dead phone as the elevator doors parted on level one. A dozen agents stared at her. She pushed through the human wall and took off on a dead run toward the parking garage.

"Did she hang up?" Kate frowned at the dead phone.

Buchner ignored her as he moved around the room, checking the windows, looking twitchy. "We need to hurry, Agent. There's not much time."

"When will you tell me what's going on?" She leaned against the wall for balance as she slipped on one sandal then the other. "How long will we be in hiding? Should I bring some things?"

"No," he answered with greater impatience than he should have. Buchner forced his voice to be quieter, he put on a smile. He tried again. "Things are happening fast. We'll get what you need later. Promise."

She eyed him cautiously as she fastened one sandal. Things felt wrong. She tested the waters. "I'm glad things worked in your favor and you're back. Shay promised she'd put in a good word for you."

"Right." His sarcasm was becoming alarmingly evident. "She fixed everything, all right. Good old Agent Cooper."

"Yeah." She was growing warier by the moment, but forced herself to remain outwardly calm. "She has quite a way with the Assistant Director."

"Actually, I talked to him myself early this morning. We worked things out." He disregarded the remaining unfastened sandal, took her arm and led her into the hallway.

Kate's feet stopped moving. "Wait—you talked to Holloway this morning?" She shook her head. "Why didn't you say so? Where is he—is he okay?"

"Home," he casually told her, tugging her arm again. She didn't budge. Buchner chuckled softly, added, "He was rather quiet when I left him."

Kate's pulse quickened, and she wondered if the agent could hear her heart hammering away in her chest. She forced a small smile, felt in her sweater pocket for her cell phone. "If you don't mind, I'm going to give my partner a quick call, tell her we're on our way."

Buchner grabbed her hand. He squeezed hard, until she cried out and dropped the phone. He slammed the heel of his boot onto it and ground it into the hallway floor.

When she looked at him again, he was pointing a gun at her.

"Actually, I do mind."

CHAPTER FORTY-FIVE

Shay Cooper called for backup as she sped along the freeway back to Pleasant. Buchner was surely on the move by now, and the further she allowed him to travel, the colder the trail would be. He'd learned from the best, after all. She raked a hand through her hair, shoved long bangs out of her face, and steered the car abruptly left, nearly launching the car off the shoulder and back into the stream of traffic.

She comforted herself with the knowledge that Kate was smart. She couldn't believe she, herself, hadn't seen it before now, but her partner surely knew by now that Buchner was their man. She'd drag out their departure, she'd utilize every drop of sweet talk she had in her, right? Shay had seen Kate in action with the Scottsdale PD—how kindly she'd wheedled the information out of them, and how nicely they'd responded.

Beauty and brains. Shay hoped like hell both of those qualities were working overtime.

She zipped past a green mileage sign. Five miles to go. Kate would leave every clue possible for Shay to find her. She only hoped it wouldn't be too late.

"No. Not the front door."

Kate had started for the foyer, but Buchner steered her toward the kitchen. He seemed to know that she'd try to create a ruckus in front of the neighbors. He jammed his gun in her back, squeezed her wrists tightly together. "Back door, move now."

Pure panic coursed throughout her, but Kate tamped it down as much as possible, focused on keeping him conversant and engaged. It might buy her some opportunity to come up with a plan for escape.

"Where are we going?" she asked, but the request fell on deaf ears as he pushed her into the kitchen. She revamped her approach, tried again. "What's really going on? What is this about?"

He didn't answer, only jammed his gun painfully between her shoulders.

Her anxiety level peaked as they neared the back door. Once she was in his car, all opportunities would be lost. She would be his to do with whatever he pleased. She tried to think quickly.

"You haven't done anything wrong yet." Her voice was high and anxious. "Shay is going to talk to Holloway and straighten this out. Please don't do anything regretful, I'm begging you."

"Number one, I happen to know for a fact that Shay will not be talking to Holloway." He hesitated, smugly amended his statement, "Well, she can talk, but he's in no shape to listen."

At once, she felt as though the blood had left her entire body. Her head was light and her hands tingled.

"And number two—" He jerked her backward, leered over her shoulder and whispered into her ear, "—since we both practice the same hostage negotiation tactics? Give it a rest."

She miraculously wriggled loose, spun around to face h̲i̲m̲

The quickness of the move made him nervous and he pressed the barrel of his gun against her forehead. She closed her eyes, blindly forged ahead.

"What happened? Was it Williams? What did he do to you?"

He pulled his gun away from her forehead, saw the red indention he'd made in her otherwise flawless skin. Keeping his gun trained on her, he looked thoughtful, downright human. He was quiet.

"It was Williams, wasn't it?" She urged him on, dipped her chin demurely, tried to find common ground. "I should have known. Tell me what the son of a bitch did to you."

He studied her a moment before bursting into a grin. "I gotta tell you, that's a balls to the walls move there, Kate Harris." He chuckled, thudded the barrel of his gun against her temple. She grimaced with pain. "That's using the old noggin. You're good at this." He again waved his gun toward the back door.

Kate didn't move just yet. "Since this is probably going to end badly for me, tell me what he did to you, James." Her eyes swam, her voice was a hoarse whisper as she added, "It's really the least you can do."

"Okay," he said, having appeared to think it over. He lowered his gun, but kept his defensive stance, watched her every breath. "Tony Williams was a total fraud."

"I know."

His expression hardened and in a split second he was back in her face, jamming her collarbone hard with his index finger. "Do *not* agree with every word I say. I find that condescending as hell." His voice wobbled, his gun shook in his tremulous grip. He swiped the beads of sweat that formed along his upper lip. "That's what Williams did. Treated me like the dirt beneath his feet—as if he was truly the brilliant guy everyone thought he was."

"He did that to me as well," Kate quietly admitted. "I was his silent partner and you were his scribe. We were nothing more to him."

"Scribe?" He shrugged, chuckled as he considered it. "But it didn't take long for me to figure out it was the time stamps. I pointed out the inaccuracy only to have him verbally annihilate me."

Kate had seen her former partner relentlessly belittle him. "He was a bully."

His eyes flicked to hers. "You never stopped him."

She conceded. "No, I didn't."

"You were drunk on his ideals of greatness, just like the others." He stared at her before launching back into his narration. "But I checked it out myself. Found a few bodies, took the news to Holloway."

At the reminder of Roger her stomach lurched. She focused on survival, suddenly interested in Holloway's role in the situation. "Holloway knew about this?"

He nodded. "But by then, he had his big old book coming out and a year to retirement. And believe me, he did not want to screw that up." Buchner laughed. "So much for Fidelity, Bravery and Integrity, huh?"

"He didn't tell you to leave it alone." She closed her eyes as if to perish the thought. Feeling sick to her stomach, she whispered, "Tell me that he didn't tell you to bury it."

"Figuratively and literally. I guess he got a whiff of the money and fame. He was probably sick of the second-hand high he was getting off Williams." He rested his gun against the kitchen island behind him. "Probably sick of the mere pittance he was getting from consulting on Williams' books."

"Christ..." Kate muttered. It felt like the bottom had fallen out of her world. She shook her head. "Why didn't you take this to someone else?"

"And wind my ass up on a slab in some morgue?" He looked incredulous, then adopted a haunted tone. "Or just...vanish?"

"No, this can't be true," she whispered.

"What's not to believe?" He took a step toward her, his voice steadied. "That Williams falsified his very existence, made millions off crimes he himself committed, and hid it all behind a childish code?" Buchner smirked. "Hell, Williams couldn't crack a fucking Sodoku."

"How did you get here, James?" Kate's earnest voice brought him back front and center. "You figured all this out. You are the one who should be getting the props, so how did you get here, right now?"

"I thought about that for a long time." He grew quiet, contemplative. "I wondered what kind of monster Williams was. Each kill seemed to empower him. He got off on taunting the people by writing about it, and no one was the wiser."

"Knowing the truth, how did that make you feel?"

"I wanted to understand him. I wanted to see what felt so damned good about it." He picked up his gun, absently checked the cartridge. When he looked at her again, his eyes sparkled. "And it did feel good."

Kate swallowed hard, felt her eyes sting with tears. No matter the breadth of their conversation, Buchner was unstable as hell. And now he was going to kill her.

He took a step, waved his gun. "Let's go."

"No—no, please." She anchored her feet to the floor with all her might as he shoved her toward the door. After she'd lost her remaining sandal from her efforts, he ended up dragging her along. She continued to beg him. "Please! I'm pregnant—don't do this!"

"Funny, but that is the very last thing that would earn any mercy out of me, Agent Harris." His face was scarlet, and spit punctuated each angry word. "Getting rid of Williams' kid would actually delight me."

"Not another step, Agent Buchner."

The intruder wore a long coat despite the summer weather. His once well-tailored suit hung on his thin body like cobwebs. Kate recognized his face from the surveillance photo from Florida.

Buchner wrenched her wrists together until she cried out in pain. He thrust her in front of him, his gun pressed to her temple.

Ortelli's hands seemed surer and more capable than the rest of his obviously deteriorating body as he gripped his gun with steadfast assurance and aimed it at Buchner.

In contrast, Buchner was rattled, with a combination of fear and anger. "Who the mother-fuck are *you?*"

Utilizing his politest demeanor, the shriveled Italian man smiled and introduced himself.

"I'm the gentleman who's going to stop you."

CHAPTER FORTY-SIX

Shay rounded the corner on two wheels and blew through another set of lights leaving an angry honking near-pileup in her wake. She counted the blocks to the large cobblestone pillars that earmarked the beginning of her quaint neighborhood. She checked the rearview mirror—it would do her heart good to see that backup. Nothing.

One last stop sign and she was in. She slammed on her brakes as a mother stepped off the curb with her baby carriage. She squealed to a stop so suddenly she spun the Jeep sideways. Gasping for breath and deferring the possibilities of what-ifs, she met the angry glare of a protective mother as the woman crossed before her. Then Shay stomped on the accelerator. Four blocks to go.

"Come any closer, and I will put a bullet in her head," Buchner warned. But Ortelli took another small step, his stare meeting the younger agent's. Clearly unnerved, Buchner asked, "Do you understand me?"

Ortelli coolly glanced in Kate's direction and then back to Buchner. "Tsk, tsk," he uttered, took another step, a look of disappointment on his face. "Shame on you, holding that woman in her condition."

"Just stay your ass over there or I will kill her right now!" Remnants of a southern accent from an earlier life trickled through his words. It always happened when he was nervous.

"Now, later..." Ortelli shrugged, even dared to smile. "What's the difference? Either way you're a cold-blooded killer."

Buchner looked perturbed, still astounded that he was talking to a strange old man in Shay Cooper's kitchen, all the while his arm wrapped tightly around the neck of his would-be victim. He actually chuckled at the insanity of it all.

"And who are you? Neighborhood-fucking-watch, old man?"

"I'm the old man with the better gun and a surer shot than you." Ortelli was obviously proud of this fact. He eyed his opponent. "What's that you've got there? A nine mil? Tiny caliber for such a big guy. Bit of a sissy pistol, if you ask me." He held out his own gun, gazed at it admiringly, as it pointed at Buchner. "I have here a .357 Magnum, hollow points, a cannon." He gave a friendly chuckle, then pretended to fire a round. "*Pow!* The bullet mushrooms upon impact, explodes your head like a melon. You see, if you shoot first, I shoot too, and my big bullet goes right through that little lady and takes you out too."

Buchner steadied his grip on his gun and up came Ortelli's gun again. They stood in a silent standoff, one decidedly surer than the other.

"Put away your sissy gun or I'll shoot you with my big-boy gun." Ortelli saw that Buchner was on the verge of filing another threat and cut him short. "If you shoot her first, I'll shoot you anyway." He shrugged nonchalantly. "Either way, it turns out bad for you. Now, which way would you like it? First or second?"

Buchner's face poured nervous sweat, he looked twitchy, glanced behind him at the kitchen door. His freedom was just beyond it. He wondered if he'd ever get there.

"Tick-tock, Agent. First or second?" Ortelli repeated with growing impatience.

Buchner's gun went to his side. He stepped forward, practically dragging Kate with him. His face was red, his voice raspy. "You do not have control here! This is mine! Do you hear me?"

"If you say." Ortelli made show of how very little he cared to even appease the man. "But if you put a bullet in the lady, I'll have no choice but to kill you."

"I'll kill you!"

"You remind me much of my own son. You crave attention at any cost." He shook his head, sounded truly regretful. "It's an awful sickness."

Buchner alternated his aim between Kate and Ortelli. Nobody was sure precisely which one he was addressing when he said, "I'm going to kill you."

Ortelli momentarily closed his eyes, smiled. "Doubtful. But I admire your positive thinking."

Shay burst through her front door with a force that reverberated throughout the house. The noise startled Buchner into making his immediate decision. He pressed his pistol against Kate, unadulterated hatred and determination in his eyes. Ortelli aimed his Magnum at the agent. "Drop your gun, Agent Buchner," he ordered. No one budged. "You give me no choice."

Shay appeared in the kitchen doorway, breathless, her service pistol trained on Buchner. "Drop your weapon, Buchner!" she yelled. Buchner pressed his eyes shut, jammed the gun into Kate's temple, causing her to cry out.

Ortelli calmly addressed Shay without looking directly at her. "I've got this, agent. No need to get involved."

"Drop your gun, Ortelli," she commanded. Shay alternated her aim between Buchner and Ortelli. She watched as Ortelli and Kate locked gazes, as if they were communicating without words. Shay swallowed hard and trained her gun on Buchner.

"Both of you—back off!" Buchner was quickly losing his cool. He glanced at the door a few feet behind him, sweat beading on his face. He cocked his gun.

The singular sound triggered Kate into action. She plunged her elbow back into Buchner with all her strength. He teetered back slightly, but enough for Kate to spin around and knee him in the groin. He doubled over in pain and dropped to his knees.

"Bitch!" he snarled. Despite his obvious distress, he grabbed her arm and made wobbly aim at her.

Two shots twanged and echoed in the kitchen, one considerably more powerful than the other.

Kate and Buchner fell together, lay in a heap on the floor.

"Kate!"

Shay ran to her, disentangled Kate from the dead agent. Fresh blood flowed from a wound in Kate's forehead. Her pulse was weak, her breathing shallow.

"Stay with me!" Shay held her close, and using her own jacket as a compress, held it against the wound. Eyelashes fluttered open and gazed up at her. Shay squeezed her more tightly, attempted to comfort her. "Help is on the way—just please! Stay with me."

Shay didn't dare investigate the wound too much, afraid of what she might find. She didn't know exactly where she'd been hit, only that there was a lot of blood—Buchner's or Kate's, she couldn't be sure. The distant sounds of sirens growing louder piqued her anxiety, she hoped they would hurry. She cradled Kate, looked dazedly up at Ortelli who was pocketing his weapon.

"You're under arrest for shooting an agent." Shay's stamina was gone and her words sounded weak. Still, she persisted. "Just stay right there, Ortelli."

"It's better this way." He sounded sad and old. He appeared to have considered their present situation and had somehow come to peace with his deadly action. His odd tone bordered on comforting. "There was no need to get you involved more than you already are."

"I'm placing you under arrest," Shay continued her obligatory ramble while rocking Kate and staunching her wound. The sirens were drawing closer. She looked at him, said desperately, "They'll be here."

"I'll be gone before that," he quietly assured her. He spent a few moments watching his only daughter cradle her badly wounded partner, then carefully stepped over Buchner's body on his way toward the door.

Shay watched him go, her eyes wide and wet. "Why...?"

Her simple inquiry represented too many questions. Ortelli looked solemn. "I can't replace what you've lost, Shay. I'm sorry for making your life hell."

"Aw, Jesus..." She heard herself lamenting. Then she exploded, "You just killed the only suspect in Williams'—*your son's*—murder!"

"I'd do it again to save my daughter." He stared at her, his intentions crystal clear. "I'll do it *every* time."

"Oh no..." she mumbled. "No, no..."

"Shay, I killed Anthony. It wasn't Agent Buchner, it was me."

"No..."

"Yes. I killed him and dumped him at a construction site, just as he did to your son—*my* grandson." A flash of fury showed in his eyes in accompaniment to his ragged whisper. She wondered how in his weakened physical state he could manage such a thing, but she believed him. Still, she shook her head.

He nodded his own head. "Yes."

He studied her, blood-covered, shaking.

The sirens cut off in front of the house, doors slamming, CIRG team assembling. Shay knew these sounds by heart.

Ortelli remained calm. "I'm sorry for the difficult life you've had. I hope you can find it in your heart to forgive an old man for trying to make it right."

She felt her partner shift slightly in her arms as Kate fought to remain conscious. Shay stroked sticky, blood-matted hair, whispered to her, "They're here. It's going to be okay, I promise."

Kate nodded, eyes droopy. Shay's tears fell upon her partner's cheek.

"I do forgive you," Shay told her father, but when she looked up again, the kitchen door was wide open, its curtain flapping lightly in the breeze. Ortelli was gone.

Kate whispered something incomprehensible and Shay leaned in close to hear her.

"It's not a partnership until everybody gets shot...right?" A small smile appeared on Kate's lips.

"Shh, just be calm. Be calm..." But Shay was the furthest from calm. She displayed every preliminary to a full-fledged breakdown. Her eyes swam, her voice sounded pitchy. "It's okay. I promise—everything's going to be all right..."

"You trying to convince me or you?" Kate asked in a scratchy voice. She winced. "Maybe you could quit your whining and wrap that jacket a little tighter so my brains don't leak out."

Shay slowly smiled. Behind them, two agents burst into the kitchen-turned-crime scene, guns first, rapidly assessing and clearing the scene before the rest of the team converged upon the place.

Buchner was lying in a dead heap. Shay rocked her partner on the kitchen floor as fresh chaos unraveled around them.

EPILOGUE

Rust-colored leaves swirled in summer's last soft breezes before feathering into a crisp, colorful carpet. Shay stood alone, taking it in, committing the moment to memory before placing a small bunch of the season's last flowers on the newly placed gravestone. She looked on approvingly, but sadly, then kissed her fingertips and traced the name. She stood and chucked her hands into jeans pockets. The wind picked up and changed, chilled her right through her sweater, sending a shiver throughout her.

After five long years, she'd given her son a place to rest in peace. Shay glanced over at the two empty plots she'd purchased in the same row with Christopher's and wondered if she'd ever be able to honor her missing mother or her wretched, rogue father with the same final dignity. She hoped so. She talked and prayed, and at last she was ready to go.

The sun felt comforting on her face and she willed it to warm her clear through as she cut across the cemetery toward her Jeep.

Kate leaned against it, waiting patiently. Her skin was radiant in the sunlight and golden hair carelessly blew around the shoulders of her long coat. She pressed a bundle against her, shielding the tiny face from the wind. Her eyes were wet, but upon seeing Shay, her lips turned up into a small smile.

Shay went to her, wrapped them both in her hug, nuzzled Kate's cheek against her own.

"Don't cry," Shay whispered. She kissed Kate's forehead, right atop the fading scar and only evidence of that nearly fatal day months earlier. Shay clasped her hand, instinctively brushing her thumb along the gold band she'd placed there. She felt stronger by the moment, knew somehow it would all be okay. "I love you both so much."

"I wish I'd known your boy," Kate whispered.

"In a way, you do." Shay looked at her shoes then back to her partner. She made a small smile. "He was a lot like me."

"Then I would have loved him very much," Kate told her.

Shay nudged her toward the Jeep, took the sleeping baby from her and secured the child in the car seat. She checked it once, twice, three times, and only when she saw Kate smiling at her overprotective behavior did she stop. Shay got in, cranked the key and thudded her gloved hands against the steering wheel looking thoughtful. "We should get a bigger car."

Kate looked over at her. "But you love the Jeep."

"Chicago doesn't love it. Too drafty in the winter, too hot in the summer."

"We'll survive." Kate added, "We've proven to be a pretty tough bunch."

Shay considered the incredible lengths they'd gone through for that proof. She didn't feel like talking about it anymore. She'd done nothing but talk about it in one official inquiry after another since that deadly day. In all, she'd lost her best friend and a half brother she hadn't even known existed. For Kate, it meant the loss of her godfather, her baby's biological father and a Buchner, a power-crazed FBI agent who had proven to be as mentally unstable as Williams.

"Maybe we should have buried Williams—"

"No." Kate cut her off. It was a discussion they'd already had several times. "Absolutely not. He's not a part of our family."

"Right." Shay nodded. "I know you're right."

Kate could tell Shay was slipping back into her jumbled thoughts, and she moved to intervene before she fell too far into that dark abyss. "You can't beat yourself up about this anymore, Shay."

"We let Buchner take the fall for all those bodies."

"We had no choice." Kate touched Shay's shoulder, demanded she look her in the eye. "Like it or not, they're right. Exposing Tony would mean exposing the Bureau. We'd lose the faith of the public. We'd lose the faith of our own trainees." She shook her head. "In the long run, it would do more harm than good."

Shay was having a tough time buying the Bureau's proposed damage control. "In the short run, a man goes to his grave publicly accused of killing dozens."

"A man who would have killed more if given the chance." Kate's voice bordered stern. "He would have made quite a murderous career for himself, including you and me. Thank God for Ortelli."

"I never thought I'd feel that way." Shay blinked. "Did we do the right thing?"

"No. But we did the only thing we could," Kate answered without hesitation.

"Fidelity, bravery, integrity..." Shay's voice trailed off. She shook her head. "Doesn't feel much like it. It's hard to know who to believe anymore."

"I believe in you," Kate whispered. "Shay, you're in charge now."

"For the price of my silence."

"No. Because you're *that* good," Kate solemnly said. "Because you'll never let such things happen on your watch."

Shay looked at her. "No. I sure as hell won't."

Kate's hand covered Shay's gloved one as it rested on the gearshift.

"We need something bigger." Shay was talking about the Jeep again. She shifted into drive and they slowly moved down the long gravel drive. She reached up and rubbed a clearing in the foggy window. "Something with a better defogger."

"Well, you certainly can afford it now."

"*We* can afford it now." Shay's tense expression softened some. She smiled. "We'll look this weekend."

"What do you have in mind?" Kate asked, happy for the subject change.

"Something with a good safety rating, couple of built-in car seats, you know."

"Couple?" Kate looked surprised. "You planning on having more kids, Cooper?"

"Well, I figured since you're taking a few years off and all..."

"Oh, you figured I'd be the stork?"

"Well, I certainly can't be the stork," Shay said, sounding as if the idea of it was completely absurd. "I drink way too much coffee and I'd never fit a baby belly behind that desk I'm going to be commandeering thanks to my big, boring promotion."

"I've seen you with too much action, Cooper. I love boring." Kate shrugged nonchalantly. "In fact, I'm crazy about it."

Shay grinned at her. "I'm crazy about you, sunshine."

Kate's laughter warmed the air around them. It was a beautiful sound.

Publications from
Bella Books, Inc.
Women. Books. Even Better Together.
P.O. Box 10543
Tallahassee, FL 32302
Phone: 800-729-4992
www.bellabooks.com

CALM BEFORE THE STORM by Peggy J. Herring. Colonel Marcel Robideaux doesn't tell and so far no one official has asked, but the amorous pursuit by Jordan McGowan has her worried for both her career and her honor.
978-0-9677753-1-9

THE WILD ONE by Lyn Denison. Rachel Weston is busy keeping home and head together after the death of her husband. Her kids need her and what she doesn't need is the confusion that Quinn Farrelly creates in her body and heart.
978-0-9677753-4-0

LESSONS IN MURDER by Claire McNab. There's a corpse in the school with a neat hole in the head and a Black & Decker drill alongside. Which teacher should Inspector Carol Ashton suspect? Unfortunately, the alluring Sybil Quade is at the top of the list. First in this highly lauded series.
978-1-931513-65-4

WHEN AN ECHO RETURNS by Linda Kay Silva. The bayou where Echo Branson found her sanity has been swept clean by a hurricane — or at least they thought. Then an evil washed up by the storm comes looking for them all, one-by-one. Second in series.
978-1-59493-225-0

DEADLY INTERSECTIONS by Ann Roberts. Everyone is lying, including her own father and her girlfriend. Leaving matters to the professionals is supposed to be easier! Third in series with *PAID IN FULL* and *WHITE OFFERINGS*.
978-1-59493-224-3

SUBSTITUTE FOR LOVE by Karin Kallmaker. No substitutes, ever again! But then Holly's heart, body and soul are captured by Reyna... Reyna with no last name and a secret life that hides a terrible bargain, one written in family blood.
978-1-931513-62-3

MAKING UP FOR LOST TIME by Karin Kallmaker. Take one Next Home Network Star and add one Little White Lie to equal mayhem in little Mendocino and a recipe for sizzling romance. This lighthearted, steamy story is a feast for the senses in a kitchen that is way too hot.
978-1-931513-61-6

2ND FIDDLE by Kate Calloway. Cassidy James's first case left her with a broken heart. At least this new case is fighting the good fight, and she can throw all her passion and energy into it.
978-1-59493-200-7

HUNTING THE WITCH by Ellen Hart. The woman she loves — used to love — offers her help, and Jane Lawless finds it hard to say no. She needs TLC for recent injuries and who better than a doctor? But Julia's jittery demeanor awakens Jane's curiosity. And Jane has never been able to resist a mystery. #9 in series and Lammy-winner.
978-1-59493-206-9

FAÇADES by Alex Marcoux. Everything Anastasia ever wanted — she has it. Sidney is the woman who helped her get it. But keeping it will require a price — the unnamed passion that simmers between them.
978-1-59493-239-7

ELENA UNDONE by Nicole Conn. The risks. The passion. The devastating choices. The ultimate rewards. Nicole Conn rocked the lesbian cinema world with Claire of the Moon and has rocked it again with Elena Undone. This is the book that tells it all...
978-1-59493-254-0

WHISPERS IN THE WIND by Frankie J. Jones. It began as a camping trip, then a simple hike. Dixon Hayes and Elizabeth Colter uncover an intriguing cave on their hike, changing their world, perhaps irrevocably.
978-1-59493-037-9

WEDDING BELL BLUES by Julia Watts. She'll do anything to save what's left of her family. Anything. It didn't seem like a bad plan...at first. Hailed by readers as Lammy-winner Julia Watts' funniest novel.
978-1-59493-199-4

WILDFIRE by Lynn James. From the moment botanist Devon McKinney meets ranger Elaine Thomas the chemistry is undeniable. Sharing — and protecting — a mountain for the length of their short assignments leads to unexpected passion in this sizzling romance by newcomer Lynn James.
978-1-59493-191-8

LEAVING L.A. by Kate Christie. Eleanor Chapin is on the way to the rest of her life when Tessa Flanaghan offers her a lucrative summer job caring for Tessa's daughter Laya. It's only temporary and everyone expects Eleanor to be leaving L.A...
978-1-59493-221-2

SOMETHING TO BELIEVE by Robbi McCoy. When Lauren and Cassie meet on a once-in-a-lifetime river journey through China their feelings are innocent...at first. Ten years later, nothing — and everything — has changed. From Golden Crown winner Robbi McCoy.
978-1-59493-214-4

DEVIL'S ROCK: THE SEARCH FOR PATRICK DOE by Gerri Hill. Deputy Andrea Sullivan and Agent Cameron Ross vow to bring a killer to justice. The killer has other plans. Gerri Hill pens another intriguing blend of mystery and romance in this page-turning thriller.
978-1-59493-218-2

SHADOW POINT by Amy Briant. Madison Maguire has just been not-quite fired, told her brother is dead and discovered she has to pick up a five-year old niece she's never met. After she makes it to Shadow Point it seems like someone—or something—doesn't want her to leave. Romance sizzles in this ghost story from Amy Briant.
978-1-59493-216-8

JUKEBOX by Gina Daggett. Debutantes in love. With each other. Two young women chafe at the constraints of parents and society with a friendship that could be more, if they can break free. Gina Daggett is best known as "Lipstick" of the columnist duo Lipstick & Dipstick.
978-1-59493-212-0

BLIND BET by Tracey Richardson. The stakes are high when Ellen Turcotte and Courtney Langford meet at the blackjack tables. Lady Luck has been smiling on Courtney but Ellen is a wild card she may not be able to handle.
978-1-59493-211-3